THE LION'S WAY

MARCO MARSAN

with PETER LLOYD

GREENLEAF
BOOK GROUP PRESS

Notice: This book is a work of fiction. Names, characters, businesses, organizations, places, events, and incidents are either a product of the author's imagination or are used factitiously. Any resemblance to actual persons, living or dead, events, or locales is entirely coincidental.

Published by Greenleaf Book Group Press, LP
4425 South Mo Pac Expwy., Suite 600
Austin, TX 78735

Copyright ©2008 by Marco Marsan

All rights reserved under all copyright conventions.

No part of this book may be reproduced, stored in a retrieval system, or transmitted by any means, electronic, mechanical, photocopying, recording, or otherwise, without written permission from the publisher.

For ordering information or special discounts for bulk purchases, please contact Greenleaf Book Group LP at: 4425 South Mo Pac Expwy., Suite 600 Austin, TX 78735, (512) 891-6100.

Design and composition by Greenleaf Book Group LP

Publisher's Cataloging-In-Publication Data
(Prepared by The Donohue Group, Inc.)

Marsan, Marco.
  The lion's way / Marco Marsan ; with Peter Lloyd. — 1st ed.
    p. ; cm.
    ISBN: 978-1-929774-46-3
1. Rome—History—Fiction. 2. Time travel—Fiction. 3. Jesus Christ—Fiction. 4. Adventure fiction. 5. Historical fiction. I. Lloyd, Peter, 1947- II. Title.
PS3613.A7736 L56 2008
813/.6

Printed in the United States of America on acid-free paper

10 09 08 07   10 9 8 7 6 5 4 3 2 1

First Edition

THE
LION'S
WAY

ROME

THE MOB WAS OF TWO MINDS. IT SCREAMED FOR BLOOD.
At the same time it raged against the soldiers who prodded the broken man
down the road. His supporters called out, "Rabbi!" and wept wildly as he
strained under the weight of the huge timber that the guards forced him to
carry on his back. Others ridiculed his bloodied face, his back shredded by the
scourge, his hair matted with drying blood. Children either spat in his direction or buried their faces in their mothers' garments, depending on how their
parents behaved.

A stone's throw away from the center of attention, Juve muscled his way
through the throng, toward the pitiful man under the timber. As he worked
his way closer, he noticed a soldierly man who also seemed determined to
reach the object of everyone's attention. Then another and another—five,
maybe six tall men forcing their way through the crowd, shoving people aside.
Their imposing statures, clean garments, and washed faces made them easy
to spot. They moved quickly and forcefully, leaving a backwash of grimy faces
bobbing in a motley wake of worn and tattered fabric.

In the next few seconds, the six converged, one by one, on the man under
the timber. Two grabbed either end of the heavy shaft and used it to push back
the crowd. Relieved of his burden, the bloodied man stood up and seemed to

protest. Guards around the rabbi responded too slowly as the remaining four big men drew long knives from under their togas and sent several to their deaths. Then the rescuers quickly formed a semicircle around the angry and bewildered rabbi, menacing anyone who dared come near.

As Juve arrived at the scene, a soldier broke through the crowd and went for one of the rescuers. Instinctively Juve threw himself into the fray. With his right fist, he grabbed the soldier. More armed soldiers arrived. A whip cracked just above Juve's head. Before he even considered his response, Juve snatched the whip from the soldier's hand. Then, holding the business end with his left hand, he struck the stunned attacker's face several times with the hard handle. The soldier stumbled into the crowd and slumped to the ground.

Almost as one, the mob greeted the new spectacle with cheers of approval. They roared as Juve slammed another soldier down onto the hardened surface of the road and broke his neck with the heel of his shoe. An odd sense of embarrassment distracted Juve for a second, when he noticed that his shoes and pants singled him out among men and women dressed in sandals and robes. He shook off the feeling and turned just in time to impale yet another soldier on the spearlike fingers of his outstretched arm.

Two more soldiers broke through the ring of the six protectors. Juve dispatched them both—one with a side kick to the bottom of the jaw, the other with a swift, knifelike chop of his hand. Three more soldiers arrived. The crowd roared as Juve's arms and legs made contact with awe-inspiring precision—a heel to a nose, a fist to a throat. Juve clutched the third soldier by his groin and face, raised him high above his head, and speared him head-first into the dust. The six rescuers gaped at each other, their open mouths expressing their bewilderment.

Suddenly another soldier rushed Juve from behind. Sensing the attack, Juve spun around and found himself looking into the surprised man's eyes. For the first time, Juve hesitated. The crowd sensed his indecision. Silence as the men stood eye to eye. There was a flaw in the soldier's left iris. Juve couldn't move, but he managed to speak. "If you move anywhere but away, I'll kill you."

The crowd urged the soldier to attack, but he remained frozen. Then, slowly, he took a step back. The remaining soldiers followed his lead. The crowd protested loudly and demanded that the soldiers continue to fight. But, one by one, they shrank back into the crowd. Thirsting for more blood, the people groaned in angry disappointment. Some picked up rocks and began to pelt the retreating soldiers. Only a few noticed the rescued rabbi speaking to Juve. "What do you think you're doing?" he demanded.

Put off, Juve declared, "I'm just trying to save your life!"

"You don't understand," the rabbi said, as if scolding a child. "I have a job to do."

Over the rabbi's shoulder, Juve saw another soldier advancing. He moved the rabbi to one side and punched the soldier directly in the nose, knocking him flat. Then he turned to the rabbi and replied, "So do I."

The rescuers converged on Juve and the rabbi. One of them, his blade still dripping with blood, hoisted the rabbi, too weak to resist, up onto the timber. The others took positions on either side of the long shaft of wood and used it to plow through the crowd. Juve hefted a section of the timber and ran with the six and their pitiful passenger. "Where are we going?" Juve shouted to the large-muscled man in front of him.

Juve woke himself with his own words. He opened his eyes and looked around. No more mob. No more long, heavy shaft of lumber. No meek and bloodied man riding to safety. It had been a dream. The same dream.

Juventus Trajan Carnifex rose and stumbled into the bathroom, still shaken by the most recent replay of the dream. Looking in the mirror, he considered again that the pitiful man in his dream might be himself. *Carnifex* meant "executioner," and the name marked him as a descendant of a long line of elite defenders of the Republic. But how often had he awakened from these dreams to see himself in the mirror and realize how much he looked like the rabbi? The same dark, curly, shoulder-length hair, the same stubble shading the chiseled lines on his umber-colored face.

"This is nuts," he snapped out loud and splashed his face with cold water. Juve had always been a vivid dreamer—awake as well as asleep. He thought and planned in realistic mental enactments. As a student, he would fail occasionally to turn in an assignment, not out of laziness, but because his richly detailed plans to do the work convinced him that he had actually completed it. His visionary imagination had helped him solve many problems, but lately he longed for just one night of undiluted slumber.

Exercise would drive this morning's dream away. He walked back to his bedroom and lay on the cool hardwood floor, extending each limb in turn to awaken his muscles. After several minutes of stretching, he plunged into a strenuous workout. He began with a hundred push-ups, and then he raised himself up on his fingertips a dozen times before switching to one arm. Next he chinned himself slowly on a bar he had fixed in a doorframe, then faster and faster, the veins in his arms engorging with blood. Sit-ups, too, he began slowly and accelerated for almost ten minutes. Finally Juve let himself collapse on his back. His belly heaved as he caught his breath. A light sheen of perspiration covered his deeply muscled torso. He felt the pulse in his throat. In no time, he was breathing slowly and steadily.

Juve's thoughts drifted back to his childhood. His father was in some sort of military force, and Juve had become accustomed to his absences. Juve was always happy when his father returned and congratulated him for his courage. When his mother began to accompany his father on trips, Juve adjusted to the absence of both parents to prove himself worthy of their praise and love.

Then, one day, when he was nine years old and his parents were away on one of their extended trips together, two highly decorated, uniformed officers stood at his door. Young Juventus held his nanny's hand as she welcomed them in. The news came crashing down on him in a few unthinkable words: "Your parents are gone, Juventus. Gone forever."

"Both of them?" Juve cried out, stunned. "Both of them?"

After a moment of hesitation, the officer dropped to one knee to look directly into the young boy's eyes. "Yes, son," he replied, his strong hands grasping Juve's upper arms, "they're both gone. I'm sorry." Despite the strong grip of the officer's big hands, Juve felt as if he had been sucked into a black and bottomless well. "You're a strong boy, Juventus," someone said, his voice echoing and fading. "You can stand up to this, son."

He cried for the next five days. His face swelled and chafed from the tears and the rubbing. Refusing to eat or talk, he noticed little of the new residence to which he was taken.

A ward of the Republic, Juve had joined similarly orphaned boys in a school that would nurture his natural abilities. At first, he hated the idea of becoming an Indomitable Lion—a member of the elite special forces devoted to the ultimate defense of the Republic and its most powerful leaders. He refused to take part in any activities for weeks, unpersuaded by merciless abuse from the other boys in his dormitory. Finally the proctor took him aside and urged him to get into line. "You're joining the ranks of your mother and father, your grandfather and his father. You come from a long line of Trajans, Juventus. It's time to stand up and follow in their footsteps."

Eventually Juventus learned to trust the Indomitable Lions, their mission, and their code of honor. Gradually he invested in their promise of personal worth and lost himself in the discipline of daily training. It was demanding training physically and mentally, meant to weed out weakness and prepare Lion recruits for unquestioning loyalty.

Juve amazed his teachers with his abilities and creativity. At the age of fourteen, he developed a way to detect when a hand was about to shoot a pistol. In a demonstration Lions would talk about forever, Juve challenged a fellow student named Auspex to point a gun at his face and fire when ready. Auspex refused to use a real bullet, so Juve pretended to substitute a blank. Juve stood in front of a tree. Auspex prepared to shoot. A semicircle of students waited. As Auspex squeezed the trigger, Juve dropped, tackled, and disarmed his friend in one smooth action. No one was more stunned than Auspex when Juve showed them the bullet hole in the tree, right where his head had been a moment before. From that moment on, Auspex's admiration for Juve grew into a close and trusting friendship.

Juve quickly rose to the top of his class, a model of physical and mental perfection, but not without burying the deepest possible resentment for the very organization that trained him. Yes, the Indomitable Lions had shaped him into the ideal of manhood, but he would give it all back for just one chance to see his mother and father alive again. He dreamed of being a father some day. Never, he promised himself, would the Lions or anyone else ever take his child away from him, or him away from his child. Juve often renewed this youthful vow, especially during his morning exercise. Something about it gave him strength. Now, rising from his reverie, he stood up and broke into a routine of blindingly swift martial arts movements—powerful kicks and punches, each announced with a loud, explosive grunt.

Finally he settled into a long series of slow, balletlike stretching exercises before stepping into his shower. "Mayhem? It's Cobra," Juve said out loud. As consultant for the Republic's Leadership Protection Service, Juve had been issued a wayfone—the latest electronic technology. A thin wafer implanted in his head just behind his ear, Juve's wayfone allowed him to receive and send calls. To call someone, he did nothing more than think of a name and wish the call to begin. Incoming calls gave him a clear sense that someone wished to speak to him. He could answer or reject the call by simply acknowledging his intention. "Have Crow and Orso commence job number eight," Juve continued. "Get it over with by the end of the week. We're done."

Juve stepped out of the shower and began to dry himself. "Cela, it's Cobra. I want Lupus and Pavo to monitor sector eleven. Yes. Done."

It had taken a couple of hours of training to get the hang of it, but now Juve could call and answer as easily as he could speak and listen. He could even juggle, swap, and merge calls. At the moment, he listened to his caller as he began to dress. "Cobra. Right. Gather the rest at point three . . ." Juve pulled on a thin vest of body armor and continued: "Okay, we'll make dinner." As he replied, he placed a knife into each of his specially designed boots. "Sure. Fausto, Caldi, and Bruté, too."

He placed three small, razor-thin knives strategically beneath his sleeves, behind his collar, and in his waistband. Finally, a Rocco-72 automatic pistol that held three twenty-four-shot ammunition clips on a revolving spool that allowed Juve to reload, if necessary, without interrupting firing. Years of practice enabled Juve to grasp and deploy any of these weapons in eight-tenths of a second or less. Still, he continued to practice as he spoke. "Got to run, Mayhem."

Juve opened the door to his apartment, checked the hall, and stepped out into the street. Already it was alive. Men and women dashed past each other. A video monitor delivered the news as Juve passed. "Authorities report that the dissident group Forza Facia has struck again. Several high-ranking Republic officials were found handcuffed to utility poles and, as usual, distastefully tattooed with the Forza signature . . ."

Juve smiled to himself as he merged into the heavily populated flow. Video monitors were spaced along the walls of buildings so that anyone could walk or ride a velocipede and take in the day's news and announcements without missing more than a few words. Another monitor picked up where the previous one had left off. "This marks the ninetieth such occurrence in the past two years. Authorities warn that Forza Facia poses a danger to the vitality of the Republic. They offer a reward to anyone providing information leading to the apprehension of any member . . ." *Ironic*, Juve thought, as the story concluded and he noticed a spray-painted icon of a face on the wall below the monitor.

FORZA FACIA

CITIZENS CIRCLED THE OUTER RING OF THE ROUNDABOUT. Between the crowd and the commotion on the center island, cars crawled, all their drivers straining to see beyond the ring of police officers. On the island stood a towering pole with six long, outstretched arms at the top. At the end of each arm the fist of a lamp dimmed as the sun began to illuminate the city. Someone in the crowd who succeeded in catching a glimpse of the base of the lighting tower reported, "He's naked!"

"What's that on his chest?" a woman asked as she craned her neck for a clearer view. "And why don't they release him?"

From the ring of police, individual officers had taken turns stepping toward the man. But every time an officer approached, the man bolted upright and cried out in agony. As a result, the police had stopped testing the perimeter in this way some time ago. Now they all faced away from the man, out of respect for his dignity and to keep an eye on the gawking motorists and the crowd beyond. A dog sniffed around the curb of the island.

"Maybe they're afraid he's rigged with a bomb," suggested a man with a tattoo of an eagle on his shoulder.

"Forza's gone too far," a large woman in a green scarf shouted with disgust.

"Yeah, this is way out of line," another voice agreed.

"Who says it's Forza?" the tattooed man argued.

"Didn't you see the face?" the woman in green shot back.

The iconic face had appeared all around the city. As it became ubiquitous, people had named it *the face* and the unknown force behind it *Fortis Faciei*, literally Force of the Face or, in the emerging slang, *Forza Facia*, which most shortened to simply *Forza*.

Inside the circle of police, the naked man raised his head and arched his back in order to stretch his shoulders. His arms, connected at their wrists, barely surrounded the tower behind his back.

"See! There on his chest. It's the face," the woman pointed.

An older, shabbily dressed man groused, "I like it better when they leave gifts. They left my cousin some fish once—plus a bag of money."

"My neighbor got a new refrigerator after waiting three weeks for a replacement from the warranty fulfillment company," said another old man, this one wearing a black cap.

"I don't mind the graffiti. Some of it's hilarious," a young man said.

The naked captive called out to the police, "What are you waiting for? Get me out of here!" He had a large nose and protruding lips. A thick mustache contributed to his overall ratlike appearance. It was easy to despise him for his looks alone, but some in the crowd saw beyond his unappealing features.

"This poor guy doesn't deserve this, no matter what he did," someone in a blue shirt said.

"I don't feel sorry for him," the woman next to him responded. "He's what's-his-name . . . you know, the advocate general."

"I don't know his name either, but he deserves what he's getting," said the man in the black cap.

"Whatever happened to a fair trial?" muttered a girl with a small dog in her arms.

"What are you talking about?" the old man with the cap protested. "He's the bastard in charge of disposing mentals."

"Come on, you don't believe those lies," the girl scoffed.

"No lie. My brother's wife knows someone who had a baby four months ago and they disposed of it."

"I don't believe it."

"Well, she had a baby. I can tell you that. Next day—no baby. Where's the baby?"

"What did they tell her?"

"They said it didn't make it."

"So what's not to believe about that?"

"It was a healthy baby. I saw it. A cute little baby boy. It just wasn't right, that's all. But it was healthy." He locked eyes with the girl for several seconds and then stormed away.

"Look. I'm sorry about the baby," the girl called to the old man, "but you're not a doctor." She looked at her dog, then at the people around her. "It doesn't sound like he knows why it died. Sometimes babies just die."

Many people, delayed by the situation at the circle, reported to their jobs late, and it would be some time before most of them got around to doing any work. At one office, a group of seven sat around a round table in the food-dispensing area. "There are no needy people in this city or any part of the Republic," a man with short hair and small, piercing eyes argued. Two of his coworkers cut him off.

"That's nonsense!" said a heavy older woman, her face worn with years of discontent, dismissing him with a wave of her hand.

"What planet do you live on?" her companion added.

A tall, well-dressed woman walked into the room. She spoke with an air of authority. "We all know people who don't have jobs. And we all know people who have trouble making ends meet. The question isn't whether or not people have needs, it's who's responsible for meeting those needs."

"No, the question is," the short-haired man retorted, "what's the point of tying a naked leader to a light pole?"

"There's no point," the tall woman replied testily. "It's just a bunch of punks getting their kicks."

The older woman taunted her. "I liked it when they surprised people with stuff they really needed."

"Apparently that wasn't enough for them to make their point," the man chimed in.

"What point?" scoffed the tall woman.

The older woman huffed. "I think they're trying to help."

The short-haired man pretended to think about it. "How do they know who needs help?" He laughed. "Would somebody please tell them I need a new dishwasher?"

Back at the base of the pole, the chained man slept. The hot sun was beginning to redden his already tanned skin. But the face on his chest still glared defiantly, mocking him. Outside the perimeter of police, the head of the police department argued with a Leadership security official, who demanded that someone walk up to the naked man, disconnect the electrodes, clip the wrist chains, and set him free. The police chief argued that he had been advised by the medical team at the site that another shock could kill the naked official. "We're working on a way to dismantle the battery," he explained. "It seems to be buried. We think we can tunnel beneath the ground from out here, and then send in a camera, see what we've got, and either blow up the battery or clip its cables through the tunnel."

"That's insane," the official sighed in exasperation. "That could take all day!"

"I'm not talking about a man-sized tunnel," retorted the police chief, holding the thumbs and fingers of both hands in a circle, "just a small tunnel big enough for robotic tools."

"You've got exactly two hours," snapped the security man. "I want him gone by noon. I'm not going to give these hoodlums a lunchtime circus."

Meanwhile, at another office, a somewhat different debate raged in a refreshment alcove. A small, middle-aged man with a mustache had the floor. "Nobody's ever challenged the power of the Republic like Forza. I can't believe they're getting away with it."

"At least they're doing some good," added a woman in a cleaning apron. "My neighborhood couldn't get along without them."

"How does hijacking trucks and distributing the cargo help?" bellowed a burly man from across the room. "I mean, sure, it makes a few people feel great for a few weeks, but it takes more than occasional pranks to feed people."

Without hesitation, the cleaning woman hollered back. "First you've got to get the Leadership to see that some people keep getting more, while the rest of us struggle just to eat. And that's exactly what hijacking does."

"They show their real motives later when they sell the truck parts for profit," replied the big man with a bit less guile.

"They've got to fund their organization," the man with the mustache quipped.

"That's right," the woman said. "I don't see anybody getting rich on hijackings."

On the island, tunneling was underway. The naked man was stretching again as a dog sniffed the boots of a police officer. Without thinking, the cop kicked the dog away, and it bolted out into the road. Tires screeched. The dog yelped and scrambled away from the cursing driver into the circle of police. The sensors responded to the four-legged intruder and sent a current coursing through the man. He went rigid and danced freakishly on his right side. One of the officers drew his pistol and killed the dog. Lying motionless on the ground, the dog no longer activated the sensors and the man dropped in a heap, crying out in agony, "Get me out of here! Get me out!" Then he slumped, sobbing pitifully.

At the University of Rome, a History of the Republic class was focused on the question of geographic expansion. The professor, Octavia Grana, had earned a reputation as the university's most inspiring teacher. On this day, though, her class seemed distracted as they listened to her scheduled lecture.

"Gradually the Republic began to run like a machine. Science and industry developed quickly but never without humanitarian restraints to protect every citizen. A culture of cooperation flourished and creative expression blossomed. Medicine made rapid advances. Everyone considered education a privilege no citizen should pass up. Businesses and professions thrived and embraced strict codes of honor and responsibility.

"In less than a thousand years from the birth of the Republic, we had circumnavigated the earth and come to terms with every society we encountered, enriching each other with language, culture, and natural resources. Still hungry for understanding, our ancestors stepped off the planet. First to the moon, then in great, intrepid leaps through the solar system.

"At the same time the Republic busied itself with incorporating new territory and embracing exotic people in every direction. Far to the east, great empires teeming with dark-haired, round-faced people eagerly shared their art, philosophy, and music with us. To the south, dark people at one with the land dazzled their visitors with vividly colored costumes and hypnotic dance. Across the Great Western Ocean, tribes of hunters who worshiped nature and thrived in a great range of climates and topographies opened their homes and shared their food, medicine, and culture.

"For the most part, these carefully and judiciously incorporated people offered no resistance as the Republic gained influence over them and their lands, because our forebears were wise enough to make sure everyone shared the benefits as resources from around the world were traded freely and shared compassionately. Life remained as good as, and often better than, it was before the Republic became each culture's ally. What's more, the Republic always did its best to embrace and adopt every beneficial habit of every people it encountered on its way around the world. Think about it—no one had to be conquered as they were at the dawn of the Republic. The advancing forces became experts in negotiation and pacification . . ."

Sensing the class's growing restlessness, Octavia paused. "All right," she said, "let's talk about Forza's latest prank."

"Forza is a bunch of thugs," yelled a smartly dressed young man. "They challenge everything we cherish."

"No one has challenged the authority of the Republic for centuries," another student argued just as passionately. "We've weathered uprisings in hundreds of colonies . . ."

He was interrupted by the most bookish-looking man in the room. "It's not the outsiders we have to worry about. We're doing far more damage to ourselves . . ."

The unkempt young woman sitting next to him broke in. "Forza's not doing the damage. They're trying to fix it. The Leadership's responsible for the real damage."

A general uproar prompted Octavia to bang on her desk and shout above the din, "One at a time! One at a time!"

She pointed to the unkempt student. "Back up your last statement, Julia."

"For one thing, we've just about trashed Empathia."

"Objection!" shouted another student in mock protest. The classroom rippled with laughter.

"Let her finish," ordered the professor.

"Empathia represents the basis for all our success in managing people. It changed the course of history. Without it, every time the Republic came across another people, it would have cost lives and prolonged war . . ."

"How have we trashed it?" the professor asked her.

"Well, at least around Rome there are some pretty suspicious cases nobody hears about in the media, because the media is controlled by the Leadership—"

"Oh, come on!" the same dissenter protested again.

"Brutus, you'll wait your turn or leave the classroom," Octavia warned.

"But she's making this up!" Brutus complained, throwing up his arms in mock resignation.

"Go on, Julia."

"My uncle led a protest five years ago over living conditions in his neighborhood, and within a week he was gone. Nobody knows what happened to him."

"We hear so many of those kinds of stories," another student challenged. "You just assume the Leadership is guilty?"

"All right, class," Octavia announced, holding up her arms for quiet. "If we're going to go off topic, let's at least do it in the learning mode."

She scanned the room. "Who wants to get us on the same page and review Empathia?"

The studious-looking man began. "Augustus Caesar directed Flavius Aurelius to find a better way to deal with dissidents."

"Why, Antonio? How were they dealing with them at the time?"

"Well, when they identified a dissident, they'd take everything they owned, which usually put them out of commission."

"And it discouraged other dissidents," Octavia added.

"Sure," Antonio agreed and continued, "If that didn't shut them up, they'd move on to torture."

"And what was wrong with that?"

"It wasn't a question of right or wrong. Augustus was looking for a more effective approach."

A surly, statuesque woman in the back chimed in, "He did his share of torture."

"Hang on, Lydia. You'll get a chance to respond," Octavia replied.

Antonio continued, "Augustus wanted to try new kinds of persuasive techniques."

"For example?"

"He'd bribe them with money and secure positions inside the government or with his friends outside of government."

"And how did that work?"

"It was more effective than torture, but the money and other awards attracted people who pretended to be dissidents. So the Leadership ended up bribing a lot of useless frauds."

"So what happened when Augustus died?"

"When he died, Tiberius continued to work with Flavius, and together they created Empathia."

"Okay, so torture and bribery didn't work." Octavia urged him on. "What was it about Empathia that they thought would be so effective in quieting dissent?"

"I think they believed they could get better results with practical persuasion."

"Okay, go on."

"Tiberius took part in the uglier side of persuasion."

"Exactly." Octavia nodded. "He knew what he was talking about, didn't he? He had been an effective interrogator. What made him so effective?"

"Wait a minute," Brutus interrupted. "There's nothing in my history book about Tiberius torturing anybody."

"Okay, class," Octavia announced. "Somebody help Brutus with his blind faith in all things printed." The classroom erupted in a wave of derisive laughter. Brutus's face darkened as he sank into his seat with his arms folded tightly across his chest. Octavia nodded for Antonio to continue.

"He took the scientific approach, I guess. I mean he kept detailed records and paid special attention to subjects he failed to break. He found that they refused to cooperate because they believed that the pain of revealing their secrets was greater than the pain of, you know, any torture he could inflict."

"Now, we're getting somewhere," the professor exclaimed. "How does what Flavius learned relate to what Forza seems to be doing today?"

"Where's this getting us?" objected the woman in the back of the room. "We've got revolution in our streets and we sit here hashing out the fine points of Empathia!"

"Thank you!" exclaimed Brutus.

"You are university students," Octavia replied. "Your job is to understand. Anyone with a mouth can fire off opinions and raise hell in the streets. We are the people who have to hash out the issues, make informed and compassionate decisions, and recommend action that will work." She had their full attention now and she took her time, milking the silence. "If you'd rather be in the street with Forza Facia or blindly defending the Republic, leave the classroom now. But in my classroom, we're going to examine the facts, thoroughly and dispassionately." She scanned the room, challenging anyone to move. "And when you've dug as deep as you can, when you've found and honestly examined what you know to be true, then and only then do you have the right to take the kind of action that affects the lives of others." All eyes were fixed on Octavia. She treasured these moments—when she had pushed her students to the edges of their tidy collections of prejudice and could feel their inclination to consider alternatives. Choosing her words judiciously, she raised her right hand. "Fair warning: If you do this. If you faithfully follow what you find, you may come to conclusions that challenge one, many, or every belief you've ever held." Octavia extended her arms, palms up, as if offering a gift. "Who wants to continue?"

THE RIVALS

BARTH FACED HIS MIRROR. HIS EYES STILL SPARKLED WITH diamondlike brilliance, colored with the light of wisdom. At ninety-two, he was proud of the fact that women still considered him desirable, if only for his easy smile, unbridled laugh, and childlike exuberance. He simmered with more stamina and confidence than people half his age. Barth was a patient and attentive listener. His eyes twinkled with interest when most people—but especially attractive women—spoke with him. Many were smitten when he would quote verbatim little things they had confided in him from years past.

Today Barth was to receive the Republic's highest scientific honor, the Order of Lucretius, for the third time. No other scientist had ever earned the Triple Laurel, that is, three Order of Lucretius awards. Barth's closest rival and former schoolmate Zachaias Acilius had won it twice.

With scientific precision, Barth extended the individual hairs of his silver goatee and measured each one against the teeth of his stainless steel comb. Any that had grown perceptibly longer than the teeth of the comb he trimmed with small scissors. Some mornings Barth would spend as much as twenty minutes making sure every hair on his signature goatee reached the prescribed length. It helped to put his thoughts in order, especially when he faced a critical project deadline.

Barth had a mind to travel—not just from one place to another but from the present into the past. He had discovered the means to do it and today he would let the world in on his discovery. Even though the award he was about to receive recognized his development of quantum computing, he would use his acceptance speech to promote the highly controversial challenge Zachaias and he had both been working on separately—a way to predict and identify what seemed to be random intersections of distant time and space. They called them Time Continuum Intersections, or TCIs.

Putting down his comb and scissors, Barth slowly shuffled away from the mirror over to the mantle across from his bed. There on the polished surface above the battered scrollwork stood a photograph of a middle-aged woman with chestnut hair, smooth skin, and a nobility expressed in her unfathomably dark eyes.

"Good morning, Sylvia," Barth whispered as he gently touched the frame. A rush of memories plunged through his soul: the warmth of Sylvia's smile, their late night conversations, the way she sprinkled brown sugar on everything she ate. Barth shook his head with a smile. "So it finally happens. Today we pass up Zachaias. Of course, we passed him long ago. They're just finally recognizing the facts. If only you could be here."

Chuckling at the picture, Barth continued, "You know, Sylvia, you are and will always be the love of my life. And you? Do you still love your old heretic?"

Smiling to himself, Barth turned and stepped away. He was as happy as he was proud of having lived with Sylvia for forty years. Proud to have hoodwinked the bureaucracy of the Republic into permitting their interracial marriage. Even though the Republic officially proclaimed the equality of all people and cultures, racial prejudice had gradually gained quiet favor among an ever-narrowing group of like-minded elite. It spread slowly, but it moved just as deliberately through government and academia as the wild vines that climbed and smothered the structures housing them. Sylvia's unmistakably non-Roman ethnicity escaped the notice of no one, yet no one voiced an objection. In the beginning, some of Barth's friends privately second-guessed his decision to marry Sylvia, but as both their marriage and his professional reputation blossomed, not a word of objection was heard. By flaunting their marriage, Barth and Sylvia felt they kept anyone from dreaming that they closeted another secret. No one had ever discovered, nor had the slightest clue, that Sylvia was an ardent follower of Chesua. Not even Zachaias, Barth's most capable competitor and the lifelong thorn in his side.

Barth had met Sylvia when he was digging up information on the Essenes, a group of Jewish celibates who lived in the sixth century. The Republic Leadership discouraged research into this less than auspicious period of its history in the interest of cultural pride. But Barth had already begun to make his mark as an outstanding student at the Republic's most highly regarded institution of higher learning, the University of Rome, and no one was willing to get in the way of his research. When several of his professors cautioned him, he simply continued his work without drawing as much attention.

He found an eager ally in Sylvia, a beautiful young student four years his junior, as courageous as she was lovely. She had no reputation to protect. She worked quietly, without publishing, without encouragement, and at the risk of losing her position as an archivist in the university library. It wasn't a glamorous position, but it gave her access to what she loved—scraps of evidence from which she had begun to piece together the life and teachings of a man named Chesua.

At first, Sylvia's obsession put him off, but the more he listened, the more fascinated he grew. And how easy it was to listen. Sylvia's dark eyes danced with a passion for her historical mentor. She spoke with an intensity that could mesmerize any man. When they were discussing Chesua, Barth felt so lucky to be the one with whom she shared her passion. Sometimes her words were like lyrics and Barth would lose himself in her song.

Soon, however, there were more people. Around Sylvia, there began to grow a trusted troupe of young men and women captivated by the teachings of Sylvia's prophet. As the group of devotees increased in number, Barth felt he had better commit her to marriage before some other lucky student became her favored discussion partner. In addition to the profound connection he felt with Sylvia, the lessons of Chesua filled a gap he found in his understanding of life. In a culture that rewarded vigorous enterprise, especially the kind that pumped out profit, Barth found the Judean prophet's philosophy refreshing.

The scientist in him tallied up the advantages: Sylvia was beautiful, intelligent, healthy, and strong. She made him laugh, listen, and sometimes cry—three things no one else in his life had been able to do. They shared a passionate interest in a philosophy that animated their conversations and bound them in common vision. On the other side of the ledger—to marry someone non-Roman, and someone undertaking such an unpopular pursuit, could ruin his career despite his growing popularity and his professors' respect. The solution was simple: downplay her roots and manage the secrecy of her research. At the same time, he would leverage his scientific success, pursue projects that brought power to already powerful people, build political alliances with those who benefited from his discoveries, and insulate Sylvia and himself from disaster.

He had begun to learn about politics. Zachaias had already positioned himself as Barth's most serious scientific rival, but as a younger student, Barth had cringed at the idea of maneuvering for assignments, pandering to the most influential professors, paying lip service to powerful university benefactors. He just wanted to study and play. Barth and a few of his colleagues had made their mark—literally—by planting harmless sodium bombs in the bathrooms of certain professors. Now, out of love for Sylvia and in pursuit of their shared passion, he would settle down, learn politics, play the game, and protect their future, but not without mischief. Instead of planting bombs, he would turn his attention to digging up evidence of Republic abuses and uncovering clues that shed light on the story of Chesua.

It wasn't long before Barth mastered the art of political intrigue. He was amazed at how simple it seemed. And now, as he headed for his desk on the day he would receive the Triple Laurel, he realized that Zachaias still did not have a clue.

Barth had continued to stun the scientific community with his intellectual prowess, while Zachaias groused endlessly over Barth's unfair advantages—so many students fawning over him, begging to help him with his work. True. Barth had never lacked willing volunteers from among the university's student population. Every new year young admirers would paper him with proposals. As time went on, the university had provided their star with a magnificent laboratory and tower of offices rimmed with balconies and brimming with greenery. A staff of seventy handpicked men and women worked eagerly under Barth's tutelage. When word of Zachaias's complaining reached Barth, he laughed out loud and replied, "He'd have help, too, if he weren't so damn mean and ugly." When Barth's response reached Zachaias, the man reportedly flew into a rage and swore revenge.

At his desk, Barth sat and surveyed his work. His desk formed the foundation for a cityscape of paper towers. Most scientists, especially those in Barth's league, had converted to paperless data processing. But Barth preferred to hold information in his hands. He loved the smells and textures of paper and pen. He claimed he could get more from a document if he could touch it and run it between his fingers and thumbs. Rough notes and sketches covered his walls, begging to be browsed. Anyone perusing Barth's walls would see formulas for life-saving drugs alongside designs for perfumed tissues with textures that would provide better comfort and cleanliness when wiping one's private parts. It was obvious that Barth scribbled ideas whenever and wherever they occurred to him. Notes on paper napkins, hotel stationery, and bar coasters were pinned to his walls. Every idea seemed to have earned a good measure of Barth's attention. Some ideas were nothing but mathematical formulas. Others were detailed three-dimensional drawings. Some were easy to read. Others appeared to be written in code or some arcane language. The surrounding montage gave the impression of a wave of information about to crash onto the shore.

When someone asked Barth how he could find anything in the mess, he always staged the same demonstration. He would leave the room after telling his visitor to select any note on any wall or on his desk. When he returned and his visitor described a note, Barth would walk over and point to it.

Barth's dedication to paper and pen also made evidence of his ideas harder to conceal, change, or destroy. As a university student and follower of Chesua, he had come to suspect that the Republic had not only forged much of history but had also intentionally buried the work of thinkers whose ideas did not support its purposes. Certainly most of his colleagues understood that the Republic had molded history to its liking. But they considered it their duty and a mark of their privileged position to go along and help keep the Republic's secrets. "Why question origins," they would argue, "when there is so much to discover about the future?" Barth believed otherwise. He argued that the truth belonged to everyone. But his shrewd political instincts let him know when to reveal what.

Everything Sylvia, Barth, and their secret society of Chesua followers discovered ran contrary to the present-day behavior of the Republic. While their discoveries inspired them to keep searching, practical considerations prompted them to keep the evidence to themselves. It didn't take long for Barth and his friends to conclude that the Republic had disposed of Chesua. This discovery drove them deeper into secrecy and bound them with greater devotion to Chesua's teachings and a greater desire to find out as much as possible about the disposal.

Today Barth was gathering up the pages of his handwritten acceptance speech when he received a call on his wayfone. "Yes, I'm on my way. Just pulling my talk together."

Barth slipped into his jacket and walked out of his office. He knew Zachaias would not only attend today's award ceremony, he'd also have to sit at the head table. His chief rival would have to smile and applaud as Barth used the award forum to needle him. "This will be so sweet," Barth gloated, recalling the words of the poet Ovid. "Some come to see. Some come to be seen."

Checking the readiness of his Rocco, Juve waited for the motosled to stop. The four-passenger vehicle whispered along just two fingers above the street. As the fat man with long, greasy hair and sunglasses opened its door and lumbered out, Juve remembered the first time he had seen a motosled. A young Auspex had stolen one and convinced Juve to help him sell it for parts. Now as he withdrew, out of view, into the alcove of the warehouse wall, Juve could hear the man waddle toward him with the help of a cane. Another six steps and the man would face the most important decision of his life.

From inside the alcove, Juve watched the cane appear, then the bulk of the man. With his next breath, the well-dressed man found himself pinned inside the shaded alcove, looking terrified into Juve's eyes.

"You're going to die now," Juve explained with a calm directness, "unless you want to spend the rest of your life in Zostok." The man's face darkened with even greater dread. "So you know Zostok," Juve smiled. "I'm in no mood to bargain with you. Make your next words count!"

"Take your hands off of me," the man sputtered, angering Juve as he felt the spittle land just above his upper lip. "I work for Bellator and . . ."

"So do I, and you've made it a lot easier for me," Juve smirked.

The man opened his mouth to speak but gasped and rolled his eyes as Juve's knife slipped expertly under his ribs and into his heart. Juve let his victim slump to the ground, then laid the fat man above the sewer grating inside the alcove. "Disposal, job sixteen." Then he wiped his face with the back of his gloved hand and walked quickly to the motosled. Before driving away, he saw that the cluttered Midland backstreet remained deserted. He waited a minute until the cleanup crew turned the corner and headed toward the alcove.

He knew about Zostok, Juve reassured himself. As he left the disintegrating Midland neighborhood, he felt relieved that he would not have to haul the fat man all the way to Zostok.

ZACHAIAS

THE MORNING GREETED ZACHAIAS ACILIUS DARKLY.
Though the sun rose brilliantly and the birds in his garden sang as merrily as
ever, Zachaias rose in dread. It took all of his energy to drag himself through
his morning ritual. His companion, Horatio, was making breakfast. Zachaias
could smell the familiar fragrances—percolating coffee, frying bacon, sizzling
eggs—but ever since the announcement of Barth's third Order of Lucretius,
not even his favorite aromas lifted his spirits.

As university students, Barth and Zachaias had caused many professors to
predict that they each would someday win the coveted Lucretius award. As
students they had collaborated on a project that came close to winning. Their
advisors urged them, for the sake of the Republic, to continue to collaborate.
Unfortunately the near-win had given each a taste of the fame and honor sure
to come. Neither liked the idea of sharing such an honor. Their remarkable
brush with glory marked the last time they would cooperate. Every achieve-
ment inflated each man's ego to the point where they could barely speak to
each other without trading taunts. Working together was unthinkable.

Zachaias stalked into the kitchen. Horatio could feel the encroaching
gloom without taking his eyes off the stove. His heart ached. Today his partner of seventy years would have to dress up, sit stoically at the head table,

and endure Barth's award ceremony. Horatio had to persuade him to measure this setback the way a good scientist should. "Good morning," he said after planting a kiss on his spouse's forehead. "I'm making your favorite." Zachaias forced a smile as he stepped up to the table, dragging his dark cloud of depression with him, and slumped into his chair.

After graduation, the careers of Barth and Zachaias dazzled their contemporaries, who began to bet which of the young scientists would be first to win the Order of Lucretius. The academic press took notice and started to keep score. The rivalry inspired imitators, and soon the imitators were placing bets. Students who bet on Barth tried to dress as neatly and act as smoothly as their hero. The opposing Zachaias faction worked at looking frumpy and acting as clumsy as their model.

Barth was polished, savvy, and charming, a crowd-pleaser. His smile and bravado bordered on arrogance, but he was likable. Zachaias, on the other hand, was all work. Despite his companion's advice, he took poor care of his personal appearance. His hair went uncombed, his fingernails collected evidence of his experiments. It was all Horatio could do to wipe the sleep from Zachaias's eyes before he left the house.

You could spot the Barts and Zakies on any campus. They engaged each other in spontaneous and formal debates. They played practical and sometimes cruel jokes on each other. Now the cruelest joke of all was on Zachaias. Barth had made a preemptive strike on his project and all the accolades that came with it. "You're a brave man, Zachaias," his partner said. "It must be next to unbearable having to face those hypocrites today."

When Zachaias continued to stare blankly at the table, Horatio spoke more sternly. "I won't let you beat yourself up over this, Zachaias. You stand heads above those fools. You received a Lucretius award only three years after you graduated. And then you were the first person to be awarded a second Lucretius award. Your time will come again!" Horatio turned back to his work at the stove and continued to coach his companion. "This is just a temporary setback. And for what? Quantum computing—a respectable next step but hardly a breakthrough."

"Thank you," Zachaias answered, "but I'm afraid I'm just not clever enough to play politics with these people."

"To hell with politics," Horatio retorted. "Let them have their little love-fest. Your achievements still outstrip Barth's by far. History will rank you far above him." The meat and eggs sizzled in the pan as Horatio tended it. "Look what you gave the world with your language chip—the ability to understand and speak any language on the planet. You've done more for human understanding than anyone in the world." Horatio turned to face his spouse, still staring, now toying with his fork. "It's a disgrace and an outrage for Barth to be considered for a Lucretius after stealing the TCI project from you. Taking it was unethical enough, but not sharing his results is criminal. Empathia guarantees . . . What's the article?"

"Right to Know," Zachaias muttered.

"Yes, Right to Know says clearly that the people make the Republic possible, and when our scientists open the doors on something new, we own it."

"I'm afraid Right to Know has deteriorated into Need to Know."

"Well, who needs to know more than other scientists?" Horatio was practically yelling. "We can't let one scientist monopolize such important information. They all need to work in the open, in the light!" Horatio felt tears coming to his eyes. "Let him gloat over his award. You've got your integrity." He turned back to his final breakfast preparations.

"Barth's in bed with Bellator. There's no telling what the two of them will do with TCIs."

"I think it's a cover. I think they're spending their time and the university's money on something else," Horatio concluded as he shoveled the breakfast onto a plate. "You're a good man, Zachaias. That's worth more than any award."

Horatio placed Zachaias's breakfast in front of him. Resting elbows on the table and his head in his hands, Zachaias stared at the plate.

CICERO CENTER

THE UNIVERSITY OF ROME FLAUNTED ITS POSITION AS THE world's preeminent institution of higher learning by erecting in the center of the expansive campus a monument to performance and spectacle—the Cicero Center. Nothing about the center was subdued or subtle. It rose five stories, then ten, then ten more, like a staircase for a giant. Great arms of traditional columns and arches embraced the lower floors. Out of this foundation emerged the shining ascension of stone and glass.

Inside, great halls yawned, dwarfing the massive monuments to Rome's greatest heroes. In any other setting, these statues would overwhelm anyone looking up at them. But in the great halls of the Cicero Center, they became almost as insignificant as their admirers. On this day, long lines of students, scientists, and government leaders had rolled in waves around statues of Julius Caesar, Marc Anthony, and Lucretius, all the way through to the more recent Roman greats as they poured into the main auditorium.

The soft glow over the audience faded as the stage lights went up. The master of ceremonies was wrapping up his introductory remarks. Before returning to the head table lined with dignitaries, he paused, and then continued. "It's difficult to conclude this introduction. Professor Barth has accomplished more than any other modern scientist we can remember. And

I have touched only the highlights. Today, having accepted the Order of Lucretius for an unprecedented third time, Professor Barth has agreed to talk about his award-winning development of quantum computing. And, as a bonus, he will also share some of his thoughts with regard to his current work on Time Continuum Intersections. Fellow citizens, I present to you Professor Barrios Barth."

The audience welcomed Barth to the dais. Nearly a third of them rose immediately to their feet in warm admiration. The rest followed their lead. Before Barth had gathered his papers and arranged them on the podium, the head table was standing as well. The last to stand, forcing a smile, was Zachaias.

"Thank you," Barth said with a satisfied smile. Then he nodded to the men and women at the table to his left, "Thank you." He looked at Zachaias to his right. "Thank all of you."

Barth began to speak. His audience listened with as much awe as respect. He could feel their admiration and eagerness to hear what he had to say. For that reason, he took his time, allowing them to feed, a spoonful at a time, from his bounty of knowledge. He knew an audience loved to have its beliefs confirmed. He knew this audience thought he was an intellectual god. Indeed, few could fully appreciate the magnitude of what he understood. So he would take this opportunity to help them appreciate the wonder of what he had discovered and use the time to infiltrate their minds with some of his beliefs.

Barth savored every moment of his audience's attention. His remarks on his award-winning accomplishment were brief, considering they represented the purpose of the event. Soon he was unfolding the story of his work on TCIs. Step by arduous step, he took them through his struggle with problems they could barely understand, much less appreciate. He gave them a taste of how it felt to end up in a scientific dead end. He had them laughing at his mistakes, even though few would ever approach the math and physics that had actually tripped him up. Finally, with his admirers hanging on his words, he brought them home. "And so it gradually became clear that far-removed points of time and space should occasionally intersect. When this happens, matter should be able to slip instantly from one point in time and space to another."

Throughout Barth's speech, Zachaias had endured his rival's gloating. But now, as Barth led them all to the top of the mountain, Zachaias absolutely seethed at having to follow. He could feel the resentment rising from his heart to his face. He feared someone would see just how much he detested everything about this fiasco. Zachaias wanted the books opened. He had come close to discovering TCIs and, when the project was swept out from beneath him, he had demanded that Barth publish his findings.

But Barth had worked with the Republic's chief counsel to have his results quarantined. Over time, the Empathia principle of Right to Know had suffered a number of amendments that gradually limited the once-cherished ideal of total openness with the idea of protecting the public from ideas that might cause confusion or alarm. "For the good of the Republic," Barth had argued.

"What an insult to Lucretius!" Zachaias had roared when he could not obtain the work. "Quarantining scientific results from the scientific community goes against everything the great man stood for."

Bellator, the Republic's powerful Second Minister, hand-picked by the First Minister, sat only a few seats away from Zachaias, but all his attention was on Barth. He grinned proudly as he listened to his friend of thirty years. The promotion of science came under Bellator's jurisdiction as chief counsel. He fancied himself something of an amateur scientist, having taught biology at the university level. He was proud of his association with the Republic's greatest genius and seldom failed to drop Barth's name whenever possible.

When he had heard that Zachaias had been assigned the task of understanding and controlling TCIs, he had summoned the scientist to his office. It was a brief interview. As soon as Zachaias sensed that Bellator's curiosity had to do with using TCIs to his own advantage, Zachaias terminated the interview. Furious, Bellator got in touch with Barth. Here he found a more agreeable audience. Barth was eager to work on TCIs, but as long as the project was assigned to Zachaias, he would lack the necessary funding. Bellator could supply the funding. In return he wanted control of TCIs. To the scientist Barth, this idea was reprehensible. To the politician Barth, it was a necessary evil. He had his own plans for TCIs, and not a lot of time to implement them.

I can convince Bellator that he has control, Barth told himself, *while I keep control.*

Now Barth would use the rest of his speech to assure his most powerful supporter that the research he was waiting for was in good hands. That the awesome power of Time Continuum Intersections would always belong first, foremost, and forever to the Republic.

"You're full of shit!" shouted the young man to the calmer youth at his side. "The Republic sells a ridiculous dream that's completely out of our reach."

"Go ahead," the other replied, "blame the government for your limitations, but I'm headed uptown."

The two continued their discussion as their friends rolled their eyes, bored with hearing the same debate Marius and Driscus eventually staged every time they disagreed on anything. Today a beggar had accosted the group of seven young men as they idled along the main street of Rome's Midland neighborhood. "If somebody has more than you," Driscus continued, pointing to a motosled silently hovering its way around the corner, "it's because they buy the dream. They've decided to go for a piece of it."

"I don't want a piece of it. I want all of it," Marius yelled, sweeping his arms to include the masses of second-rate buildings surrounding them. He eyed the approaching motosled—the latest and most expensive version—now followed by a second.

"That's why you'll always be wanting," Driscus explained condescendingly. "You can be a part of a bigger and better thing or you can be all of nothing." All of the young men followed the motosleds with a mixture of envy and resentment.

"Look at those assholes," Marius hollered, loud enough for the first motosled's passengers to hear. Then, with a gesture of defiance, he called out to them, invisible behind darkened glass, "If we were Forza, you'd get your butt beat."

"And tattooed," added another member of the gang. Driscus backed away, anticipating trouble. A couple more members of the group did the same. The remainder followed Marius as he stepped toward the lead motosled. "Hey!" he jeered. "You hear us? Forza would take that piece of shit, sell it for parts, and give the money to someone who needs it." Marius walked up to the driver's side of the first motosled and kicked it savagely. The vehicle rocked subtly side to side.

Inside the first vehicle, Auspex turned to Juve. "Time to teach these punks a lesson."

Juve smiled and shook his head. "Keep going."

Emboldened when the vehicles failed to even slow down, Marius and his part of the gang surrounded the motosled carrying Juve and Auspex. Both vehicles stopped, and immediately Pavo, Orso, and Crow jumped out of the second. Within seconds, Orso grabbed and lifted Marius into the air. Suspended horizontally above Orso's head, the young Midland street tough saw only the backs of his fleeing mates as well as Juve and Auspex emerging from their motosled. To the terrified young man's surprise, Juve seemed amused and ordered Orso to put Marius back on his feet.

"Let him go?" Orso protested.

"Yes, let him go," Juve repeated, giving Orso a signal with his eyes. "Didn't you hear him threaten us with the wrath of Forza?"

"Oh, no, not Forza," Orso replied in mock surprise as he placed his captive back on his feet.

Marius pulled himself together and challenged Orso. "That's right, fat boy. In this neighborhood, we don't drive motosleds, we chop them up for parts."

"Do you know anyone from Forza?" Orso asked him, his right fist clenching as his eyes marked the young challenger's nose.

"No, but they take care of us just the same," Marius replied confidently. Surrounding the first motosled, Auspex and Crow monitored the neighborhood. They were attracting attention.

"Time to go," Crow said to Juve, who signaled the crew to move out.

As a student of Forza's activities, Marius had read much of the information Forza made available on paper and electronically throughout the neighborhood, including instructions on how to break into the information and control banks of the Republic's treasury and the treasuries of certain corporations and move their funds into the accounts of citizens in need. He had studied as well earlier missives from Forza, which identified the most corrupt members of the Leadership. And he admired their policy of always striking upward at power and refusing to harm anyone weaker than themselves. *Of course!* he scolded himself angrily, *they weren't showing off in those motosleds. They stole them. They're on their way to sell them for parts.*

Orso joined Juve in the first motosled. As they glided toward the dismantling garage not far from where the Marius stood, Juve was explaining to his friend. "I let him go because he's on our side. As long as those little punks are doing our work, let them try to rough us up. If nothing else, it keeps us honest. Besides, that kid, if he isn't already, will be helping the same people we help someday. It's really this simple, Orso—they're either for us or against us."

THE FORUM

THE ASSIGNMENT WAS SIMPLE. MARIA MUST LEARN TO appear more confident. Anyone looking at her would wonder how a young woman as beautiful as Maria could lack confidence. Her face was framed with dark, wavy hair that flowed softly over her shoulders. The color of her eyes shifted between a rich emerald green and a deep earthy brown. The color changed with her expression and even, it seemed, with the position of the sun in the sky or humidity in the air.

Cato, Maria's acting coach, looked into her eyes as he gave her strict instructions on how to raise her confidence to a higher, professional level. "Maria, if I can't see it in your eyes, they won't see it in your face. You've got to convince your audience you have something to say to them."

"Okay, tell me what I have to do," she challenged him.

"I want you to be able to walk up to any stranger anywhere in the city and engage them in a conversation."

"I can do that."

"Not just once. Anybody can do that. You have to do it over and over again until absolutely no one intimidates you."

"Okay," she replied a little less enthusiastically.

"Not so sure about it now, are you?"

"I admit, it's a little intimidating, but I'll do whatever I have to do. I told you I want the anchor position, Cato."

"We'll see how badly you want it. Why don't you spend the afternoon looking around the university campus? You don't have to engage anyone today. Just get an idea of what it's going to take. Then I'll prepare you for the real thing tomorrow."

After graduating with advanced journalism and world history degrees, Maria had become a candidate for a position as news elocutor for Republic World, the official public source of news and information.

"What do you mean, prepare me?"

"There are techniques you can use to make random engagement easier. It's a skill, like anything else. You can learn it and get good at it." Cato studied Maria's face, waiting for her reaction.

"Do you understand why you have to do this?" he asked.

"Yes, I think I know," she answered testily.

"Why?"

"Because as a Republic World elocutor I'll have to interview some of the most intimidating people in the world."

"That's the easy part," Cato replied smugly. "They will be the cooperative ones. As an elocutor, you'll have to engage virtually everybody in the Republic, including some not-so-agreeable subjects."

"I think I'm tougher than you think I am, Cato."

"I'm not questioning your toughness. It's your credibility—your ability to appear authoritative and, at the same time, approachable. The public will accept you and believe you only if they see you as someone who could engage them casually on the street. You can't fake that attitude. You have to learn it. You have to earn it."

The wall behind Cato showcased pictures of him with the students who had made the grade—Republic World's most respected faces. Cato paused and studied Maria's reaction again.

"I have to learn it." She hesitated. "I have to earn it?" She echoed his instructions with a touch of sarcasm.

"Are you repeating everything I say just to be a smartass?"

Maria looked at her coach and with a wry, inquisitive look, replied, "Smartass?"

They both laughed and embraced warmly like old friends.

As she left Cato's office, Maria thought the university campus would be perfect. It always seemed to be alive with people near her age. Friendly, curious people, open to engagement. Yet Maria felt that she was wading into unfamiliar waters. Making friends had never been difficult for her. It just came naturally. But now that it was an assignment, now that she might actually fail at it, she questioned her ability.

As she approached the center of the campus, an open area called the Forum, she could feel her pulse quicken. Her mouth felt dry and her heart seemed to move up into her throat. She tried to concentrate on her mission, on the perfect day, the cloudless, bright blue sky. She could hear the comforting hiss of the Forum Fountain, a fastidiously preserved but technologically updated relic of Rome's earliest days. A shaft of white water as thick as a large tree crescendoed high above the heads of the campus community as they crisscrossed each other's paths. As if it vied for their attention, the water cascaded down and crashed into the surrounding pool. But only a few took time now and then to stop and enjoy its power and beauty. Maria noticed a young couple, their arms around each other's shoulders, seated on a bench, gazing into the liquid turbulence. They certainly didn't want to be interrupted.

If I'm not the kind of person who can contribute something to their experience, here in person, Maria asked herself, *how can I hold their attention on Republic World? I have to make myself believe I have something to say to everyone.* Nevertheless, she found herself avoiding several more opportunities to engage strangers. Annoyed with her reticence, Maria remembered that Cato had advised her to cut her teeth on someone not so intimidating, then to move on to more difficult subjects. A spry old man in a smart jacket strode toward her. She looked him in the eyes and smiled as he passed. He didn't even break his stride. He didn't seem to notice her pleasant smile. *Okay,* she told herself, *I'm going to speak to the next person I pass.*

She stopped and looked around and noticed that her security personnel—at least three men—each a few dozen paces away, had come to a halt as well. Turning to elude them, she tumbled into the arms of a surprised stranger. "There you go," he said, almost laughing as he set her back on her feet and propped her up for a second. "Just learning to walk?"

"Yes," Maria answered just as playfully. Quickly brushing her hair back, she added, "How am I doing?"

Intrigued by her beauty and friendliness, the young man replied somewhat warily, "Not bad."

Without hesitating, she continued trying to seem as engaging as possible. "Where are you headed?"

Now the man's eyes squinted, questioningly. "Not interested. Thanks." He turned to walk away and recognized an undercover Republic security guard watching them. The guard turned away guiltily.

"Hey, wait! I'm not a soother. If that's what you think."

He stopped, turned around, and saw Maria standing defiantly with a hand on her hip. Over her shoulder, he thought he detected another man observing them.

"How do you know about soothers?" he asked as he glanced away, scanning his surroundings.

"My name is Maria. I'm in the final auditions for Republic World."

"They call me Juve," he replied, studying Maria as she tried to hold his attention. "Does that explain the security?" he asked, indicating the men watching them.

"I need to meet someone." Maria smiled, ignoring Juve's question. "It's part of my training . . . to work on my credibility, which I don't really think I need to work on, but that's beside the point."

"I agree. Your confidence is fine. But how do you know about soothers?"

"Everybody knows about soothers."

"Hardly everybody."

"I don't like the idea of people faking kindness. Or anything else, for that matter."

"Even if it improves civil order?" Juve challenged her.

"Yes," she snapped back. "Too much order makes people weak and dependent."

"Are they happier when they have to sort through all the crap life throws at them and figure out for themselves what—"

Maria interrupted, hoping Juve was just testing her. "Fake kindness is bullshit, whether it's soothers hired by the Republic to make people smile, or pandering doctors who let dying people think they're going to live forever, or any other kind of smooth talker."

"I agree," Juve said with his second smile of the encounter. "And that's why you want to be a Republic World elocutor? To tell the truth?"

"I think I could bring integrity to the news."

"I'm sure you could."

"The tough part is keeping someone, anyone interested in what I have to say."

"Well, I'm not a soother either and I'm definitely interested," Juve assured her, "but I have to be somewhere." He smiled an uneasy smile, not quite sure of his next move. Maria returned the smile. He was surprised at the warm glow it aroused in his chest.

"Want to see the Verona Game?" Maria blurted out.

"Sure."

"I mean, tomorrow night, with me?"

Juve looked in the direction of where he knew he had to be. The security guards had disappeared. He turned back to Maria. He felt another wave of attraction, but reminded himself that he had sworn off romantic entanglements.

"What's the matter?" she challenged him. "Are you interested or not?"

"Of course," he answered bluntly. The thought of allowing this lovely woman into his life made his mind race with all the problems he knew would arise, but he still found it impossible to turn her down. "Tomorrow it is. Meet you there?"

"No. Let's go together. We'll meet at Theodosius station, Arch XII, around seven."

"Seven it is."

BARTH TOWER

"WHILE WE ARE ABLE TO PREDICT THE TIME AND LOCATION of Time Continuum Intersections, it would be much too dangerous at this point to do anything more than observe what may or may not appear or disappear from our time and place in the universe or arrive from some other place and time." A restrained but audible tremor of awe arose from the audience. Bellator began to nod subtly in approval. "Besides, our calculations lead us to believe that intentionally sending individuals back in time to tamper with past events could create catastrophic consequences. We currently describe these anticipated disasters as quantum cataclysms. Such events could cause irreparable interruptions in the smooth flow of time and space. Therefore any kind of work in this area must be strictly monitored and remain entirely secret. Knowing as little as we do about these mysterious phenomena, any unsupervised experimentation would be recklessly irresponsible, if not criminal."

The first to applaud was Bellator. The audience followed. As the applause subsided, Barth knew what he was about to say would infuriate Zachaias, because he had heard Zachaias say it. "This kind of secrecy goes against everything I've been taught," Barth said, trying to catch Zachaias's reaction out of the corner of his eye. Then he added the thought he knew would unnerve Zachaias and, if it were possible, tighten his bond with Bellator. "But nothing so potentially dangerous has ever come into the hands of the human race. Or, if I may quote our poet Pubilius Syrus, 'It's too late to ask advice when danger comes.'" Bellator rose to his feet in passionate approval. The audience followed suit. Barth drank in their approval and stepped down from the dais. He walked through the rest of the event as if in a dream. The familiarity of it all was very satisfying. After accepting his award and sitting through the conclusion of the ceremony, he waded through the adoring crowd, worked his way out the door, and walked across campus toward the office building built in his honor.

At first glance, Barth Tower appeared to be a simple, round, twenty-five-floor cylinder ringed with wide walkways. It was obviously a neat stack of offices, each opening onto the walkways and looking out over Rome and its surrounding hills. Upon closer examination, however, it became clear that the exterior walkways were not exactly level or perpendicular to the vertical thrust of the tower. They were more like string wrapped around a spool. An even more surprising effect met the eye inside. The twenty-five rings of offices also looked into the cavernous Barth Tower atrium, which was crisscrossed by a spectacular web of catwalks. None of the catwalks crossed over to the same floor or made a line through the center of the atrium. Each ascended or descended a floor or two above or below its opposite end at an almost awkward angle. Barth had insisted on this tribute to whimsy. It would force his people to respect the randomness of nature, he explained to his architects. "The way to understand nature is anything but orderly," he contended, "and an orderly environment is an awful distraction."

Barth further insisted that none of the floors or rooms be given numbers. This decision heightened each resident's sense of exploration, just as Barth had predicted it would. After a brief period of confusion and grumbling, Barth's people grew to respect the anarchy. They created names for every floor and catwalk. They prided themselves on learning and debating over the best routes from one point to another. Newcomers found the maze of walkways challenging and the directions from place to place daunting. "Take the catwalk two doors down from the office of Marius Antius over to the Juniper floor. Turn right and follow the balcony to the next catwalk and take it up to Virgo. Go left until you get to the first red door . . ." It was like finding your way through a jungle.

Barth assigned offices so that people who worked together were separated by several floors. The old man would reassign rooms whimsically on a regular basis. He wanted his people to move around and run into each other unpredictably. "That's the way nature works," he would say, "and nobody has ever surpassed the inventive power of nature."

Barth arrived, stepped into the main foyer, and looked up through the web of catwalks. His staff, all loyal supporters, were cheering him wildly, from seasoned scientists to eager students. They had watched his speech at the Cicero Center on the huge video monitors scattered about the rotunda at the bottom of the atrium. Barth nodded and bowed to his supporters, smiling broadly as the applause and cheers rolled over him. Waving his hands with both arms in the air, he made a complete circle, scanning the balconies. He could not escape, he realized, without sharing his thoughts with them.

When their applause settled to a spattering of pops and cracks, Barth gently stroked his goatee, unconsciously checking its length. "We all share the glory of this great day . . . ," he began, only to be silenced by an eruption of cheering and more applause. Barth accepted the love of his devoted staff with a twinge of sadness, knowing that his experiments with TCIs might cause him to leave them—maybe soon. He realized how rare it was to find support from so many intelligent and talented people. In the past six months, the old professor had created a labyrinth of clues that would ultimately lead some clever and trusted colleague on a step-by-step discovery of the research and conclusions from his extensive work.

When he could be heard again, he continued. "There's more work to do. I know you expected no less. As much work on safeguarding what we now know as what we will learn as we go forward. People will debate the prospects, the tremendous opportunities that await, and, of course, the potential for catastrophe that looms." He paused to let his words have their effect. "We stand at the crossroads, my friends, just as many of our great forebears have stood. With the great power we have at hand comes awesome responsibility. That's why it's our job as scientists to answer all questions about TCIs before they are raised to us. But I'm not going to lecture you today. This is a day for us to relish our victory but not to rest on our laurels." Barth made a motion with his right arm and from the wings on every level came waiters with bottles of wine and empty glasses. He raised his arms and his voice. "Today we play!"

For the rest of the afternoon, the finest Prosecco from the north of Rome sparkled and flowed freely. Barth reached out his hand. Someone placed a glass in it. He raised his glass to a thunderous downpour of appreciation. He emptied his glass and let both the admiration and the alcohol warm him. Even under the influence of both sedatives, he could not stop from reminding himself that time was running out. *What will they think if I disappear?* he wondered. *Will they put it all together?*

Everyone associated with Barth admired his devotion to his late wife. Most members of his staff sensed that he was guided by a set of principles more demanding than standard, professional ethics. Very few were privy to the source of Barth's principles—namely, the informal and secret society he and Sylvia had built around the scraped-together teachings of Chesua. While everyone working on his staff came under strict security clearance, Barth imposed even greater secrecy demands on his Chesuan confidants. He had a way of fathoming a person's depth of idealism and humanity, and invited into this exclusive circle only his most trusted friends. Recently he had started to watch a woman known to Barth as Octavia Grana, a professor at the University of Rome. She had worked with him for fifteen years and become one of his most trusted colleagues. Several months before this day's award celebration, Barth had taken Octavia to dinner and begun to introduce her to Chesuan principles, without naming them as such. Now he wondered if she were ready for the next step.

In the heat of the award celebration, Octavia caught Barth's attention. The noise made it difficult to hear, which made it easy to speak unheard. She shouted in his ear, "I've been thinking a lot about what we talked about a while ago."

Barth took Octavia by the arm and walked her to an alcove where they could hear each other. "Would you care to join me in my office?" he asked her.

"Of course," Octavia replied.

THE VERONA GAME

ARRIVING FIVE MINUTES EARLY WOULDN'T BE A PROBLEM, Juve told himself. A half hour early would be a problem. That would come off as too eager. But then, unless she was a half hour early, who would know? *This is ridiculous*, he scolded himself. *I've killed men in my sleep. Why am I worried about what this woman thinks?* Juve's thoughts were interrupted by the architectural beauty in front of him—Arch XII, a sweeping tribute to Roman art, engineering, and ingenuity. It looked a lot like the other eleven arches lining Theodosius station, but this evening, as Juve regarded its grace and stability, he found himself considering the work that must have gone into it. At the same time, he realized why he was unusually observant and sensitive to this time and place. He had to admit it. He very much wanted to see Maria. He fought against the aching feeling that she might have changed her mind. Every second felt like a minute. The scents, colors, and textures of everything around him were magnified and intensified. He could not remember ever wrestling with this kind of anticipation. Now he examined the intricate mosaic patterns in front of him. As he passed his hand over their irregular surface, Maria touched his shoulder. The beauty of the arch became irrelevant.

"Have I kept you waiting?" she asked with just the right touch of concern.

Even though his stomach tightened, Juve maintained his calm exterior. "No, I just arrived," he replied.

The train ride began with stolen glances, anxiety made sweet with the exhilaration of blossoming friendship. Juve broke the ice with news of a possible sciopero—not exactly a strike, but a slowdown by the transportation workers. Maria's response caught him by surprise.

"Yes, I heard," she said. "That's why I booked a room."

"You booked a room?"

"Not for us—for me."

"Oh . . ." Juve was nonplussed.

"At *least* for me." He was temporarily speechless. "If you play your cards right," Maria said, smiling, "I might let you sleep on the floor."

"Thanks," Juve said. "And exactly what card game are we playing?"

"No games." Maria laughed at Juve's tone. "I always book a backup room when I ride the train. You never know when there's going to be a sciopero. Especially when they've got the leverage of such a big game."

Maria was charming him with her easy repartee. *She's got spirit*, he thought, but decided to move the conversation away from sleeping arrangements. "I love the way these workers play the system." When she did not reply immediately, he added, "There are so many procedural rules they have to follow and, at the same time, there's the pressure to make their schedules." Maria nodded in agreement. "So when they want to stick it to management, all they have to do is go by the book, and suddenly the system's choked."

"It's brilliant," she said. "They start slowing down knowing that when they approach about ten percent efficiency, it's all over."

"And you can tell where every one of the passengers stands. The big shots get all hot and pissy, while the sympathizers kick back and enjoy the chaos."

"Verona's perfect for a sciopero, too. There's so much to do. All the shops and gelaterias. I love all the old Roman architecture."

When they arrived in Verona an hour later, Juve knew he was stricken. He hoped she felt as elated as he did as they walked to the stadium and learned from passersby that the transportation workers did intend to stage a sciopero that evening.

At the stadium they quickly found their section. Maria led the way with a gentle tug on Juve's hand. As they descended toward their seats, they could feel the crowd's anticipation. Everyone expected an unforgettable match. The two teams had fought their way to this championship game in an elimination tournament that lasted half the year. Now each player could almost feel the smooth, gold Republic Cup in his hands. The great tradition of raising it to the skies with teammates in tow was every boy's dream. Today the two finest teams were there to determine who was more worthy of the precious victory.

Juve had followed Sparta, "the team of destiny," not as a fan so much as a student of their fierce determination to always finish strongly no matter the odds. The Spartans were known for their ability to wrestle victory from the clutches of the most hopeless situations. Their opponents, München, were formidable. No one player stood out as a superstar. The team was built on discipline and tradition, every player big, strong, and capable.

Maria took stock of the size of München's players as they took their seats, close enough to hear the team psych themselves up. "You're as big as they are," she observed as they sat down. "Did you ever dream of playing?"

Juve smiled, glad that Maria refrained from marveling too much at the team's masculinity. "Of course I did, just like every other boy in the Republic. But I had other priorities."

Maria let the subject drop and turned her attention to the spectacle of the opening ceremonies. The sound and color of the patriotic display struck Juve as both glorious and vain. He was stirred with pride and anger—pride for the Republic's heritage, but anger at its present corruption. He didn't say anything, but he noticed Maria's jaw clench slightly as the most self-congratulatory stage of banner waving began.

The game of spheres was played with two inflated balls about the size of a man's head. Using only their feet, each team of nine players worked to kick a ball through one of two spheres, not much bigger than the ball, positioned three meters off the ground at either end of the turf field, a hundred meters long by thirty meters wide. Play began with both balls in the center of the field. Only the first ball through a sphere scored a point. After each score, play resumed with both balls in the center of the field.

A great variety of strategies came into play. A team might decide to control and drive both balls toward one goal or drive each ball toward opposite goals. Either way, the object was to get one ball through one sphere before its opponent scored on the opposite or same goal. A race to score at opposite goals became a breathtaking test of speed and shooting accuracy. Racing toward the same goal added layers of quickly shifting offensive and defensive tactics. A team could drive one ball toward one goal to force the other team to defend or steal the ball, while one player broke off toward the undefended opposite goal with the second ball.

As the balls were kicked off, Juve and Maria were swept up in the excitement and grew more and more delighted with the contest. As they cheered and exchanged comments, Juve was happy to find that Maria understood the game well enough to make it interesting and not enough to challenge Juve's own knowledge.

"I was here three years ago," she said at one point.

"When Demetrius made that eighty-five-meter run?" Juve asked.

"Yes," she exclaimed, "it was unbelievable. No one could catch him!"

"I know," Juve agreed. "I can't believe anyone could label him a liability to Sparta."

"How could anyone say that? That wasn't the only time he proved that he was invaluable. He always plays with such determination."

"I agree. It was his coach," Juve began to explain. "He and the Spartan coach didn't get along. He tried to hold Demetrius down. I can see if he had been hurting the team with his arrogance or something like that. I mean, in that case it's a coach's job to put him in his place. But the way he held Demetrius down—just for the sake of humbling him—I think that was bad for the team."

"And look what it did to them that season," Maria agreed.

The sports banter was endearing both of the spectators to each other. Their involvement went beyond cheering for great plays and complaining of errors. Maria was seeing in Juve a surprising level of sensitivity to the human side of the game. She could tell he saw the game as a reflection of life and that he possessed a well-developed appreciation for personal struggle and team spirit. Juve was charmed by Maria's appreciation for the outstanding stamina and highly developed skills of the players. She could tell a hard kick from a finessed shot.

As the two rode the highs and lows of the game with the rest of the stadium, the game teetering many times on the brink of giving one team a winning advantage, time finally ran out. Each team showed one point on the scoreboard. An extended period of play followed almost immediately. The first to score would win the game. One mistake at this point would cost one of the teams the Republic Cup—and one moment of inspiration could win it. Juve looked over at Maria and saw that she was completely absorbed in the game. At the same time, he noticed Orso and Auspex trailing a Leadership official up toward the restrooms or concessions.

Auspex and Orso followed the man to the restroom and waited outside, where Pavo stood guard. A nod from Pavo let the other two know that the man was alone. When they heard a toilet flush, Auspex and Orso pulled on masks and slipped inside. In a series of precisely choreographed moves, Auspex stepped behind the man and clutched his neck in a way that immobilized and silenced him. Then Orso threw the full weight of his massive body into a volley of precision punches the astonished Leadership official would never forget. "Remember," Auspex whispered sternly into the man's ear, "we don't rule the world, we just adjust the ones who do!" With a chop to the man's neck, he knocked him out. As Orso helped him carry the unconscious man over to a urinal, Auspex removed the victim's wallet and keys. Orso pulled the man's pants to his ankles, while Auspex handcuffed him to the urinal. Then, with his handheld tattoo gun, Orso branded the Forza face on their victim's rump. In the next second, the two had removed their masks and were casually leaving the restroom.

On the field, each team took a ball and raced to opposite goals with eight men. The ninth man on each team ran with the opposing team in an attempt to interfere with their shot at the goal. München shot first and missed. Sparta was about to shoot when the München defender snatched the ball and drove with a kick just beyond the middle of the field. Now both balls were at the goal to the left of Juve and Maria. With everyone in the stadium standing and screaming, a München player snagged the incoming ball and shot it at the left goal. Another miss. In seconds all eighteen players were scrambling over two balls—all except one München player, who hung back near the center. One of his teammates heard his signal and drove the ball to the center. All alone, the München player ran toward the right goal and set up his shot. While seventeen players fought for control of the other ball, the München player shot. As his ball arched, certain to be swallowed by the right goal, Demetrius fired the other ball from within the melee of players. His ball moved faster with a shorter distance to travel. It hit its mark a split second before the München ball.

"See!" Juve screamed. "See what I mean about Demetrius?"

"Yes! He's unbelievable!" Maria screamed as they joined the celebration pouring onto the field from all corners of the stadium.

THE SOUFFLÉ

"HAVE A SEAT," BARTH SAID, WARMLY GESTURING OCTAVIA TO the chair at the side of his desk. "Tell me what's on your mind."

"Did you hear what the dissidents have done in the last couple of days?" she asked.

"Another Forza scherzo, I understand," Barth answered, his gaze drifting to the office windows to his right. "Pretty nasty, they tell me."

"Yes, they got the advocate general."

The old man sprung from his chair and took three steps over to the window overlooking the campus. A wasp had attracted his attention, flying repeatedly into the windowpane from the outside. It stopped, climbed up and down in an erratic pattern, then attempted to fly through the window again. Barth tapped his finger on the glass where the wasp attacked the other side. "I'm a little hungry and I don't want to eat with the crowd out there," he said distantly. He dismissed his impromptu wasp experiment. "Why don't we whip something up in my kitchen while we talk about this?"

"Why not," Octavia replied with just as much enthusiasm as she followed Barth from his office into the next room. A sense of privilege raised her spirits as she surveyed the simple but very serviceable kitchen. No one she knew had ever bragged about an invitation into Barth's kitchen. Yet here she was. The room was clean and sparse, white and silver, with plenty of working space. On one wall near a round table hung a writing board peppered with notes. A tall window over the sink looked out on the campus.

As soon as she got home after that dinner with Barth a few months ago, Octavia—or Cela, as her comrades in Forza knew her—had reported the scientist's revolutionary conversation to Juve, the leader of the group. She had told him she thought he and Barth were kindred spirits. As she had expected, Juve had urged caution. But over the intervening weeks, Octavia had built her case for bringing the Republic's most celebrated scientist into the confidence of Forza Facia. "There's virtually no limit to the ways he could help us," she had insisted. Finally Juve had agreed to let Octavia build a bridge to Barth if and when she judged the time was right.

"I can tell you, Octavia, and it may surprise you, that I'm inclined to support these rebels," Barth offered as if their conversation in the office had not been interrupted. "I mean, I understand them."

It took Octavia a second to realize what he was talking about. "No, I'm not really surprised," she replied, watching Barth pull down a large, worn book from the shelf over a long counter.

"You're a good judge of character, then," Barth observed. He stared at the ceiling while he fussed over his goatee with his right hand. "I've watched our Republic's greatest principles get whittled away by vain, unscrupulous, over-ambitious thugs lining their nests at the expense of the public." Barth stopped fussing with his goatee, looked at Octavia, and suggested brightly, "Let's make a soufflé?"

"A little tricky, but sure," she agreed, pleased with the selection.

Barth moved to the counter and continued as if he were lecturing a class. "These . . . these insurgent troublemakers are much more than just pranksters. They're getting at something, though I haven't quite figured it out yet." He looked at Octavia and remembered what it had been like to wrestle over these kinds of questions with his wife. He spoke fondly. "What do you make of them, my dear?"

Octavia considered and chose her words carefully. "If they do nothing else, they're letting the rest of us know we don't have to settle for not having what we need."

"I agree," Barth replied, delighted with her observation. "Especially not in a society as prosperous as ours." He began to arrange ingredients on the counter. "Would you get us four eggs, please? And it looks like now they're putting some people on notice."

Octavia felt her caution giving way as she opened the refrigerator and scanned its contents. The box was well stocked, clean, and neatly arranged. "Does someone take care of your kitchen, Professor, or are you this organized?"

"Yes, I have help. And please call me Barth," the great scientist requested as he pulled a canister down from the cupboard over the counter. Octavia gazed warmly at the man working at the counter. It was time to let Barth know more, she decided, as he struggled with the canister lid.

Octavia selected four eggs from the refrigerator shelf and brought them over to her host. Barth popped the stubborn lid off the canister just as she was about to offer help. As she placed the eggs among the other ingredients, Barth stopped and admired her endearing, youthful beauty. Octavia's short, red-brown hair flowed in a subtle curve from the top of her head, framing her intense green eyes, until it bounced playfully around the nape of her lightly freckled neck. Tiny freckles began around her eyes and disappeared from her cheeks, only to reassert themselves on her neck and shoulders before they retreated under her blouse. Barth found it difficult not to admire her lively, feminine features. There were plenty of intelligent young women willing to spend time with the old professor. Many were willing to share more than their time. But he had taught himself some time ago to guide his waning lust toward inspired admiration. It was often difficult. This afternoon, his spirits riding high, it was more difficult than usual.

"These dissidents remind me of the man my wife and I have studied and admired over the years." Barth brought a mixing bowl to his workspace. "You've heard me talk about Chesua, no doubt."

"Yes, of course," Octavia replied. "And I'm intrigued."

"The story of Chesua," he began as he dipped several spoons of sugar into the mixing bowl, "has been obscured by the centuries, I'm afraid. In the first place, there is no official written record. Chesua was one of many prophetlike characters who rebelled against the established way of running things a few thousand years ago."

Octavia understood that she was about to hear a lecture from the great scientist. She decided to hear him out as she quickly scanned the recipe on the face of the old, open book. She would gladly have sat through a lecture on some arcane branch of physics, but she was about to hear Barth speak on a richly human and thoroughly understandable subject, a subject the old man pursued with a singular passion. His enthusiasm was intoxicating. As she listened she resolved to make the soufflé project run as smoothly as possible. Seeing that the recipe called for vanilla, she began opening cupboards until she found a collection of spices from which she retrieved a bottle.

"While the Empire, under Augustus, was establishing the Principate, Judea was teeming with prophets. Some attracted great, devoted bands of followers. All of these groups offered some kind of mental escape, some mysterious set of ideas that offered psychological relief as a kind of remedy for the general misery of their followers." Barth walked over to the oven and entered a series of commands into its control panel. Octavia began to spread butter over the inside of the soufflé bowl.

"Our official history glosses over it, but it's a fact—we were pretty rough on the people we ruled before Flavius Aurelius and Empathia. And in the case of Judea and the Jews, we were downright heavy-handed. We had this convenient technique for silencing the most dangerous dissidents, called crucifixion. You've heard of it?"

"That's where they nailed people to crossed beams of wood," the young woman answered as she handed him the prepared bowl.

"Exactly," Barth replied, taking the bowl, inspecting it, and nodding his approval. "We'd hang them right out in the open for everyone to see. It was effective for keeping some would-be troublemakers in line, but for every dissident we crucified, ten more were born. And the population would always go with them. 'If we can't have heaven,' they seemed to say, 'we'll raise hell.' I think that's from Virgil."

Barth spoke into the refrigerator as he selected cheese. "Of course, none of them really wanted to be crucified, so every new wave of reformers came up with better ways to rebel. Some were more effective than others. But the point is, we lost generations of men and women who could have been productive citizens. We guaranteed that they would never wholeheartedly cooperate with the Republic." Barth emerged with a block of cheese and a grater and walked over to Octavia, who was carefully separating egg whites from their yolks, and answered the question she was about to ask. "It was a quick and easy fix. Cruelty is the first symptom of lazy leadership. And crucifixion actually did help keep the Jewish leadership in line. It persuaded them to encourage social order and cooperation. Even though they quietly despised their occupiers, they wanted to protect their people. So they urged them to lie low and keep quiet."

"More lazy leadership," Octavia interjected.

"Precisely!" Barth agreed. Octavia could tell her cooking partner was pleased with her insight as well as her ability to separate eggs. He began whipping her egg whites with a passion. "So, as usual, the impetus for reform came from the people who had the least to lose—the people who had lost brothers, sons, and fathers to the crucifix. They came up with all kinds of reactions. Some worked alone, ambushing soldiers, poisoning food, burning buildings." He paused to test the expanding mixture, then continued whipping. "Some tried to escape into alternative subcultures and occupied themselves with drugs and orgies."

Barth looked at Octavia, raised his eyebrows, and allowed her to glimpse the glint in his eye. She was delighted to see him play with the idea of drugs and orgies with such childlike innocence. "Others went the other way," Barth continued, "cloistered themselves in secret societies, and lived horrible lives of self-denial, celibacy, prayer, fasting, and a search for personal enlightenment." He took a break to test the mixture, saw that it needed more work, and resumed his whipping. "Of course, none of the reactions, as you can imagine, had anything to do with embracing the Republic or learning how to cooperate."

"So the Republic lost on every level," Octavia observed. "Everything we were doing raised the level of dissent. Kind of like today."

"Except that a thousand or so years ago," Barth replied, again examining the egg-white mixture, "we had Flavius Aurelius—someone smart enough to express why it was counterproductive to keep tightening the screws."

Barth dipped his whisk into the mixture and raised it slowly. Tips of white froth clung to the whisk, broke away as the whisk stretched them to their limit, and stood up straight. The soufflé makers smiled brightly at each other. Barth made his next point with a shake of the white-tipped whisk. "Flavius saw that the Republic was fighting ideas. And that some of the ideas they were up against were stronger than all the brutality the Republic could dish out."

"Isn't that always the case with new ideas?"

"Absolutely. Flavius struggled for years just to get Empathia adopted by Tiberius. And then, nothing really changed. You have to completely discredit the old ideas that get in the way of the new idea. Cicero said, 'Sticking to what they think has never helped political leaders.' Today we rule the world, but back then we ruled only the known world. And it's what we didn't know that kept us from implementing Empathia. It wasn't until 1345, when we came across the Incas and saw something like Empathia actually working . . ."

Octavia interrupted, "Hold on! The Incas?"

"Yes, yes, the Incas," Barth assured her. "Schools no longer teach this, but when we discovered the Great Western Continent, we encountered people as advanced in many ways as we were. The Incas were way behind us in many ways. They were claiming to communicate with gods under the influence of hallucinogens, for example. On the other hand, when the Incas encountered a new culture, they shared their gods, and treated the people remarkably well." The professor posed now, imitating an Incan general, holding up a spatula like some official staff of authority. "If we fail to spare our enemies, it will be our loss. They and all that belong to them will soon be ours, so treat all of it as if it already is."

"Makes perfect sense," Octavia noted.

"Still, it took twenty years for the Great East-West Alliance and another thirty before Rome started to apply Empathia as policy universally."

"But didn't Flavius put it in writing five hundred years earlier?" Octavia knew her question was more of a comment, so she took it a step further. "How do you think Flavius managed to come up with ideas so ahead of his time?"

"My wife Sylvia asked herself the same question," Barth replied warmly as he gently guided the freshly whipped mixture with a spatula into the bowl Octavia had buttered and now held for him. "We were taught that Flavius was inspired by Stoics like Seneca the Younger and some of the Greeks . . ."

"Yes, but none of them go nearly as far as Flavius ended up going," Octavia added as she held out her hand to request the spatula from Barth.

"That's correct," he agreed, handing her the spatula. "Sylvia was convinced that it was just too big of a leap for even a great thinker like Flavius. There was just no reason for Flavius to go so far without some extraordinary external influence."

Octavia smoothed the top of the final concoction with tender, circular motions. "And that's what sent her off looking for the source."

"Yes," Barth answered as he seemed to lose himself in the hypnotic motion of Octavia's spatula. "'Think about it,' she would say, 'We're doing just fine. The Jews are troublesome, but they're contained. We face similar uprisings here and there throughout the empire, but we're able to keep a lid on all of it. Then, all of a sudden, his boss Tiberius comes up with a set of principles advocating the direct opposite of what had gotten the Republic to where it was.'" Barth turned to Octavia with the warm glow of nostalgia still in his eyes. "Sure, there were some strategies having to do with accommodating conquered people to some degree or another, but nothing like Empathia," he said, walking over to the oven. "Have you come across the Code of Isaac in your studies?"

"Never heard of it."

"Well, it's where Empathia gets the Blood Ballot, for example. I realize it's meaningless today, but in its original version, adopted from the Hebrew tradition, every Roman senator who voted for any kind of combat action had to have a son or daughter—a blood relative—among the fighting forces." Barth paused and posed again, "Tiberius was the first to say, 'It only gets better if we all go together.'"

"And if they had no children?"

"They weren't eligible to vote for war or any operation that might involve bloodshed. Although, they could still vote against," Barth said as he marched the bowl containing the soufflé to the oven. "Mind you, over the years the Blood Ballot was gradually downgraded. The blood relation phrase was stretched to include more and more distant relatives, and then adopted children. Senators paid mercenaries to become adopted children. At one point all they had to do was donate a drop of blood in order to vote yes. I think today one member of the senate must have one child in some kind of public service. It means nothing anymore."

Octavia opened the oven door. "In any case," Barth concluded, "you might give a man like Flavius some credit for something like Empathia, but you have to wonder where he came up with the ideas like the Blood Ballot. Do you realize that Flavius even included limits on the disparity of personal income!" Barth placed the soufflé preparation on the rack. "Sylvia used to say it seemed to come out of nowhere. 'Whose shoulder was he looking over?' I remember her asking me in those days. She believed that if she could find the sources of Empathia, we'd have something powerful in our hands—something we could use to get the Republic back on track."

"Is Chesua the source of Empathia?" Octavia asked as she closed the oven door and he set the oven controls.

There wasn't an immediate answer from Barth. He hesitated, proud of his new accomplice. "Maybe," he replied mysteriously. "Sylvia uncovered the Essenes—one of those celibacy cults—in the work of Pliny the Elder and others. Their ideas resembled Empathia, but not closely enough for Sylvia. She kept digging until she found references to Chesua in some notes written by Flavius. It seems that he may have spent some time with Chesua. If not Chesua, then someone who followed him. In any case, it's not until after these references to Chesua that his notes show his first really revolutionary thinking."

"Could be coincidence."

"Spoken like a true scientist, Octavia," Barth replied admiringly. They both sat at the kitchen table. "That sequence alone would never have convinced us either." He placed his hand invitingly on his young guest's arm. "Would you care for an apéritif?"

"That would be nice. Yes."

Barth went to a cabinet and returned with a bottle and two glasses. "Well, we searched everything we could find about anyone who might have known Flavius." He carefully poured two drinks. "Eventually we turned up a small group of people who made reference to Chesua and his teachings. Sylvia collected and sorted it all out and came up with a set of Chesuan principles. When you compare them to the principles Flavius outlines in Empathia, you can't miss the resemblance." Barth raised his glass.

"Still . . . ," Octavia paused before raising her glass to challenge the central premise of Barth's beliefs, "a lot of similar ideas must have been floating around in those days."

"Indeed." Barth nodded approvingly. Octavia touched her glass to Barth's. "To Lucretius."

"Yes, good old Lucretius. Thank you."

They sipped and Barth sighed before continuing. "We think Chesua absorbed a lot of ideas from the Essenes. It seems that if you wanted to hold onto a following in those days, your belief system had to have a few mandatory tenets. Your prophet or messiah had to have a certain pedigree, had to be a man, had to be born of a virgin, and you had to promise eternal life after death."

"That's a pretty tall order." Already she could feel the glow of the alcohol.

"Not really." Barth began to count on his fingers as he made each point. "There were no real birth and death records, so you could claim just about any kind of lineage."

"So why wasn't there a messiah on every corner? Or was there?"

Barth paused to let the apéritif do its work for a few seconds. His smile indicated his approval of the drink. "The job had no real benefits. If you enjoyed any adulation, you certainly attracted as much ridicule. There were not very many perks and you could end up dead. Messiahs had to be truly driven by incredibly strong beliefs and a fiercely determined sense of mission."

"Or crazy." She sipped again, taking in the rare aroma of the fine drink.

"Oh, they all had to be delusional. No doubt. But their madness or, more kindly, their peculiarity only enhanced their charisma. Which won them lots of fawning followers, which bolstered their confidence and gave them more charisma, which made their followers more susceptible to all kinds of seduction."

"That's a lot of power for one man to handle."

"Most men couldn't earn that kind of following unless they were utterly dedicated. Although we did dig up some charlatans. But, for the most part, the messiahs were a pretty crazed bunch. And we think Chesua was exceptional this way."

"Exceptional in what way?"

"Chesua advocated a simplified and a more humanized interpretation of the Hebrew law. He boiled it down to loving your fellow man, including your enemies."

It was quiet for a minute as Barth and Octavia looked at each other. Barth smiled. Octavia was ready to let him in on Forza. The brandy had made both of them feel even more at ease with each other, but she decided to let him tell her more about Chesua before suggesting that he meet Juve. Besides, Barth was in high gear. Teaching was as natural to him as breathing. She enjoyed learning from him and loved to watch him practically dance as his ideas formed, churned, and flourished in front of her.

"First, we have to understand one thing about nature," Barth asserted as he walked to the kitchen writing board. He wiped it clean with wild, dashing strokes, then wrote, "Nothing changes without pain," as high on the board as he could reach. He read his own words out loud as he underlined the entire statement and circled the word *pain*.

What does this have to do with Chesua? Octavia thought.

As if he could read her mind, Barth turned to her and answered, "To appreciate Chesua, we really need to set him in his context." He drew a horizontal line across the board. "And that will take us to Judea almost eight hundred years after the founding of Rome." He made a short mark across the horizontal line near its left end. "We think Chesua was born around 750." Again he marked the line. "So he's just a boy when Augustus dies and Tiberius succeeds him." The board bore several marks and the names *Augustus* and *Tiberius* along what was becoming a time line of early Roman history. Completely in his element, Barth lost himself in pedagogy.

"Remember how Augustus tried to legislate morality? He instituted laws to discourage ostentatious displays of wealth. He punished childlessness as well as adultery. There was something afoot that our official history doesn't really address. The arts flourished as never before. We were given Virgil, Horace, Ovid, and Livy . . . and, of course, Flavius."

The aroma of the soufflé began to play with Octavia's nose. She drew a deep breath and felt her stomach respond with an urgency to eat.

"Under Tiberius, Flavius approached Empathia from the angle of pain." Barth also took a deep breath. "That smells good, doesn't it?"

"Yes, it does." Octavia's answer betrayed her hunger. "How much longer?"

Barth went over to the stove and read the control panel. "Nine more minutes. Let's get something to hold us over." He opened the refrigerator door and scouted the shelves. Octavia got up and joined him in his search. Standing side by side with the cool air rolling over their feet and the brandy running through their brains, the two began to feel indifferent to everything but food.

"Nine more minutes," Octavia repeated. Barth looked over at the stove. "Eight." They both laughed without taking their eyes off the contents of the refrigerator. Barth put his arm around Octavia and squeezed her shoulder. She reached around his back and rested her hand on his hip. "Well, Octavia, see anything you like?" Barth asked.

"Well, Barth . . . ," Octavia began. She chuckled, "That feels okay—calling you *Barth*, that is. I thought it would feel strange, but it doesn't."

"Octavia." Barth pronounced the name slowly and carefully. "Now that's a beautiful name."

"You can call me Cela, if you like. It may not sound like a big deal, but it is."

They both gazed silently into the refrigerator for another minute. Barth tried out the new name. "Cela . . . how do you get that from Octavia?"

"It doesn't come from Octavia. It's a code name."

"What do you mean, a code name?"

She turned and looked her new confidant in the eyes. "Nobody knows my code name but you . . . ," she prepared herself for his reaction, "and all the members of Forza Facia."

Barth froze for a second, utterly taken aback. "Oh, I see," he said as he reached into the refrigerator, pulled out a covered dish, and led Octavia over to the table. She watched his face as he placed the dish on the table, let her take her seat, and eased himself into the chair next to her. When he looked up, he was beaming. She returned his smile with a great sense of unburdening. Barth lifted the lid off the dish and uncovered an array of crisp vegetables, slices of meat, fish, sausage, and cheeses. Even cold, she could smell their fresh aromas infused with tantalizing spices. "Dig in, Cela!" Barth commanded and she obeyed, hungrily grabbing one delicacy after another. Her host got up and returned with plates and napkins. "Five more minutes," he reported on his way past the oven. Barth interrupted their foraging by raising his glass of brandy for a toast. Octavia complied. "To your health, Octavia!" he proclaimed as their glasses touched. "If you don't mind, I prefer to call you Octavia."

"To yours!" rejoined Octavia, "whatever you choose to call me." They both emptied their glasses and Barth poured a second round. Then, as if nothing had happened, he continued his exposition of Chesua.

"You know, Octavia, we see all sorts of pragmatic justifications pointing to Empathia long before Flavius committed it to writing. But nothing urged anything as revolutionary."

By the time they had discussed the letters of Tiberius to his peers and how he had always encouraged them to use restraint and compassion in governing,

Barth had mitted his hands and was pulling a perfectly bloomed soufflé from the oven. Octavia sang its praises as he served it steaming and exploding with rich fragrance. They both ate slowly, savoring each bite. Barth had opened a gloriously harmonious wine, which they shared as they dined and delved into the fine points of winning over dissidents and incorporating conquered people. They discussed the present-day Republic and the role of Forza. Then they moved to General Tullia and the early Roman Principate coming to terms with an expanding empire. Then they pushed aside their dinnerware and focused on the wine and conversation.

"Tullia contended that for Rome to succeed as ruler of the world, she would have to do more than satisfy the physical needs of the people it brought into her realm," Barth continued. "Conquest was insufficient. People could not live without a sense of hope and the feeling that they had some say about their future."

Barth jumped up and wiped away everything he had written from the board. Holding his wine in one hand, he wrote furiously with the other. Octavia watched contentedly and settled in to enjoy the music of Barth's amazing mind. Before he began, he looked at her with a boyish grin. "Cela, eh?" he said, and then he shook his head as if he had made a discovery.

STREETS OF VERONA

"TELL ME ABOUT SCHOOL," JUVE ASKED MARIA AS THEY walked from the game to the hotel where they would stay. Maria tried to get Juve to talk about his work. He was generally evasive, which made her a little uncomfortable, so she decided that candidness on her part might disarm him. Going first had always been her way. While others would make a tiresome game of getting to know each other, Maria always opened up easily with someone she liked.

"Right now I'm finishing my thesis," she reported. "If you care to know more about the Roman incorporation of Islam, I can probably put you to sleep."

"Actually, I'm interested."

"How interested?" Maria replied, looking at Juve with a wry smile. Juve caught himself laughing and looked away, surprised at how quickly he was warming up to this woman. A warm breeze lifted the leaves on a row of trees along the walkway to their left. Juve was pleased that the people they passed took so little notice of Maria and him as a couple. How that contrasted with the way he felt. He wanted to tell every stranger what it felt like to walk with her, but he wasn't sure he could find the words. It was difficult enough dredging up facts from his Roman history classes in order to respond to Maria's question.

"Well, as I remember, as the Republic moved east, it found people around the Euphrates River area who were more resistant to incorporation than most," Juve began. "If this is a history test, I'm warning you, I've got a general sense for things but not specifics. I might fail."

"No, but I'd like to see what you know, so I know what to fill in."

"You could probably fill all night."

"Don't worry about it," Maria assured him with a hand on his shoulder. "Most people know so little about the history of our Republic. That's why I love digging around in it."

Juve gave her a quizzical look. Before he could ask, she answered his question. "No, it's more that I want to help set the record straight. Believe me, it matters. So what were you taught about how we incorporated the Muslims?"

"Not much. Just that we eventually conquered them, but I'm not sure I know how. Tell me about it."

Maria hoped silently that Juve's interest was sincere. She had been seduced into spilling her guts before, only to find her listener had ulterior motives. "So you are familiar with Incorporation?"

"Yeah, after Flavian, right?" Juve offered.

"Flavius."

"Under Tiberius."

"Yes, Tiberius made it happen. He was emperor," Maria explained, "but Flavius devised Incorporation and worked out all of the theory."

"That's right, Incorporation comes under Empathia."

"See, you know what's going on," she teased.

Juve felt himself more deeply attracted to Maria as she expounded so effortlessly. Her eyes let him know she was interested only in sharing what she had learned and not at all in showing off what she knew. He drank it up. It was as if she was filling an empty part of him, the part he had neglected. Until now, he had been interested only in what went on around him, not much in why. "That's all I was taught. I'm sure there's more," he said, his tone encouraging her to continue.

"After Tiberius, we no longer conquered anybody in the old-fashioned way. You know, marching in and killing anybody who resisted. Instead, we began to incorporate them, following Empathia doctrine." It suddenly occurred to Juve that Maria not only knew things he didn't know, but also that what she knew was about to plow up and till a big, empty chunk of terrain in his mental landscape. "But the Muslims put up the greatest challenge," Maria continued. "They were fiercely tribal and fanatical believers, each clinging to his own version of their creed."

The two young amblers had arrived at the hotel, but at the door, Juve suggested they visit a gelato vendor stationed across the street and take a few more turns around the neighborhood before checking in. Maria's face broke into a smile that told him he had made a romantically wonderful suggestion. They hurried across the street. The vendor recognized immediately that he was serving a pair of new lovers and easily talked them both into taking bigger servings than they would have ordered. As Maria and Juve wandered away with their small mountains of gelato in crisp shells of baked sugar, she resumed her lecture on Roman history.

"It was a brilliant plan, really. Maybe the best execution of Incorporation ever. The First Minister, Petrus Marcus, sent in emissaries, who met with the top Islamic scholars, respectfully and humbly asking to be schooled in the Qur'an and the Sunna—Islam's principal sources of revelation and interpretation." Maria stopped in her tracks to emphasize her point. "This is where it gets good," she said as she licked a little stream of melting gelato from the back of her hand and walked on. Juve watched her enjoy her treat and smiled secretly to himself as she continued. "The emissaries quickly identified a number of contradictory interpretations in the Muslim doctrine. Remember, it's a new religion. They're making it up as they go. They see the Jews around them with one, all-powerful God, so they've got to have one, all-powerful God. They see a flood and a set of commandments, and a creation story—the works. But they're not agreeing among themselves yet. The different tribes each have their own ethnic traditions and they've already begun to teach their followers different ways to wash their hands . . ."

"Wash their hands? You mean literally wash their hands?" Juve questioned Maria as he, too, was forced to lick the gelato running down the back of his thumb.

"Yes, literally, wash their hands," Maria explained, grabbing Juve's hand. She pretended to wash one of his hands with her free hand and got some of his gelato on her fingers. "It was crazy before we brought science to some of these people." Maria licked Juve's streams of gelato off her fingers but stopped to hold up her hand—a gesture meant to prevent him from interrupting while she cleaned her hand. "The Jews wouldn't eat pork," she continued, "so the Muslims banned it, too." As she finished licking her fingers, he took her moist hand and pretended to inspect it, but she continued, "You wouldn't believe some of the rules primitive people followed before we came in. The Muslims even banned alcohol."

"Based on what?" Juve asked, now forced to take a big bite of cold gelato to stanch a river of sweet cream from running down his arm. Playfully Maria ran her finger up the river on Juve's arm, stopping at his wrist. After sucking her finger clean, she went on. "Based on what their holy books said. Believe me, that's not the strangest part. Before science, people would make women stay in a room during their periods. Their husbands couldn't even touch them."

"That's nuts." Juve thought for a moment, as fascinated with what he was learning as he was occupied controlling the flow of gelato in his hand. "We probably have some dumb rules that have survived scrutiny," he observed.

"I think you're right," Maria agreed. "That's the good thing about Incorporation. We took a big burden off some of these people. On the other hand, we also took whatever they had that we could use."

"Took?" Juve asked, trying to measure just how Maria felt about the more larcenous aspects of Incorporation.

"Okay, assimilated," she offered, and welcomed Juve's nod of approval. "We got our numbers from the Arab Muslims. Did you ever try to multiply with old Roman numerals?"

They had drifted into a part of the city where the streets were still well lit, but groups of people were fewer and farther apart. Juve knew Verona was safe, but he still felt like Maria's protector. Still savoring his gelato, it occurred to him that Maria was offering something that could protect him. *She's like the streetlights*, he thought, *illuminating my picture of the world, showing me how to subdue a people without military force*. "People only do wrong in the dark," he blurted out.

"What do you mean?"

"I'm sorry." Juve caught himself. "I interrupted you."

Maria paused. They both heard the shuffle of feet and playful laughter of several young voices. As they turned the next corner, they saw a fresh new Forza face on a wall. The discarded spray can still wobbled and came to rest by the time they spied it. "But what did you say?" Maria probed, still gazing upon the Forza face, "about people in the dark?"

"I was thinking about the streetlights and how, when everything's out in the open, people tend to behave."

"Yes, exactly!" she exclaimed, almost tossing away her gelato as she raised her hands in agreement. "That's what I want to do on Republic World. There's so much that needs to be exposed. It's not like we have to grab people, take them out, and rough them up. If we just show everybody what they're doing . . ." Maria switched her gaze from the still wet graffiti image to Juve's face. "When the lights are on," she continued, "not just on the street, but on people's ideas, you can see them for what they are. The ideas. You can test them and prove them right or wrong. Sort of like what these Forza characters are all about."

"Forza?" Juve asked, a little surprised.

"Yes, I like what they're doing," Maria confided as she returned her attention to her runny treat.

"You like them? Why?" Juve asked, warily watching her enjoy her gelato.

"They're imaginative and effective," Maria explained. "Did you hear what happened to the advocate general—the man they chained to the pole the other day?"

"What happened?"

"He resigned, and I think he's going to inform on a whole bunch of higher-ups."

"No kidding!" Juve had not heard this news and was genuinely pleased.

"Which is a trick taken right from the playbook of General Tullia. When her emissaries to the Muslims came back to her with their findings, she devised a brilliant plan."

Juve stared at the clear sky. Many times before, the starry night sky had made him feel small and insignificant. But tonight, Maria had opened a vault in which, he began to realize, waited broader and deeper night skies. Someone could slug him in the stomach and he might not notice. "She let them conquer themselves," Juve observed.

"Not only that," Maria said, delighted with the way Juve summarized the strategy. "She not only let a whole series of Islamic Wars run their course, she patiently waited, offering her ambassadors as referees from time to time."

Maria stopped, turned, and blocked Juve in his tracks. "She waited until all the battling factions were begging for intervention. The beauty of Tullia's plan was patience—patience and precision timing. At the perfect moment, she placed in front of the rival parties a proposal. It was written in language so eloquent that it read just like their own sacred texts." Maria began to walk. "After that, it's back to the textbooks. The rest was easy."

Juve snatched Maria's hand, feeling how cold and sticky it had become. Bringing it to his mouth, he kissed her knuckles, watching her eyes brighten with delight. As he raised his lips away from her hand, Maria stepped forward. They stood now with their bodies just touching. Juve took a deep breath, opened Maria's hand, slowly spread her fingers, and gently began to lick away the drops of sweetness between her fingers.

"We're back at the hotel," Juve whispered, his eyes still lost in Maria's.

"So we are," Maria sighed, allowing a hint of a suggestive smile.

"Are you tired?"

"I am but I'm not," she answered, as they walked hand in hand through the hotel lobby, talking quietly, wandering from history to the stories of their own lives long into the night, first in separate beds, then together in Juve's bed, where they fell asleep fully dressed and loosely tangled in each other's arms.

It was beautiful, a smooth nugget of red-gold amber, made even more precious by its rare inclusion—a most unusual insect, suspended as if in flight with its wings spread. The several colors of the delicate, long-legged creature were forever altered by the amber, creating rich hues of gold, purple, and shimmering emerald. Now, a few weeks after their first night together, Juve held it up for Maria to admire and to display the almost imperceptible sparks of light that flashed from a metallic carapace just behind the insect's eyes. "It's beautiful, Juve!" Maria marveled. "I've never seen anything like it."

"That's a rare sort of wasp in there, I'm told," Juve explained. "A female."

"Naturally."

"She's able to reproduce every other year without the help of a male."

"No kidding . . . ," Maria teased. "That could come in handy."

"That's not why I chose it. Look on the back," Juve said with a glint of special pride in his eyes as he pointed to a small symbolic impression.

"Oh, my!" Maria gasped. "Is that what I think it is?"

"I don't know. What do you think it is?"

"It's the mark of Tiberius?"

"Yes."

"A controlled antiquity . . . You could be locked up for a long time, my friend."

Juve beamed and nodded his head as he placed the gift at the center of Maria's neck, brought the delicate white-gold chain around, and fastened it beneath her hair. "Let's hope not," Juve replied with a wry smile.

Maria looked at him with amusement and curiosity as he admired his gift. "I know I shouldn't ask . . ."

"You're right, you shouldn't."

"But . . ."

"But you're going to, so I'll tell you." Juve studied her face. Her intense need to know pleased him and fanned the flames of his growing desire for her. He decided at that moment to cultivate and harvest her curiosity for a long time. "Let's just call it a trade."

"Well, it's beautiful." Maria continued to gaze at the gift, as she furrowed her brow. "Does your job make it easy to find this kind of thing?"

"Yes."

"What else can you get?"

"You name it. Any kind of coral, ivory, wild boar tusks, ebony, teak, sapphire, diamonds, all kinds of rare stones . . ."

"At great risk to yourself."

"I believe it's wrong to imprison such beautiful things for the sole enjoyment of one class of people."

"I agree," Maria said, touching her finger to Juve's lips. She looked directly into his eyes and told him without a word that now was the time.

Later that evening, the new lovers lay drowsily under gentle waves of cool wind drifting over their naked bodies. Juve had thrown off a tremendous weight of care by letting his pure desire for Maria take him away, and he found Maria just as hungry for release. Now, mesmerized by the gentle flow of the wind in the sheer white curtains and the warmth of Maria's arm draped across the small of his back, he thought about his gift and Maria's graciously inquisitive acceptance. Trained to extract information from what seemed to be casual conversation, Juve had found out what he wanted to know. Maria was not so sheltered after all.

She was surprised that I could get contraband, but she knows more about it than she's letting on, Juve thought. He was proud of himself and his cool undercover work, but Maria had learned just as much, if not more. As they drifted off to sleep that night, they both understood that it was time for a break. They had come crashing into each other, and now they needed to catch their breath.

Juve slept lightly, always aware of his surroundings. Tonight he heard Maria whimper softly in her sleep. Her body trembled slightly and she murmured. *A dream is upsetting her,* Juve thought sleepily. He reached over to console her, placing his hand on her shoulder, then caressing the small of her back in a careful sweeping motion. Just enough pressure to reassure her, not too much to wake or tickle her. His attention seemed to relieve her fretfulness and she fell back into a deep sleep. But now he was awake.

It's not that I don't have it in me, Juve thought, *but these feelings for Maria come so naturally.* His ascent into love was thus far both liberating and frightening. *They call it falling in love,* Juve chuckled to himself, *but it's so uplifting!*

Maria was locked in his heart and yet he was her prisoner. He was intoxicated by her. He couldn't get enough. Everything about her was new. The small mole on her back, the temperature of her body, the way she scrunched her pillow . . . *Now that has to have some significance,* he thought, because as he had come to conclude, Maria was perfect. The shape of her nose had become the model for the perfect nose. Her perfection, he believed, must have significance, but the only reason his lovestruck brain could devise—*because it's Maria.* He felt protective. He thought about her constantly, his mind teetering over admiration for her strength and vulnerability.

Outside the window, Juve saw Sarenta, a star he had known since the day of his parents' funeral. He had often thought of it as a friend, something he could rely on, something that would never go away. Juve gazed at Sarenta and repeated the words he prayed whenever he saw it, "Mother, Father, you're in my heart." Then he modified the prayer. "I've tried to be everything you intended, but I've grown calloused, hard, and mean with the knowledge of life and its limits. Calloused to protect myself from ever being disappointed. Now I've met someone who makes me want to change every plan I've ever made." As he drifted drowsily, his thoughts gently broke into fragments and he was asleep.

When he awoke, Juve was awash in guilt for neglecting Forza. He had been a hands-on leader for the past decade, and now, with a critical mission on the horizon, his mind was wandering. He had always checked and rechecked his plans. Now they didn't seem as important. Lately his first thought each morning was how and when to see Maria, but today he faced a Forza planning session. As Maria rose, she seemed similarly distracted. They dressed, following their own routines, then faced each other smiling, relieved that neither seemed to have found the flaw that would open the crack and change everything.

"I'll see you in a couple of days," Juve announced to Maria. To his relief, she agreed. There, he had his answer. She, too, had other plans, and didn't press him for details. Juve left her with a hurried and friendly kiss. As he walked, he worried, arguing with himself over this unexpected, uninvited development in his life.

PREPARATIONS

WHEN JUVE ARRIVED AT THE ABANDONED LOFT, CELA WAS waiting for him, sitting alone at a table near the back of the room, studying a page from among the clutter of paper in front of her. At the sound of Juve's footsteps, she looked up. "You're late."

"Octavia . . . ," Juve began before he checked his agitation, "not now."

Cela's eyes widened in surprise at hearing Juve call her by her given name. "Octavia? You haven't called me Octavia since before we started Forza."

"Sorry. Cela." Dropping himself into the chair across the table from his cohort, Juve made no effort to disguise his foul mood. Each knew the other well enough to make room for bad humor, to let time diffuse tension. Their deep respect for each other was as old as Forza, born on the day Octavia's father Lathius was dropped from the ranks of the Republic's elite leadership. In response to his sacking, Lathius had staged a one-man protest, walking naked around the block that housed his former office. To anyone who would listen, the humiliated man poured out his grievances. He was quickly arrested and never seen again.

It was Juve who had drawn the job of arresting Lathius. Ordered to execute him, the young Indomitable Lion broke rank for the first time. Instead of killing him, he had arranged to hide him permanently, but the old man had died

soon after they reached Zostok, a remote sanctuary for the Republic's unde-
sirables that Juve and Octavia would eventually convert to a Forza-friendly
outpost.

This first act of disobedience had given Juve and Octavia the impetus for
embarking on their life of rebellion. They had founded Forza together, determined to slow the corruption of the power-mad state. Now they were at a
crossroads, facing the most divisive decision they'd addressed since they had
begun.

"You know, I have to tell you, Juve," Cela began in a tone that told Juve she
was ready to argue, "I don't see the point. It's just not us. The moment we kill,
we should expect to be killed. Even worse, we forfeit our authority to condemn anyone killing—us or anybody else." When she was convinced that Juve
was not going to answer, Cela pushed her papers aside, stood up, and walked
away. She stood with her back to him for a few seconds, and then faced him.
"Remember I told you I wanted you to meet Professor Barth?"

"Another father," Juve groused, "just what we need." Juve and Octavia were
already good friends when Lathius had welcomed Juve into his house as his
daughter's suitor. Impressed with the boy's intelligence and ambition, her
father had done his best to carefully expose the naïve and impetuous Lion
to the creeping growth of abuse within the government the boy had sworn
to defend. Lathius had schooled both Juve and his daughter in the beauty of
Empathia, whenever he could get them to sit still for it.

"He's not my father, though he is older and wiser." As she answered, Cela
remembered fondly Juve's swaggering dismissal of her father's lessons. Lathius
preached patiently, and, eventually, he gained their interest and attention. The
two young converts soon bridled at each new story of corruption and abuse
Lathius exposed, both growing eager to take corrective action. "Pick your
battles carefully," Lathius had cautioned them. "Choose your plan of action
only after you know your enemy ten times better than he knows you."

"He's all over the news," Juve said to Cela. "We don't need to get involved
with someone that popular right now." He spoke of Barth, but Juve was thinking of Cela's naked father, wrapped in a blanket, sitting blank-eyed in front
of him. It embarrassed Juve even now to remember how he scolded Lathius
sarcastically with "Pick your battles carefully," the very words of advice both
he and Octavia had taken to heart. Octavia's father had sat silently as Juve

complained how the old man's crazy prank had stalled his and Octavia's plans. "We've started to build an underground organization to redress the wrongs of the Republic using Empathia as our guide," Juve remembered grumbling. Then, heaping his frustration on Lathius, he shouted, "Now this!" Angrily pacing the small dimensions of the hideout he had quickly improvised, Juve went back to shuffling his options and measuring their consequences. It was clear to Juve that he needed more resources to handle unexpected situations just like this one. No matter how carefully they planned, he and Octavia would always have to be ready to hide people, equipment, and evidence.

"He agreed to meet you," Cela announced.

Awakened from his reverie, Juve blurted, "Who?"

"Barth. I think you should meet him."

"Remember, Cela." Juve stood up and walked over to her. "Remember when your father died? Remember how unprepared we were after he was gone?"

"You thought we were unprepared," she snapped, turning away from Juve.

"We were," he insisted. "We had no plans for half of what we were about to run into."

"Everything we planned after he was gone—the way we recruit, the way we train, the independence of the units, the way they form and dissolve with each scherzo—all my father."

"Some of it."

"Most of it."

"Okay, most of it," Juve conceded.

"And he never would have agreed to assassination."

"Would Barth?"

"No."

"I didn't think so."

"He's with us," Cela insisted. "His whole life has been revolutionary, in his own way, fighting from within."

"And where has it gotten anybody?"

"Where is murder going to get us? It makes us no better than they are."

"So give me a better way," Juve said with a clear air of exasperation.

"Barth—he can pull strings. He has influence. Even though Bellator is his biggest supporter, he's confided in me about his plans to remove him from power. What would it hurt to add his influence to what we've been doing?"

Juve clapped both of his hands down on the desk. "Okay, so we enlist Bart."

"Barth."

"What do we want this guy to do? Why would he want to help us? Why wouldn't he turn us in? There's a bounty on our heads, remember? And a bigger one after the assassination!" As Juve leaned forward, resting his head in his hands, he grumbled to himself in frustration. Cela stormed around to Juve's side of the table. She sat against the table, her feet on the floor, her arms folded defiantly. As Juve sat up, the back of his arm brushed along the curve of Cela's hip. He remembered how close they had come to becoming lovers before her father died. Looking into Cela's eyes, he saw Octavia, the girl who had served up his first taste of passion.

Recognizing the look in Juve's eyes, Cela suppressed the tender feelings his look engendered. "What's eating you, Juve?" she asked. "Barth is trustworthy. He could be an asset. But I really don't think he'll help us if we go through with the assassination."

"So much for Bart, then."

"Barth."

"Fuck Barth!" He stopped himself, checked his anger. A wry smile came to his face as he realized how ridiculous he was beginning to sound.

"Besides, killing Bellator is letting him off too easy," Cela continued, ignoring Juve's outburst. "I mean, breaking into his banquet and getting away, that's enough to . . ." Seeing that she was failing to lead Juve out of his fog, she changed her tack. "Look, Juve, Barth can help Forza—and I mean real help, not hit-and-run adolescent delinquency—and you blow it off. It's time for you, me, and Forza to grow up. I don't want to be a punk for the rest of my life. My father's memory is worth more than that, and, frankly, I refuse to allow it. I want remedies. I want profound change. I want to clarify our message and take it to the people. We started out to reestablish Empathia. Now you want to throw Empathia itself out the window with an assassination!"

Juve slapped both hands on the table and exhaled, "You're right."

"Don't patronize me with that tone of voice," Cela warned as she went to the papers on the desk and snatched the page she had been reading when Juve had arrived. "I'm not asking you to back off from our principles. I'm asking you to abide by them. How can we demand the Reciprocity principle if we assassinate? Blood Ballot?" Now Cela was reading from the page in her hand.

"The pillars of Empathia—Equal Access, Freedom of Expression, Dignity for All . . ."

Beneath the drone of Cela's litany, Juve sat silently. Something seemed to have snapped inside his head. He'd felt this snap before. But it had always launched him into violent action. This was different. It snapped and he felt as if he had been dropped into a cushion. "Maybe I'm a thug for life, Cela. Maybe I'm so used to getting whatever I want with force that I can't change. You've always been the brains of this outfit and I know you're right now. But almost every day a Lion gets an order from Bellator to kill someone—men like your father. The lucky ones get me for their assassin. I at least give them the option of going to Zostok, but the place is filling up. We're running out of space. I can't dump many more of Bellator's victims in there. He's out of control. It's time to stop the problem at the source!"

"I can't see an end to it," Cela argued. "I agree that killing Bellator will temporarily eliminate a lot of our problems, but where will the killing end?"

"When we eliminate Bellator," Juve argued more ardently, "we eliminate the major disease. He's behind everything—at least the worst of it. When his sympathizers see him go, they'll scatter. Most of them want him gone."

"Do you really think no one will take his place?"

"It may take more than one shot . . . ," Juve conceded. "One or two more . . ."

"One or two? Four or five? They'll never give in and we'll never stop killing. We're making progress, Juve. At least our pranks amuse the population. They undermine the dignity and authority of the Leadership. If we start killing, we'll lose the support of the people and without their support, we're dead. Right now, we're moving slowly but steadily—like rust. We've begun the consumption and there's no stopping it." They both sat quietly for a few moments. Then Cela added, "What about Barth?"

"What about him?"

"Will you at least talk to him?"

Juve stood up and held Cela by her shoulders. "I'm willing to hear what he has to say."

"But he won't help us if we assassinate Bellator."

In Cela's eyes Juve saw the same intensity that burned when she learned of her father's demise. Understanding that her love for her father made her devotion to Forza possibly stronger and truer than his own, he spoke patiently. "Okay, even if Barth comes up with some great plan to dethrone Bellator, how long will it take?" Cela shook her head in weary frustration with Juve's inability to act on what she was sure he must understand. "People are suffering today," Juve continued. "What? Let them suffer while we help Barth with his brilliant internal coup? I can do that *too*, but I can't do that *only*. I have to fend for those who can't fend for themselves. It's what I am."

"I can't do both. We become corrupt if we kill."

"I understand that, but they can pile on wrongs faster than we can right them. We've got a responsibility for *now*. The people have come to depend on us. We've become the guard dogs. We have to attack injustice, any injustice, anywhere we smell it."

Cela shrugged her shoulders and stepped away. "I heard some very interesting ideas last night."

"From Barth?"

"Yes. He's discovered something. He thinks he's found the thinking—actually, the thinker—behind Empathia."

"Flavius."

"No. Flavius was looking over somebody's shoulder." She turned to face Juve. "A man who disappeared from history, or at least from the history books."

"What's this got to do with us, Cela?"

"The heart of Empathia comes from this man. His thinking is deeper and richer than what ended up in Empathia. Barth is convinced that his principles are even more powerful—that if we could get to the real source of Empathia, we'd have an even more effective weapon against people like Bellator."

"What kind of weapon?"

Cela chose her words carefully. "A way to deal with people like Bellator."

"I know how to deal with Bellator," Juve snapped impatiently.

"I know," Cela replied with disarming patience, "but I'm talking about a response that's ludicrous on its face, but if you imagine what would happen if you actually did it . . ."

"What are you trying to say?"

"Imagine what would happen if, instead of attacking our enemies, we met them with the same respect we give the people we love."

Cela's words stunned Juve. They recalled his first visit to Zostok. Auspex had been with him when they had attempted to hide Cela's raving father. It looked ugly and smelled awful. Filth fell everywhere. The snow was gray, and the air almost too cold to breathe, so heavy you could taste it.

How can these people stand to live here? Juve wondered as he and Auspex had approached the lonely collection of hovels that made up the town. Officially classified Z-1 through Z-20, Zostok's inhabitants were mentally retarded, chemically dependent, physically challenged, hideously malformed, or psychologically deranged. Half-witted volunteers or hard-case prisoners made up the governing bodies and public security force. Eventually Juve pulled strings and was assigned the thankless job of managing the security force. Gradually he would populate Zostok with Forza recruits and make it their haven for people they would refuse to execute.

"My enemies?" Juve began. "On my first trip to Zostok I understood who my enemies were and why I could never love them. They were people like Bellator who filled Zostok and a few other hellholes with nature's mistakes. These places are still the dumping ground for people the Leadership doesn't want to see in Rome or any other civilized city. These people do work no normal person would consider. I couldn't get Zostok out of my mind. I never told anyone this, Cela, but you know what I thought of those people? They disgusted me! They were ugly and they smelled—even in the bitter cold. They drooled, they beat each other, they shit their pants, they fucked in the streets, they howled and bayed at the moon. I hated myself for feeling the way I did. I hated myself for the weakness in my stomach. I fought it. I demanded to know how I could feel this way about human beings. I realized that the enemy is also me. It's you, Cela. It's anyone who lets the weak suffer, anyone who perpetuates the suffering. There's something ugly in all of us! You know how I finally got rid of that feeling?" Juve didn't wait for Cela's reply. "I made myself understand that their wretchedness is not their fault."

"You already knew that," she said.

"No, not in the way that changed my attitude," Juve explained. "I had to put myself in their place and ask a lot of hard questions. I had to make myself feel unable to express or to even form any kind of uplifting thought." He gave Cela an inquiring look. "You know what I mean?"

"Yes, I do," Cela replied. "I can't imagine not having that power. How could I despise someone who doesn't have it?"

"Exactly. If they can't appreciate the better things, those of us who can have no call to condemn them. We need to protect them. At best, we replace the system that disposes of them, that feeds itself more than it can consume and keeps grasping for more." Juve paused. "I'm sorry, Cela, I don't need to preach to you."

"You need to get it out of your system," she replied with a smile.

"Cela, sometimes I think I'm in this for the thrills. I love bolting some fat, naked bastard to a pole. When kids paint the silhouette all over the walls, it feels good. I admit it. But if Forza weren't around, what would some of these people do? I have to go through with this. If you want out, I understand. And if Barth won't help us after the assassination, too bad. Playing by the rules just isn't going to get it done."

They looked at each other for a moment. Finally, Juve spoke. "When do I see Barth?"

Cela had arranged for Barth and Juve to meet in the professor's office that same afternoon. Juve arrived on time. Face to face, the two men began to size each other up immediately and came to their conclusions quickly. Neither could disguise his respect for the other and each man took warmly to the admiration he sensed coming from the other. Barth was the first to acknowledge his respect. "You've created a formidable source of rebellion. Just what we need in these times, I'm afraid."

"I'm flattered that someone in your position appreciates our work, Professor," Juve replied.

"Please, call me Barth. And thank you. May I call you Juve?"

"Of course."

"What I do, Juve, requires little more than painstaking concentration. I'm good at what I do, because at the point where most people throw their arms up in frustration, I hunker down and keep plodding along."

"You're being too modest, Professor. I'm sorry . . . Barth."

"No modesty. I'm leveling with you. Basically my work requires little more than a high tolerance for pain. And some intelligence, but that simply shortens the length of the ordeal. The key ingredient to success in science, or any enterprise, I'm sure you agree, is passion. If you don't have the passion, you can't take the pain."

"Well put." Juve smiled.

Within the first few minutes of small talk, the two men were speaking less guardedly and, eventually, from their hearts. The initial awkwardness faded quickly and gave way to genuine and mutual interest. Finally, to signal that it was time to get down to business, Barth went to his desk, sat down, and offered Juve a chair. "We're lucky, you and I, Juve." Barth leaned back in his chair, folded his hands behind his head, and studied the ceiling.

"What do you mean, lucky?" Juve asked as he, too, sat down.

Barth rocked forward, leaned on his desk, and looked Juve directly in the eyes. "We're possessed with a passion few people have the privilege of even tasting. And I suspect we share the same passion. Our approaches may be very different, but I think we're after the same thing."

"Tell me what you mean."

"I mean that we detest injustice. We see corruption and we hate it, because we know that fair and honest people could do so much better."

"You said it better than I could," Juve admitted.

"When I say our approaches are very different—and I hope you don't take this the wrong way—I'd like to suggest that while your method is active and forceful, it's equally negative and destructive."

"I have no problem with that."

"When you burn down a house, for example, you no longer see the house, but it's still there. It's ashes, gas, light, and heat, but nothing is really destroyed except the view of the house. I'm using this example because I want to suggest that your efforts, as outstanding as they appear to be—"

"So what's the point of doing anything?"

"Precisely!" Barth exclaimed. "You have a way of getting right to the point and that saves me an awful lot of jaw work. I may be a professor and I do love to hear myself talk, but I prefer talking to quicker minds. We can get a lot further . . ."

"So why don't you just tell me what's on your mind, Professor?"

Barth took a deep breath. "You've heard of my work with Time Continuum Intersections?"

"Of course. Who hasn't?"

"I'm about to run my first test, Juve, and I'd like some help."

"What kind of test?"

"I need to take something about as big as a human being—a big dog or maybe a calf—and see if I can send it back in time." Juve gave the old man an incredulous look. "It's not quite that easy," Barth explained. "The TCI limits your options. Each window to the past occurs at a specific time and place and delivers you to the same place in another time. My discoveries may have unraveled the schedule of these events, these intersections of time."

"And you want me to help."

"Yes, if you like," Barth replied, unfazed. "I certainly can't manage an animal as big as a man."

"What about one of your students?"

"I want to limit the number of people who see the results of this experiment to the absolute minimum. If this works—if the animal disappears—I want the person who witnesses this to be the same person who eventually goes with me on an actual journey back in time."

Juve raised his arms. "Wait a minute," he interrupted. "You're going back in time—something no one has ever done—and you want me to go with you?"

"Take it easy, son," the professor replied. "The chances of this actually working are incredibly slim. It's one of those things that looks good on paper, but in reality—"

"I think you *believe* it will work."

"I *hope* it will work," Barth replied calmly. "I will try to go back. I'm an old man and I would increase my chances of success if I were with someone who can handle himself in challenging situations."

"Challenging situations?" Juve leaned back in his chair and smiled. "You're right. This isn't like going out for a loaf of bread or something."

"We could find ourselves . . . who knows?"

"So, if the test animal disappears," Juve proposed, "you want to do this to yourself?"

"That's correct. And if the animal goes nowhere, or if it comes to some unfortunate fate . . ."

"Then it's back to the drawing board."

"Exactly."

"What if the animal doesn't *appear* to go anywhere?" Juve paused before continuing. "How do you know it hasn't gone somewhere, spent some time there, and returned?"

"That's a distinct possibility," Barth conceded, "but as long as the animal appears to be unharmed, it's probably worth going ahead."

"I see," Juve agreed, then added, "but if the animal disappears, there may be no way back?"

"If we go, I think there's a way back."

"Wait a minute," Juve cautioned. "You *think* there's a way back?"

"I have plans for a return, yes," Barth answered unconvincingly. "We should be able to return."

Juve looked at Barth incredulously. Trying not to laugh, he declared, "Barth, you're an interesting old man, and your proposition is incredible. Cela was right. I like you. We share some of the same beliefs, but that's where it ends." He grabbed the professor by his shoulders with a firm grip. "But I'm going to continue fighting my way—here, in the present."

Barth looked at Juve and nodded. "It was a long shot," he said with a smile. "I still hope you will give it serious thought over the next few days. To get where I want to go, I have to run my test in the next few weeks. If the results are positive, I need to move fast."

"Then I suggest you travel with another scientist."

"No," Barth declared firmly. "Another scientist would be redundant. Besides, the mission I have in mind, should time travel be possible, requires someone as daring, clever, and resourceful as you."

"And just what is your mission?" Juve asked.

Barth moved his chair directly in front of his guest and leaned forward. "I want to go back to find out why Chesua disappeared from history. Then, I'm going to do whatever I can to change his fate."

"Who's Chesua?"

"Were you a good history student?" Barth asked as he rose and began to pace.

"I was interested some of the time. But most of my teachers bored me."

"I'm sure you learned about Flavius Aurelius in school."

"Of course," Juve replied, following Barth with his eyes as the giant of science continued to pace more briskly now.

"And your teachers must have given you some general idea of how the Roman Empire came to be."

"You mean Romulus and Remus?" Juve joked.

"Well, I certainly hope you got beyond the legends."

"I was raised in the Lions' camp. I gave up on legends long ago."

"So did I, Juve." Barth stopped and pointed to himself. "I rejected all the gods of Rome when I was very young. I've always lived my life holding the belief that nothing would go unexplained forever. My desire to unlock the secrets of nature was all I needed to motivate me." The professor turned his back to Juve and paced, leaning forward, his hands clasped behind his back. "My wife Sylvia was my perfect opposite. Everything struck her as some kind of miracle. 'How could it be a coincidence,' she would ask me, 'that the creations of your imagination and your mathematics describe so perfectly what actually exists?'" He stood twenty paces away and turned to the younger man. "I still ponder that question, Juve."

He resumed his lecture. "Sylvia spent her life uncovering the teachings of a man whom official history has attempted to bury. To her, he was a life guide. To me, a messenger, another source of data, until she showed me that this man, this Chesua, must have inspired the work of Flavius Aurelius. It was then I saw, for the first time, that my life could actually benefit from a guide."

Juve's face was discernibly perplexed. The men had just met, exchanged little more than small talk, and now they were talking about a forgotten figure from history as some kind of personal guide. For the first time, Juve began to wonder about the sanity of the famous scientist.

"When you're a child, your parents guide you . . ."

"I wouldn't know about that," Juve interrupted, annoyed at the direction of the conversation. "My parents were snatched from me at age nine."

"I'm sorry to hear that. What happened to them?"

"They were assigned to a mission and given a total identity change."

"Where are they now?"

"I've been assured that they both died in the line of duty."

"Do you believe that?"

"Do I have any choice?"

"Why didn't they take someone without kids?" Barth asked.

"Because I was already scheduled to be extracted and raised by the Lions. That was decided at my birth."

"Did they know? Your parents. Did they know they would have to give you up?"

"Yes. They conceived me in hopes of producing a Lion. Producing warriors for the Republic was a great honor to my parents' generation."

Barth seemed to absorb and share Juve's anger, his face darkening with indignation. "Honor? What kind of honor is there in abandoning a child?"

"Don't be too hard on them," Juve warned defensively. "Sometimes it's almost impossible to run against the herd. But if you want to go back twenty years, let me know. There are some things I'd like to change."

Barth tilted his head to one side and smiled at Juve. "I may be one of the cleverest men in the Republic, Juve, but I'm about to venture into unfriendly territory. What better company could I choose than the leader of Forza—a man with the ingenuity and courage to challenge the authority of the world's masters?"

Hearing Barth refer to him as "the leader of Forza," Juve reminded himself of the risk of taking Barth into his confidence. Even though he trusted Cela's judgment, caution prompted him to bring their discussion to an end. "Do you really think it's possible to do something in the past that alters the future?"

"It's a long, long shot. I'll know a lot more after the test."

Juve held up two fingers, one pressed tightly against the other. "I've heard that genius and insanity are like this." Then, smiling at the professor, he moved his paired fingers apart and concluded, "I'm not sure which you are." Barth laughed and Juve continued. "Your proposition interests me, I have to admit. Thank you for inviting me, Barth." Juve stood and walked away from the seated professor toward the office door. Looking back at his new friend, he left him with "But I have work to do here and now—today. People depend on me."

ASSASSINATION

ORSO PICKED UP A BANANA, HELD IT AGAINST HIS TROUSERS, and walked behind Pavo, his favorite joke victim, as Pavo, seated among his fellow Forza members, continued the story. "Orso's holding the kid up over his head, while the little fucker keeps going on about how he's going to tattoo *us* with the Forza tag . . ." Pavo felt something bump against the back of his head. He turned to see the banana and said, "I've seen you naked, Orso. Either get a smaller banana or grab a string bean."

Instantly the crew joined in with laughter and more suggestions. Crow suggested that Orso give his string bean a matching pair of capers. Orso, feigning innocent disinterest, methodically peeled the banana, allowing his audience to wait and wonder what he would do next. Stuffing the banana all the way into his mouth, he dropped the peel on Pavo's head and loudly mumbled, "Bite me!" Jumping away from Pavo's lunging attack, Orso burst out laughing. Wet lumps of chewed banana spewed from his mouth, instigating a boisterous rumble that grew as more crew showed up for the meeting.

Juve arrived as the tumult was losing momentum and surveyed the room. The forty-seven men and women clowning around in the loft were, in Juve's mind, the most dedicated and devoted group ever assembled—his dedicated tifosi, he called them. His heart filled with a quiet pride. In the past decade,

Forza had evolved from a band of rowdy teenagers into a worldwide voice of dissent. To say that Forza was loosely organized would understate the spontaneous spirit that inspired imitation and gave its members the appearance of organization. Binding the hearts and minds of all those who called themselves Forza Facia was the understood objective of embarrassing, harassing, and intimidating the Leadership of the Republic until they completely reestablished the principles of Empathia in their original form and interpretation.

While Juve was generally recognized as the group's leader, and tales abounded extolling his courage and exploits, no one could prove that Forza's operations were in any way centralized. Forza members frustrated attempts at being identified by operating as needed as ad hoc crews, never meeting in the same place more than a few times. Patience was their primary advantage. The Republic was forced to defend an infinite number of fronts. Forza needed to find only one chink in their defense to wreak havoc. If a member of Forza was ever captured, all of that crew's plans were dropped. No top-down orders had ever been intercepted, despite diligent Leadership eavesdropping on all forms of communication.

Recruiting was a cinch. Imitators seemed to arise spontaneously around the world, inspired by news of Forza scherzi—especially the mischief staged in Rome against the highest levels of the Leadership. Naturally, the official news from Republic World exaggerated the maliciousness of Forza's pranks. In response, there emerged a style of music and a body of songs that retold every event, making no apologies for exaggerating the story in the other direction. These "shouts," as they were called, were recorded in bedrooms, basements, garages, wherever possible. Even though shout recordings were distributed electronically and from hand to hand, for the most part songs were passed from performer to performer, sung in school corridors and on street corners.

The Forza family Juve looked on with pride this afternoon was responsible for the greatest part of the success of the movement, each member uniquely qualified to carry out a part of Forza's mission. Pavo, the peacock, was best known for a break-in gone awry. Two years before, Forza had been ransacking a Leadership household, looking for money and jewelry to distribute to the less fortunate, when the woman of the house surprised them. She was frightened at first and began to call the authorities with her wayfone. But the suave and handsome Pavo changed her mind. They would leave without taking anything, he assured her, and leave her unharmed. She agreed. Pavo ordered his crew to leave. As the others withdrew, Pavo watched the woman's demeanor change from fear to acceptance to invitation. When they were alone, Pavo turned to go, telling her with his disarming smile that, if she asked, he would stay.

"Why do you have to leave?" she asked before he had taken three steps. Pavo spent the night, and the woman voluntarily gave him a small fortune for the cause—far more than they could have stolen and fenced. Pavo turned most of it over to Forza. He bragged that he deserved to hold on to some of it as payment for his stellar performance.

Cela was the strategist of the organization and its conscience. Her association with Barth and her expertise in history and physics made her indispensable to the team. Perhaps no one was as dedicated to the ideals and the mission of Forza. She worked tirelessly, researching and evaluating the organizational strategies of effective groups past and present. Using unassailable data and incisive logic, she could win any debate in which she decided to engage. However, she deployed her mental magic so judiciously and dismantled opposing arguments so deftly that those who disagreed with her almost always came over to her side, willingly and often adamantly.

Auspex was the member Juve held up as an example to all the others. He was strongly built, hard, and rugged looking, with close-cut blond hair. His word was gold, rarely wasted, and always genuine. No one could match his devotion to Forza. Juve's vision and clandestine celebrity made Forza famous and attractive to recruits and imitators, but it was Auspex who had forged most of the alliances with other dissident organizations. His no-nonsense approach was also charismatic. He could convince with strong, fair diplomacy. The other members called him "the Silk Anvil."

Orso, the Bear, broke bricks just to amuse himself and to keep his hands as hard as steel. He always woke to a breakfast of six to eight egg whites. A former spheres player, the powerful Orso had won world-class competitions of pure strength and, years before, had enjoyed the title of Republic's strongest man before quietly devoting his energy to Forza. He was distinctively, powerfully built, always with a wad of cocoa-chew in his mouth.

Lupus and Crow were a couple in the truest sense of the word. He, Lupus, sported a thick, unruly head of bright red hair and collected garbage in the district of Rome that had become the home of top-level Leadership. Despite the fact that the residents had been warned to watch what they disposed of from their homes, Lupus successfully mined the weekly refuse to Forza's advantage. Crow drove the truck that Lupus loaded every morning. She could be counted on to find ways to make her truck available for Forza's purposes as well. They volunteered more often than any of the Rome-based crew and carried out their assignments with speed and precision. As the eyes and ears of Forza on the streets, they regularly recruited sympathizers, who helped Forza identify people in need.

Three popular musicians—Caldi, Fausto, and Bruté—also lived together and formed a group called, unpretentiously, CFB. Their artistic camaraderie and constant companionship helped them make plans and coordinate their efforts with the highest level of precision. Each had been recruited from the ranks of the Indomitable Lions. Like all Lions, they possessed superb fighting skills, but it was their celebrity that provided Forza a unique set of assets, including access to powerful people and secluded places. Ironically, the Leadership operated under the illusion that the trio was making just such inroads for them. Caldi, Fausto, and Bruté played a dangerous game of keeping the Leadership convinced they were infiltrating the young population to spread their ideas, while actually doing so for Forza. Every path CFB greased for their comrades, they sabotaged another for the Republic Leadership. They especially enjoyed writing and performing the shouts that made them famous. It had become a game of balancing double meanings and weaving allegories into their lyrics, making particularly savvy use of the ever-evolving street slang of the day. The fact that both supporters and detractors of the Leadership quoted CFB lyrics spoke to their success as this double agency.

"All right, tifosi," Juve called out above the restless rumble of voices, "we've gone over the plan enough times. We have it down. I just want to hit the most important points one more time." He scanned the room. Everyone was riveted with attention. "Remember," Juve continued, "after we take out the guards in the banquet room, we've got fifty seconds before the backup response teams arrive. Listen to Auspex's countdown. You know your numbers. Make sure you get your job done on your number. The dais is on the interior wall, so Auspex and I will be coming up the center of the room to take out Bellator." Juve paused. "Does anyone have any questions? Has anyone found any flaws?"

There was no response. "As you know, Cela and a few others will sit this one out. Anybody else have any second thoughts about completing this particular mission?"

There was silence out of respect for the decision of the dissenters. Juve looked around the room. "I guess this means the rest of us are in accord. One more thing—the abort signal." Juve sliced his hand across his throat. "This means no assassination and go to plan B. There was some talk that the hall windows have been reinforced. I spoke with Crow and she assures me they have not. Just make sure you hit the glass with your ankles crossed. You can ask Fausto if you want to know what it feels like to take out a window frame with your nuts."

Fausto took a barrage of catcalls and flashed back a hand signal that suggested the recipient consider engaging in an unnatural act more suitably performed in private.

The banquet hall was wrapped on three sides with tall windows, perfect for filling the room with light, and even better for Forza's break-in. On the roof, a half dozen security guards lay bound and blindfolded with reinforced packing tape. They lay passive as Juve and his men got into position around the perimeter of the building. The men and women of Forza walked quietly, aware that below them Bellator's banquet was underway. Juve nodded to his crew. Intently focused on their tasks, they all secured their ropes to the building's façade. In a matter of minutes, all forty were lined up on the edge of the roof, one above each window, ready to leap. Juve walked past as they secured themselves, giving each a slap on the shoulder. They counted on this traditional signal of encouragement. Now they waited for his signal to proceed.

Inside, Bellator stepped up to the dais to offer a few remarks to the audience of two hundred and fifty well-dressed men and women. On either side of him sat members of his family and friends finishing their desserts.

Juve raised his hand, spreading all five fingers for all jumpers to see. Then he showed four, three . . . down went forty masks over forty faces . . . two, one. As Juve's hand became a fist, he leaped straight off the roof in unison with his crew. Two seconds later they plunged as one through the windows below. The sound of breaking glass rattled throughout the room. As the Forza team crashed to the floor, Auspex yelled, "Fifty!" Guests screamed, dishes shattered, food splattered, drinks spilled, tables cracked, glass rained, and chairs tumbled across the floor. Terrified people shot off in all directions, while the band of party crashers leaped to their assigned positions. All the guards on the periph ery were quickly disarmed. The guards at the ends of the dais managed to fire one shot each before they were subdued, but no one seemed to have taken their bullets.

"That's a plan flaw," Juve remarked to Auspex as they shouldered and kneed their way up the center of the room.

"Forty-five," Auspex cried above the din.

As he plowed toward the dais, Juve made a complete circle and was pleased to see his plan unfolding perfectly, except for the two gunshots. At both entrances Forza members were using guards as shields in anticipation of incoming security forces. And then, an unexpected treat. At the doors to the left of the dais, a Republic minister tried to play hero. Pavo not only subdued him and forced his face to the floor, but also exposed the minister's bare but-tocks, displaying the Forza tattoo he had earned a year ago.

"Thirty-five!"

Juve was two strides from the dais when his eyes met Bellator's. "You punks won't get away with this!" Bellator screamed at Juve, loud enough to ensure that everyone in the room witnessed his courage under fire as he stood tall, shielding a young woman behind his back. "I'll run down each one of you and personally whip your hides!"

"Twenty-five!"

"You arrogant bastard!" Juve growled as he sprang to the head table and announced to Bellator in a voice that filled the room. "You won't do a thing from your grave." He drew his knife, then froze in astonishment. Maria jumped up from behind Bellator and threw her arms around her father. Looking over her shoulder, she was eye-to-eye with Juve. He checked his mask. The band of intruders held their positions, waiting. Juve stood speechless as Maria peered even closer into his eyes.

"Fifteen!"

With a hand gesture, his hand across his throat, Juve abruptly aborted the mission. He turned away from Maria and tried to disguise his voice as he announced to the entire room, "We can kill you anytime we want!"

"Ten!"

The assassins vanished as quickly as they had appeared.

Bellator shook as he screamed, "I want anyone who looks like them, or says good things about them, or so much as whispers the name Forza with even a shade of approval . . . I want them dead! Today!"

His assistant, Rowan, had grown accustomed to Bellator's outbursts, but tonight, in the rubble-riddled banquet hall, the Second Minister rose to a new level of rage. Rowan instinctively assumed the voice of reason. "But, sir," Rowan calmly pointed out, "that would be half of the population."

"I don't care," Bellator roared. "We're going to end this right now!" His voice broke like a clap of thunder and echoed around the hall. For a brief moment the cleanup crew and police investigators froze before resuming their work. "Letting this nonsense go on under my nose—that was my first mistake. Now it's personal. I want these shitbags eradicated! I don't care what we have to do!"

Rowan watched the veins in Bellator's neck. They looked as if they were ready to burst.

"And all of my bodyguards on duty last night—they're all fired. All of them."

"Yes, sir. I'll get the Indomitable Lions on it immediately, sir."

"I want the best of the best Lions on this assignment, Rowan."

"Absolutely, sir."

"And not just one. Get me two . . . No, make it six."

"Yes, sir. Six."

Rowan hurried from the hall. Alone with his fury, the Second Minister stormed over to a window, looked out over the city, and hissed through his teeth, "Where are you, you miserable sons of a bitches? We're going back to the old ways of dealing with you fuckers."

Juve was alone in his apartment analyzing his situation, weighing his options, evaluating his moves. He had voluntarily isolated himself, devastated by what had happened. Forcing himself to focus on what to do next, he banished his embarrassment from his thoughts. He knew Bellator would send Lions after him. They'd assign the best, which meant they were sure to call him. *Orders to kill myself,* he smirked. *Should I accept? Why not?* he answered himself. *If I turn them down, it will just raise questions.*

Every time he had been ordered to kill, Juve had accepted. But he evaluated every assignment. If the assassination would benefit Forza, he carried it out. If it meant harm to Forza or great advantage to the Republic, he devised and executed an alternative plan. At great personal risk, Juve had not only faked certain assassination jobs, he had also arranged to give the intended victim a new identity. The Leadership always assumed that their orders had been carried out. Indomitable Lion training was so thorough and intense that the word of a Lion was rarely doubted. Lions cherished and protected their word and knew that if they ever broke it, they were dead. And when it came to assassination, the pragmatic Republic Leadership was satisfied as long as their assassination targets no longer caused them any concern. Their arrogant belief in their own power prevented them from seriously considering that an order might not have been carried out. The order to kill Juve, however, would not be handled in the usual manner. It would come, encrypted as always, but there would be no name, just a directive to locate the leader of Forza and eliminate him. Juve knew that as few as three Lions might be assigned—and as many as six.

AFTERMATH

FORZA'S BRAZEN DEMONSTRATION DOMINATED THE NEWS on Republic World—the Banquet Prank, they called it. "Seven Members of Forza Facia in Custody," the headlines lied. They exaggerated as well the failure of the leader to dispatch their target. All the chatter on public transportation and every office bull session was devoted to it. Public opinion polls registered mixed support for the outrageous mischiefmakers. Forza's history of benevolence and now their formidable ability to make anything happen gave citizens new respect for their principled spectacles. Forza tags multiplied throughout the Republic. The Leadership called an emergency meeting on how to deal with this most recent incident.

The mood was somber in Forza's hideaway the morning after the attack. "You compromised our mission," Auspex told Juve, though it obviously pained him. "You've lost your focus. If Forza isn't the most important thing in your life, you can't lead us."

Auspex is right, Juve admitted to himself as he watched his oldest friend and most trusted comrade lead the review of the night's mission. As hard as he tried to listen to the lecture, his thoughts went elsewhere. Juve nodded in agreement with Auspex, but he was seeing Maria. Juve kept replaying the ghastly moment when he looked up to see Maria embracing and protecting Bellator—

his target, her father. Over and over, he replayed it. Each time the sick feeling in his stomach intensified. *She knows it's me,* he kept telling himself.

So many thoughts. Should he hate her for living with Bellator, the enemy? Or should he love her more for growing up so beautifully in his home? *How can she relate to such a tyrant?* he wondered. *How can she relate to me?* He couldn't stop his racing mind. *I've compromised more than the mission,* he thought. *I've compromised my crew. I've put my personal interests over the interests of Forza. Unforgivable. Even if we did pull off the most dramatic political statement in our organization's history.*

Juve listened for a moment to Auspex. *He's taking it easy on me,* he thought. Then his mind hurried back to Maria and the next time he'd see her. He didn't know where she lived, or he would have shown up at her door. He knew Lupus and Crow could locate her. *Right! Rub salt in their wounds by asking Lupus and Crow to find the woman who caused me to botch our first lethal mission.*

"Juve," Auspex concluded, "you are my lifelong friend, but you hesitated. Enough of us went into this with doubts that kept us up at night. We were about to move into new territory. If we let you stay in charge, we'll go into our next mission with doubt. We can't have that. It's time to take a break, Juve. Someone else needs to take over."

"You know, Auspex," Juve replied, measuring his words and shaking his head, "I'm doubting everything. I admit it." He threw up his hands in frustration. "Cela can run things. Or you." Juve sat up straight and spoke to the assembled crew. "Vote on it. I'm through." Enough protest came from the assembled crew for Juve to raise his hands and continue: "Ten years ago I had no hesitation. I've never let you down until now. But today I'm distracted. Cela said it was time for me to grow up. If this is growing up—becoming indecisive . . . No, I'll call it what it is—impotent! You need a new leader."

"Take some time off, Juve," Auspex advised. "You'll get your edge back." He walked over to his friend. Juve stood. The two embraced as the others made their way to join them. Auspex whispered to Juve, "Coffee?"

"Sure. Tomorrow?"

"Tomorrow. Café Fiorentina," Auspex suggested. Juve nodded, broke from Auspex's embrace, and warmly hugged each of the others as he made his way out the door to a second appointment with Barth.

As Juve hurried along, Bellator's orders were being carried out. Juve noticed workers scrubbing and blasting Forza tags from city walls, leaving conspicuous clean spots on the grimy walls. The directive to end Forza's existence had been set in motion.

Their principal target found his new friend Barth at the appointed corner. The great scientist greeted the young rebel with a beaming smile and immediately began to heap on praise for the previous night's scherzo at Bellator's banquet. Juve endured the old man's adulation as they walked. When he could endure it no longer, he interrupted Barth with a peevish denial. "It wasn't a prank. I meant to kill him."

Barth stopped and put a hand on one of Juve's shoulders. "Kill him?" He studied Juve's sullen and silent face. "Juve, most of the city thinks you pulled off the most amazing demonstration. It was stunning . . ." The older man could see that Juve was not impressed with the city's adulation and changed his approach. "Why didn't you kill him, if that was your goal?"

"Complications."

Juve and Barth walked along the Tiber River. As they headed for a square dedicated to the great Flavius Aurelius, Barth said, "Imagine what the world would be like if everybody—or even just a few more angry people—demonstrated their dissatisfaction the way you almost did."

"The point is, they don't," Juve retorted. "People follow. Too few take a stand. They want to be led. They have to be led. I have no respect for most people. They can't be good to each other, Barth, unless you prod them. Given the chance, they'll always take advantage of one another. Have you ever been to Zostok?"

"No, but I'm well aware of what goes on there."

"But you haven't seen it."

"No."

"You have to see it. You have to smell it to appreciate real inhumanity." They turned away from the river and headed toward the center of the city.

"Everything is collapsing around you right now," Barth commented, "and that's good."

Juve laughed. "What's good about it?"

Barth smiled. "Everything in your world will collapse, Juve. The sooner you learn that, the better. Losing your parents gave you most of the motivation you needed to become a Lion. Didn't it?"

"Sure, but I'd give it all up," Juve snapped, "to have lived a quiet, normal childhood with them."

"I'm sure you don't mean that."

Juve hesitated. "You're right," he reluctantly agreed.

They walked on as Barth continued, "Everything we see and hear and smell and touch is temporary. In a sense, it's just an illusion. All of it. None of it will last forever. And none of it has to be the way it is. This is important to keep in mind, especially for someone like you, so passionate about fixing things that can't be fixed." Barth raised his hand and shook his finger for emphasis. "You're reaching for justice, Juve, and justice is beyond your reach." The two took a few more steps before Barth spoke again. "You remind me of Flavius, Juve. He struggled to find a set of principles that would save Rome from its decline. The reign of Tiberius represented a high point in our history—a departure from the conquer-and-subjugate policies of Augustus. But now, in part because of you, it's clear to a good number of people that we've been heading back in the wrong direction for a long time."

They arrived at the Piazza de Flavius. Barth pointed to the statue towering over the center of a broad square. People milled and mixed and hurried around the pedestal supporting the statue of Flavius. Juve contemplated the noble figure wrapped in old Roman garb. In his left hand, the author held his time-honored work, *Empathia*. His right arm rested at his side as he gazed to the east and beyond the horizon. On a ribbon wrapping a scroll in his right hand, Juve noticed the inscription "XXXVII."

"For all the statues and squares named after Flavius, there really ought to be a dozen or so for Chesua," Barth sighed. Juve contemplated the statue as the professor went on. "I believe he was on the verge of changing the world for the better. Not just for a time, mind you, but forever. Let's go over there and sit for a few minutes," Barth suggested, pointing at a group of unoccupied benches.

"It wasn't completely original," Barth said as they headed for the seats. "Much of it can be traced back to other Roman writers, some groups we call mystery cults, and to one group in particular known as the Essenes."

Juve sat back and thought to himself, *Give this old geezer a chance. Hear him out. He's supposed to be the most brilliant man in the world. Besides, what have you got to lose?*

After a while, Barth had telescoped through a history of the Republic and Juve's head was spinning. The old man was an animated teacher and his stories took on lifelike color and texture in Juve's susceptible mind. He could feel the old man's love of history. Every character leaped into Juve's imagination and played his part as Barth described it. The professor gripped Juve's arm to emphasize certain points and leaped out of his seat to illustrate the importance of a watershed event. Finally, Barth said, "There's a place I like around the corner. Do you want to have a late breakfast?"

"Lead the way," Juve replied agreeably.

On the way, Barth began to probe. "What has Octavia told you about our dinner discussion?"

"We just touched on it."

The restaurant bustled with late-morning diners. Barth and Juve could hear talk of the banquet caper as they walked to the table Barth had reserved with his wayfone on their way over. He was a favorite customer of the restaurant staff, and the two men received immediate and deferential treatment.

As they ate, Barth considered what kind of companion he'd find in Juve, even if it were not possible to bring him along on his journey through time in the TCI. *Only a few more days*, he reminded himself.

Maria sat down to dinner with her father. The past twenty-four hours had been hellish. She looked across the table at the man her Juve had failed to kill. How could she love someone who could do something so reprehensible? Juve had come so close to doing the very thing that made her despise her father.

What is it about men? she seethed inwardly. *What makes them want to solve their problems with force?* Was Juve to be admired or reviled? He did, when he saw her, change his mind and spare her father. Did Juve really intend to kill him? If so, she had saved her father's life! And now, she was sure, her father would kill Juve, if he could find him.

Maria refused to answer Juve's calls to her wayfone. She had too much to say, too many questions. Each time he called she shook her head no as if he were actually there. She wondered if her father had noticed her strange behavior.

More than once she'd wished her father were someone else. He stood for everything she detested—the worst of the Republic. She had enjoyed a life full of opportunity and privilege, but as she grew she had come to understand the price others had to pay for her father's wealth and power.

Maria's mother had died when Maria was ten years old. She and her father had grown very close, so close that he now confided in her as he had with his wife. She had learned about soothers, the Indomitable Lions, and how her father in especially difficult times had circumvented and abused his power to advance his personal aims. More than once she had heard him issue orders for someone to be killed. She had tried not to dwell on these kinds of memories. Most of what her father did, she had believed, was good for the Republic. Yet in recent years she had begun to distance herself from him and from her privileged position. Her disenchantment with her father's dishonesty prompted her to pursue her dream of bringing honesty to the Republic as a voice on Republic World. It was one of the reasons she was so attracted to Juve.

Maria knew she would eventually talk to Juve. She realized she was sending him a message by not answering his calls. *Is that the message I really want to leave?* she asked herself.

The house staff served bread with honey as her father opened a bottle of twenty-year-old Falernian wine. The conversation, as expected, began with Forza. Maria allowed Bellator to vent. She knew the wine would either send him off on a jag of self-righteous pity or lift his spirits to the point that he spoke freely to her as the father she remembered loving as a little girl. Either way, she made up her mind to guide the conversation toward what she wanted to know—had her father identified Juve as the leader of Forza? And if so, could she persuade him not to kill the man she loved?

"I'm curious, Father," she began. "What did the Leadership do in the past when it confronted these kinds of problems?"

"It's never been this out of control. We've never had such a selfish, ungrateful pack of pampered citizens!" he complained, taking a drink from his glass of wine. The servants brought in plates of lamb, pork, more bread and honey, and bowls of fresh figs, dates, and apricots. "The old ways worked in the past, because decent people held up their end of the bargain. They worked hard and they cooperated willingly."

The truth, Maria wanted to explain, was that people worked just as hard today. *What do you think ninety-eight percent employment means?* she wanted to reply angrily. "What percent of the people are working?" she asked instead, with measured curiosity.

"Hell, it's somewhere around ninety-four percent." Bellator shoveled a large morsel of lamb into his mouth with his fingers and spoke as he chewed. "Our people have it too good. That's the problem."

Why can't he detect his own contradictions? Maria asked herself. She sipped her wine, wondering if it was a good idea to drink, since she was already feeling light-headed.

"It was literally too good to last," her father continued. "The problem is, our social decline has been imperceptible to almost everyone."

"Reminds me of a cruel science experiment," Maria said. "Do you know that you can boil a frog in a pot with no lid?" Bellator knit his eyebrows and looked at his daughter quizzically. "Our science teacher put a frog in a pot of cool water," she explained. "No lid. Then he turned on the flame and heated up the pot very, very slowly. The frog just sat there even as the water began to boil. Boiled alive!" Bellator drank more wine and seemed to take satisfaction from the story. "Frogs are cold-blooded," Maria explained. "They don't perceive the change."

"My point exactly," Bellator exclaimed, proud of his daughter's grasp. "If you do it slowly enough, you can go to hell without a hint."

"And that's what we're doing?" she asked.

"That's what we're doing," he answered smugly. "I remember when our Primo di Augusto celebrations were one-hundred-percent positive affirmations of our pride in our greatness, in our traditions . . . Now, ever since that shameful demonstration in the East? Ever since then, our principal holiday—it's become a forum for dissidents reminding us of our flaws. What was I supposed to do, let those students take over the center of the city? After seven days of it—the local economy shutting down, the soldiers taking all kinds of abuse, the gutters full of shit—what was I supposed to do?" Bellator pretended to wait for an answer, then continued, "All our Primo di Augusto parades used to be uplifting and proud. Now every other float is a peace bird or a shout group whining about their pimples and the police. And they get more applause from the sidelines than the patriotic displays and the military bands!" Bellator pointed his finger at Maria. "That's a bad sign, Maria. And I choose not to ignore it." He stuffed his mouth with another helping of dinner and chewed it as he spoke. "And just like your frog experiment, it happened slowly, almost imperceptibly—to hell without a hint. Yes, to hell without a hint."

As the conversation heated, it was beginning to feel to Maria as though she were interviewing a controversial guest on Republic World. Suddenly she realized her challenge was to draw her father out as she would a guest in an interview. Could she do it without making him angry? She posed her next question with all the innocent wonder she could muster. "Wouldn't some people say that the Leadership has not always held up their end of the bargain?"

"Oh, sure, we've had less than perfect leaders, no doubt," he admitted with a proud sort of candor. "But I'd have to say, for the most part . . . for the greatest part of my time at least, Republic Leadership has done its very best. I can honestly say that. Before my time, we slavishly followed the law of the Blood Ballot. You couldn't vote for war without your own blood on the battlefield—a son, a daughter. When I was young, they let you at least send an adopted kid. Let me tell you, that started a run on adoptions. By the time I was working my way up the ranks of the Leadership, we started seeing a few breakaway provinces thinking they could work outside the jurisdiction and scrutiny of the Republic. Island provinces thinking they could start marching to their own beat. We couldn't wait to respond, and we couldn't have responded at all if we'd had to adhere to the idiotic Blood Ballot."

Maria thought her father sounded like he was giving a speech. Maybe the speech he had planned to give at the banquet. She took another sip of wine and framed her next question. "How long has it been this way? Was there ever a better time?"

Her father looked at her with admiration. He loved the way she was presenting her questions. He positively glowed with pride and wine. "My darling Maria," he began as he examined his glass of wine, admiring the deep color and the embers of light inside. He twirled the glass by its stem between his thick fingers and admired the legs of the wine as they descended. He brought the drink to his lips, inhaled, and closed his eyes in order to swim in the effect. "We are not perfect," he continued as he set his glass on the table and looked at his daughter to let her know that he had just made a profound observation. "Only gradually did the happy citizens of the Republic begin to ignore the lessons of our untidy past—the dictators, wars, and corruption."

Bellator went back to his dinner, but Maria could tell he had just begun a long, fatherly pronouncement. Maria wanted to make sure he followed the thought he had just planted. "I know what you mean," she interjected. "We learned nothing about dictators in school."

"Do you still remember that poem you used to recite to us? The one about Julius Caesar?"

"Yes," she laughed.

"Of course, there's nothing wrong with instilling love of country in children, but Caesar wasn't anything like the poem."

"How did we get away with altering history?"

"Over time, I suppose, the older the history, the less important our dark side seemed to be. It's not like somebody came along one day and tore certain pages out of all the history books. It was more like a silent, self-congratulatory conspiracy." Bellator smiled, pleased with his turn of phrase. "Everybody wanted to love everything about the Republic. We were all wrapped up in the new world we were creating together. So we just conveniently forgot the bad stuff."

"But wouldn't that mean actually wiping out all kinds of official records?"

"No, nothing was ever officially destroyed—just ignored, pushed aside, and after a time, discarded. I remember, it was when I was in school, we stopped referring to the old Republic as the Roman Empire from 750 back to year one. I grew up thinking we were always some kind of enlightened people who emerged triumphantly out of some prehistoric gloom."

"Tell me if I'm wrong," she stated as demurely as possible, "but this innocent self-deception . . . couldn't it be dangerous? I mean, couldn't it make it difficult for us to avoid repeating our mistakes?"

"In a word, yes. And there were archivists who refused to revise, mind you. Just like you, they argued that the uglier side of history must be preserved, if only as a warning to the future. Unfortunately they got to be a pain in the ass and were shuffled off to the sidelines." Bellator had finished his first glass of wine and didn't want to lose the soft effect he was enjoying, if only as an antidote to recent events. He motioned for the dining-room attendant to top off Maria's glass and to fill his own. "Look, my dear, I don't want you wandering around in the world with stars in your eyes, especially when it comes to your government. You'll get torn apart." He drank from his freshly filled glass. "So you should know that as our civilization has become more and more complex and demanding, we've had to do without some of the high and mighty principles that got us to where we are.

"Try to see it this way, sweetheart," he said, leaning toward her. "Does it really matter that one's occupation is determined by DNA analysis and aptitude metrics? Yes, it encourages class. Yes, it puts people in silos. I know that. But what difference does it make? Everyone has what they need. Hell, we all have a little more than we need. I've got more than I ever expected. And we'd have a lot less if we hadn't adjusted that ridiculous Income Parity business in Empathia."

Maria had argued angrily with her father when the gap between what the highest- and lowest-paid were allowed to earn was adjusted few years ago. Since Income Parity was adopted in 1395—a date memorized by every student—the gap had been allowed to widen gradually. In the beginning no one could ever earn more than ten times the income of the lowest-paid citizen. But it wasn't long before monetary awards for breakthrough inventions and discoveries were overlooked as income. Then awards for wildly popular artists and entertainers, then for outstanding athletes, then for the best in just about any field. These exceptions seemed to encourage innovation, and eventually higher incomes were paid as awards on a regular basis. "We've made a mockery of Income Parity," she had screamed at her father when the gap was raised from a factor of one hundred to five hundred. But now she listened patiently to the same man gloat over the results.

"Now we can have what we deserve. I break my back executing the directives of the First Minister. I know, I know—a well-equipped and more-than-comfortable home is not what life is all about. Labor-saving appliances eliminate drudgery but at the same time make us lazy. Big-screen monitors, cozy couches—every home becomes an oasis of relaxation. Theaters and stadiums—when are they ever dark?"

Maria wanted to scream, "You don't see even the edge of misery in your fairytale city!" But she held her tongue. Instead she smiled at her father, whom she loved and pitied. She hardly noticed that he was still waxing his self-justification.

"The baths stay open all day and all night. Life is too good." He paused. As if the demonstration at the banquet had actually delivered a message to him, he added in a less congratulatory tone, "Something's got to give! And do you know where it's going to start?" Bellator didn't give Maria a chance to answer, even if she dared. "Right at the head of Forza," he announced and locked his eyes on Maria's. His unexpected gambit caught her off guard.

She looked away. *He knows that I know Juve*, she told herself, feeling like a child again, caught by her father. "You mean the man with the knife?" she remarked as casually as she could. "Are you sure he *meant* to kill you?"

Bellator sat erect and gripped the table, looking at his daughter with the kind of parental arrogance that made her crazy with resentment. "My dear daughter," he said sarcastically, "I could see the blood in his eyes."

The silence was like thunder. Maria waited for it to end. *Go ahead, say it*, she thought. *Go ahead and say, "Until he recognized you!"* Struggling with her composure, she started to coach herself. *Don't look at him. You'll give yourself away.* Maria weighed her options as she pretended not to unravel. She scooped up some pork with a piece of dark bread and considered faking ignorance. *You don't think I know him.* Or, *You don't think I know him?* She considered offering an offhand explanation like "Maybe he didn't have it in him." Finally she said, "They've never killed anybody; they're just pranksters."

"What about the knife?" her father demanded.

"Just for show," Maria offered, "to frighten you."

It came off as weak and phony. *Pull yourself together, Maria,* she scolded herself, *Juve's life is at stake!*

"So why do you think he didn't go through with it?" she asked.

"Something stopped him," Bellator replied, confident now. From the time she could talk, she had seen him study her, as he studied every other person he needed to manipulate. He knew the meaning of the movement of every muscle in her face.

"Something stopped him?" she asked weakly.

"Yes. He recognized you," Bellator answered, his voice level. His words hit her like a blast of cold wind. "He's been calling you all day, hasn't he?"

Nobody spoke for half a minute. Nobody had to speak. Bellator let his daughter weigh her choices as he finished his meal and his second glass of wine. Maria knew she was trapped. She looked around the room, avoiding her father's eyes. Then her father lost his patience. He slammed his hand on the table. The dinnerware leaped into the air and came clattering down.

"You know who he is," he bellowed, "and you know *me*! If you don't tell me who he is, he's a dead man." He let the fact burn through her for a second and continued in a moderated tone of voice, "But if you tell me, he has a chance to live."

The thought of killing her own father flared in her until she forced herself to put the thought away and think clearly again. *Options. I need options. What options do I have?*

"You have no options," her father reminded her, sending a chill through her. "I could use your help, but I'll find him with or without it."

"Well, then, that's how it's going to have to be," Maria replied, watching her father's reaction. She had never been able to call his bluff, but now she pretended to be more interested in her dinner than in her father's answer. Bellator played along, and they ate quietly for a minute. "Of course, I'm willing to give something for finding him immediately," he proposed at last.

"I will not help you unless I have your absolute assurance that you will spare his life."

Bellator's eyes softened momentarily. Even Maria could hear the tone in her voice that told him she was in love. But he shook his head and returned to the perspective his job demanded of him. "He has insulted a lot of people, ridiculed and humiliated some very close friends of mine. And, of course, he intended to kill me."

"But if I hadn't known him . . ."

"Yes, my daughter, you saved my life," Bellator almost chuckled as he leaned back in his chair. "How ironic! He would have killed me if it weren't for you. So I suppose I owe you something for that, too."

Maria felt on the verge of tears, but her abated anger and fierce determination to save Juve kept her from breaking down.

"All right," he promised, "I won't kill him, if you lead me to him tomorrow."

"Give me your word," she replied, pretending that she would comply.

"I'll do better than that." Bellator made a motion with his head and spoke through his wayfone, "Come in here, Rowan."

As her father pulled a notebook and pen from his coat pocket, it all struck Maria as too smooth, too prepared. *I'll never lead them to Juve,* she thought, *but how will I get word to him?*

Rowan entered and presented himself to Bellator. "Yes, sir?"

Bellator wrote in his notebook as he spoke. "Maria will arrange with you to identify the leader of Forza tomorrow." He folded the note and handed it to Rowan. "Forward these orders to capture but not to harm the man she identifies. Is that clear?"

"Yes, sir," Rowan replied, taking the order, "capture with no harm."

Bellator looked at Maria. "The two of you will speak after dinner." He turned back to Rowan. "That's all."

CAFÉ FIORENTINA

BARTH'S OLD HEART COULD NOT KEEP HIM FROM HIS Saturday-morning walk in the park. Ever since Sylvia's death, it had become a ritual he treasured. There were pigeons to be fed and flowers to be gathered to adorn her grave. His favorite vendors greeted him every week: "Where have you been? I expected you earlier!" Every week they brought a smile to his face. Barth would buy a coffee from the same vendor and sip it with the same calculation he applied to his work. He knew how to ration his sips so that he would have just enough coffee to get to his favorite view of the city—the spot that captured his feeling about his wife, his life—and enjoy draining the cup there. Sometimes he'd revel in memory for a while, other times he would just acknowledge the spot and walk on. Today he sat for a long time.

He arrived at Sylvia's resting place, his breathing deepened, emerging emotion churned in his stomach, and Barth felt his purpose, as always. He leaned down to clean around the stone, dutifully removing the week-old weeds that had started to envelop the name on the stone. He tore at the plants with defiance, as if to say, "Don't you dare cover her name." As he worked, Barth looked down at his gnarled and discolored hands. He wiped them when he finished weeding and commenced his graveside ritual, reciting the same passage from his first love letter to Sylvia, pausing at the words that meant the most to him.

Like the bow of a great, stone ship, the ancient structure housing the Café Fiorentina split the narrow Strada Fiorentina into two, equally slender avenues. Juve and Auspex sat and talked at the point in the outdoor patio, two cups of coffee on their tiny, wrought-iron table. Their moods were upbeat, despite the fact that each had received orders to find and kill the leader of Forza.

"Forza has motivated me for the last ten years," Juve was saying. "For ten years—four thousand mornings—I couldn't wait to wake up and wreak havoc. I couldn't wait to see what we could do to try to create change. Now, each morning I wake up to the thought of Maria and what she means to me. It doesn't make Forza less important, just less important to me."

"Well then, Juve, I guess I'm just going to have to kill you," Auspex joked.

"Sorry, Auspex, you're the leader of Forza now," Juve replied. "It's you Bellator wants dead."

"Actually, my friend, Bellator's order may literally read, 'Kill the leader,' but you have to admit that when he wrote it, he had in mind the guy who held a knife under his nose."

"I see your point, tifoso, and I think I have a solution. We will kill each other simultaneously."

"If there's anyone I'd trust with my life, it would be you, Juve. But, I don't know. When it comes to my own death, I think I'd actually rather do it myself."

"What?" Juve exclaimed in mock astonishment. "You'd break the Indomitable Lion injunction against self-destruction?"

"Except . . . ," Auspex countered, his finger poised in the air, "except, as we both were taught, 'when honor-tied, we shall abide.'"

"Aha! You agree with me, then," Juve replied with a satisfied air of victory. "The orders are to kill you, not me, as you declared at the beginning of this ridiculous debate!"

Auspex threw up his hands in amused frustration and declared, "You know, they could have made this a whole lot easier on both of us, if they had just given us a name."

"Let's go see Bellator, then," Juve suggested. "I'll ask him, 'Do you want me to kill Auspex here, the most recently elected leader of Forza? Or would you prefer that he kill me, the punk who crashed your party and made you shit your pants in front of your daughter?'"

Auspex and Juve spilled over their table with laughter. Most of the café patrons couldn't help but smile, but several let it be known that they resented the minor uproar. The two young men eventually assumed a more sober tone. Auspex broached a question that had been nagging him. "I have to ask, Juve." He looked into his empty cup. "How long have you known Bellator's daughter?"

"Can she be trusted? That's what you want to ask," Juve answered. "It's a fair question." Juve picked up his cup, considered it for a few seconds, and continued, "I tell you, Auspex, it's like nothing I've ever known. Maybe she clouds my judgment. But I trust her. I trust her with my life." Juve took the last sip of his coffee and added, "Let's ask her when she gets here."

"I think we should. You know I can smell a lie on the other side of the horizon."

"Don't worry, she'll pass. You'll see. I'm more concerned about how many Lions Bellator put on this job."

"Good point. If it's just you and me, no problem."

"We kinda pissed him off," Juve chuckled. "So he probably covered himself."

"Here's another question—What makes Bellator think we know who leads Forza?"

"I wouldn't worry about that. He tagged us, because we're the best."

Juve saw Maria approach along Strada Fiorentina. Auspex followed Juve's line of sight and spotted her. He instinctively grabbed a free chair, placed it between himself and Juve, then tried to get the attention of a waiter. When he looked back, Juve was standing, his eyes trained on Maria. She saw Juve now and walked more quickly toward him. Juve stepped around the table and walked into the street to meet her. Auspex felt the hair on the back of his neck bristle. He scanned the street, shops, and windows but failed to identify the source of his alarm.

"Damn it, Juve, watch your periphery!" he hissed under his breath. From the point of the intersection, Auspex glanced down both forks of the divided street. When he looked back toward his friend, he saw the kind of motion he had been trained to spot and avoid—two bodies were converging, headed for the place where Maria and Juve stood embracing each other. Someone touched Auspex on the shoulder. He spun and held the man by his neck a few inches off the ground. "Sorry," Auspex said as he released the stunned waiter and darted into the street toward Juve and Maria. "Alert!" Auspex cried as he ran.

Instantly Juve sensed the impending attack. He glared at Maria. Speechless, she gaped as he reached, without averting his eyes from hers, and stabbed the approaching attacker in the voice box with the steeled fingers of his right hand. The enemy on his left went down with a blow from Auspex just below his ear. Juve's eyes, still locked on Maria's in violent disbelief, searched for a clue to her innocence. His eyes begged for an explanation as a bloody gash appeared below her left collarbone in sync with the muffled report of a silenced weapon from behind Juve. Maria's expression barely changed as she sank into Juve's arms.

Another shot whispered from the left as Juve went down, covering Maria. Auspex collapsed, lifeless, on top of them. *The first shot was meant for me,* Juve realized. *The second for Auspex.*

As the pedestrians scattered, Juve feigned lifelessness long enough to convince any other attackers that they had succeeded and could disappear. Then he rolled Auspex off his back. He was dead. Maria was alive, but too much blood ran from the front and back of her limp frame. "Why did you do this?" he whispered.

Maria struggled to keep her eyes open and breathed, "I thought I could elude them." She took a painful breath and exhaled again, "I was so sure I wasn't being followed."

"Stay with me," Juve pleaded. "Help will be here soon."

Maria replied with a flicker of a smile, then grimaced as she lifted her right arm and let her hand drop on her stomach. She opened her mouth and formed the breathless words "Our baby."

Juve struggled to take in what he thought Maria had just said. "Our baby?" Maria was struggling to nod as a smile drifted across her face and the light faded from her eyes. Juve pressed his hand to her body and felt a breath rise, then fall. It was her last.

Juve's world went white. His ears pounded with a cottony silence. The dry weight of a roaring ocean seemed to press and numb him from all sides.

He lifted Maria and cradled her gently like a baby but could not feel her. He pressed her tightly as if to squeeze her into himself. He wanted to go with Maria—and their baby!—wherever they were going. But now he felt his heart pounding in his chest, in his arms and neck. It refused to die. With its primitive, drumming thunder it racked his head and demanded to live. "No!" Juve screamed with all the rage he could muster. "No! No! No!" he screamed, in an all-out attempt to kill his defiant heart.

As the crowd gathered around him, stood and pitied the shuddering body wrapped around the lifeless woman, a rescue vehicle cleaved the gathering crowd and its medical team raced to Juve's side.

"Maria!" a miserable voice cried from the outside of the crowd. The cry snapped Juve back to his senses. He carefully arranged Maria's body on the street. A few seconds later, Bellator was standing next to Juve. He had tailed one of the assassins, hoping for the pleasure of seeing his banquet attacker go down. Bellator's eyes, bloodshot and watery, confirmed what he feared. His sniper team had failed. Sobbing and shaking, the chief counsel reached weakly for his daughter as Juve rose from her side. Face to face with Bellator, Juve wondered why, instead of hating, he now pitied the man. Because he saw in Bellator's face the seeds of Maria's beauty? Because he understood that just below this foul man's skin ran Maria's blood? Because nothing was worth killing for anymore?

"Live with what you've done," Juve said to the broken man with a calmness he had never heard in his own voice. Then he walked away. Bellator dropped to his knees, his head in his hands, sobbing.

BRAINSTORM

ON HIS OWN, BEFORE BARTH HAD TAKEN OVER THE TCI program, Zachaias had come very close to solving the riddle of how time and space collide and open doors to each other's realms. So close, in fact, that it didn't take him very long to catch up. At every step along the way to his solution, Zachaias made himself miserable fuming over Barth's advantages—how he was attacking Time Continuum Intersections straight on, backed by a staff of brilliant researchers and more than enough funding from his champion Bellator, the way he had used his political ties to advance his scientific career. Recently Horatio had convinced him to approach the problem from another angle. "Any angle," Horatio answered when Zachaias had scoffed at his suggestion. "You can't solve it conventionally. You don't have the resources. So come in a side door."

Then, not more than a few days ago, a colleague let Zachaias in on Barth's interest in Chesua and his long conspiracy with Sylvia and other devotees. When Zachaias mentioned this to Horatio, neither one of them knew what to do with the information. Now Zachaias felt that there might be a connection with Barth's TCI work. Over the past two days, writing on the board that covered his office wall, Zachaias had made two lists. On the left he summarized what he knew about the science of time and space and on the right what he needed to know. Between the two columns he scrawled Barth's name. Now he sat and stared at it. He stood and wrote *Chesua* below Barth's name. This, he sensed, was the stepping-stone to what he needed to know.

"I've exhausted every other resource available to me. I need to understand Barth's motives. He plans to use a TCI to his own advantage. Go with that," he said out loud as he circled the pair of names. "Let's assume he has already predicted when a TCI will occur. If he knows how the mechanism works, he can predict an event."

Zachaias saw a window. He knew now that if he could deduce when and where a TCI would take place, he could crack the secret of how they worked. It was the back door, but it was a way in. "If he knows when and where it will happen, he's sure to be there," Zachaias figured and wrote *when* and *where* under the names. "So I follow him around?" He scoffed at his own suggestion.

He stared at the names for a moment and remembered something Horatio had brought up a few days ago. "Why would he want to go through a TCI?" Zachaias had asked his partner.

"Forget why!" Horatio had replied. "You need to know where he wants to go."

"No, I need why to get me to where." Zachaias listed all his conjectures in an angry scrawl. "He wants to be young again? He wants to be with Sylvia? He wants to relive his life, and this time he'll beat me to the language chip . . ." He underlined *language chip* as he said the words. He stared at the board.

Suddenly, something else Horatio had said came to mind. "It's not about you." Zachaias drew another line from Barth's name and prepared to list the things that would motivate Barth. He was about to write *Sylvia* when it hit him.

"Of course!" Zachaias cried loud enough for Horatio to hear from the next room.

"Of course, what?" his partner inquired.

"He's going to meet Chesua."

"Who?"

Zachaias explained as he entered the room where Horatio was reading. "I told you about the Hebrew prophet my colleague in the language department told me about?"

"Chesh-something . . ."

"Chesua," Zachaias corrected. "He was complaining about a missing language chip—ancient Aramaic. We were trying to figure out who would want it. All he could come up with was Barth's secret fascination with this forgotten Judean philosopher named Chesua. I'm thinking Barth might want to go back and meet his mentor." Flushed with the ecstasy of oncoming solution, Zachaias disappeared back into his study. Horatio smiled to himself and continued reading. He had seen Zachaias succumb to the throes of creative intuition many times. It was one of the man's most attractive features.

On the board Zachaias quickly calculated backwards from a number of time and position coordinates situated in and around Judea. Several started to fit. He drew lines under several coordinate pairs—the five that he quickly estimated would calculate back to somewhere close to the present time. He made more detailed estimates of the first set of coordinates. Without the detailed math, it looked like the first location, deep in the desert east of the Roman Sea, connected to a TCI that should have occurred about a year ago. "Missed the train," Zachaias said, and he moved to the second set of coordinates. These were south of the city of Jerusalem—now a historic vacation spot and once a hotbed of religious activity. His second pass at the math put this TCI event a few months from now. Zachaias circled it. The third set of coordinates were useless. He realized he had included them by mistake. They were nowhere near Judea. But the fourth sent Zachaias's heart pounding. The event would take place on the eastern shore of the Dead Sea and in the next few days.

Within a few minutes Zachaias would have everything he needed. It was all over, except for the finer calculations. He went over to his desk, carefully entered the data into his computer, checking and double-checking each entry. Now his finger was poised to set the formula into motion. "Go!" he commanded. In a matter of seconds he had his solution. "Amazing! Simply amazing!" the scientist exclaimed. Horatio came into the study and looked over Zachaias's shoulder. The numbers and symbols meant nothing to him, yet he could sense their beauty, if only because his dearest friend sat gazing at the figures almost in tears.

As the two men celebrated that evening, Zachaias explained to Horatio that once he knew where Barth might be headed, he had what he needed. "The time and place of a proximate TCI cinched it," he declared victoriously.

"It's the only thing Barth had that I lacked. He got it by solving the problem head-on. Now I've got it by working back from the solution."

"Tell me if I understand this, Zach. If Barth goes to the proper place at the proper time, he'll simply stand there and suddenly find himself transported to another time and place?"

"Same place, different time. In this case, Judea in the year 787."

"How did you figure out that he's going to Judea?"

"That's where Chesua lived," Zachaias explained. "He's a devotee and one of the few people who could have gotten into the language department to steal the missing Aramaic chip."

"That's Chesua's language."

"Yes. So I worked from the assumption that he wanted to go see his hero. TCIs have to occur—can only occur—within limited arrangements of space and time. I posited the place and calculated the possible times. There's a TCI about to take whoever wants to go to Judea 787."

"So let me see if I understand," Horatio said, holding up his hands in a gesture that said slow down. "Whoever is at this place you've identified at the right time will go back in time and live in the past."

"If he survives," Zachaias cautioned. "We don't know what happens, except that he won't be here and now any longer."

"But if Barth goes back in time and survives it, couldn't he do something in the past—his present, our past—that alters the future? That is, his new future—our present."

"According to one theory, yes. But another theory says you can't do anything that will change the future, because it's impossible. You can't kill your father, for example, because that would mean you never existed and could not have come back to kill your father."

"Does that explain why we don't always feel in control of our actions?"

"That's an interesting way to put it. It could be that there may be a future in which time travel is possible and there could be time travelers among us. Except that, technically, there is no future or past, Horatio. Only the present exists, that is, if the present isn't an illusion."

"Well, then, at the other end of a TCI, there's something? Or not?"

"The math says yes, but the mind boggles."

"Do you really think Barth is going to attempt to travel in a TCI?"

"Why wouldn't he? He's triumphed with his Triple Laurel. He's a breath away from death. His wife has been dead for twenty years, and if my calculations are correct, we'll witness . . ."

"Witness?" Horatio scolded. "Why witness? You've got to stop him!"

"Why? It will be enough to see the look on his face when he sees me there."

"No, here's what you have to do, Zachaias." Horatio was firm. "I've watched you take second place to Barth all your life. Enough is enough. He stole the TCI project from you and you're going to take it back!"

"How?" Zachaias replied, taken aback by Horatio's sudden adamancy.

"Go to Bellator. Tell him how Barth is about to betray him. How he's going to make a fool of him. Show him the evidence."

"What if Bellator's in on this? What if they're planning some time-travel spectacle?"

"Then go over Bellator's head. Expose him, Zachaias! He's got to be stopped."

THE TIBER

JUVE TOOK TO THE ALLEYS. HE KNEW THAT TO KILL himself, he would have to make a decision, but he was too tired to decide, too spent to be angry, too angry to cry. His mind slogged with the thought of Maria. *You have to care about killing yourself to pull it off*, he thought, *and I really don't care whether I live or die*. It was difficult enough to put one foot in front of the other, and it took real effort to choose right or left when his path offered the choice. Yet he managed to always choose the darker, lonelier option. The night was cool and a single tear set a chill path down his cheek. Up ahead, a cat raced across the path of a man approaching slowly, hunched forward.

Have my instincts dulled, or is this man not a threat? Juve wondered. He couldn't keep his trained mind from calculating, *How many assassins did Bellator assign? Four in the square. The two we dispatched and the two shooters. He used Maria to mark me* . . . Juve couldn't stop his thoughts from returning to Maria—Maria and the baby. *If this man is going to kill me*, he thought with a shrug, *let him. I've killed enough*. The man ahead seemed unaware of Juve's presence. *Maybe he doesn't think I'm a threat*, Juve snickered to himself. *We can change that delusion real fast. Why not take him with me?*

Juve was now close enough that he could see the man's face. He appeared to be crying. Hands at his sides. No tension. No anticipation. Not intoxicated. Suddenly the man noticed Juve, stopped and looked pitifully into his eyes, raised the palms of his empty hands, shook his head and passed by. Juve stood still and watched the man depart into the dark. As he was swallowed in the distance, Juve played over and over Maria's last words. Her final glance and smile were seared into his soul. He tried to empty his head but it was impossible.

Juve mounted a bridge a hundred meters above the Tiber and stopped to look over the side. His whole body tingled with a sense of anticipation as the night took on an eerie, otherworldly pallor. Watching the inky water relentlessly slap and nudge the rocks under the bridge, he began to feel as though the Tiber were coaxing him to jump.

The door rattled furiously. Barth could tell that the banging was not going to stop, so he eventually conceded that he would have to answer the door.

"Barth! Open up!"

Recognizing the voice, Barth opened the door. The two men stood facing each other equally surprised. Juve opened his mouth to speak but found himself at a loss for words. Before him stood a ninety-year-old man in a yellow crash helmet, body padding, skin-tight camouflage pants, green swimming fins, an oxygen adapter, and a white parachute. The parachute sat atop a red backpack stuffed with supplies. From his waist hung a collection of climbing tools and several bottles of water.

"Juve," Barth said as he pulled up his sunglasses and assessed Juve's bloodied clothes and disheveled appearance. "What happened to you?"

"I want to go with you . . ." Juve hesitated. Then he shook his head and scowled, "But not if you're dressed like that."

"What happened to you?" Barth repeated.

"Too much to tell you," Juve answered. "Let's just leave it at I've lost everything, I'm ready to go with you."

"Not looking like that," Barth scolded, shaking his head. "You look horrible."

"You look ridiculous," Juve said as he walked around and inspected Barth's gear.

"We're not going anywhere until you tell me what happened to you," the older man insisted.

Juve considered the demand for a moment. "Okay, but don't spend a lot of time consoling me," Juve warned his friend. "If you're ready to go, I don't want to slow you down."

"Agreed."

"Maria and Auspex—my best friend—they've been killed."

Despite his promise, Barth was immobilized by his emotions. "What happened?" he gasped.

"Her father sent men out after me. They meant to get me." Juve spoke as if he were reading a script. Barth recognized Juve's façade—the self-protective emotional repression of a highly disciplined soldier. Barth stepped up to hug his young friend, but his equipment made the embrace awkward. One of Barth's swimming fins slid up along Juve's shin. A climbing hammer poked his ribs. "Oh, Juve, I'm so sorry . . . ," Barth began as he squeezed and patted Juve on the back. Juve returned the gesture, clumsily slapping Barth's oxygen tank.

As they withdrew from their embrace, Juve could see that Barth had been hit hard by the news. He grabbed a cord dangling from Barth's chest. "What's this?" Juve asked as he gave it a sharp tug. Immediately Barth's parachute deployed with a loud whoosh, slapped against the ceiling, and settled over the old man. "I'll have you know that I was prepared for anything," Barth scolded Juve as he fought back his tears and struggled to extricate himself from the parachute tent.

"What about public ridicule?" Juve let his friend find his own way out, giving him some more time to compose himself.

"I plan to ditch all this protective stuff as soon as I arrive, depending on how I arrive," Barth explained as he emerged from the chute and began to struggle with his backpack. "Help me get this off." With Juve assisting him, Barth continued, "I've got everything I might need. It's all in here." Juve helped his friend pull one arm out from behind a shoulder strap. The two managed to unload the backpack to the floor. It hit with a solid thump.

"How far do you think you would get with this load?" Juve asked.

"Far enough," Barth replied defensively as he unbuckled the pack and removed several packages of compressed food, a couple of bananas, a small camera, a grooming kit, and a hand computer. Then he drew out a full-length robe made of coarse material and held it up in front of his body.

"I'm impressed," Juve admitted. "Looks real. Is this what they wore back then?"

"Believe me, it's as authentic as you'll ever find. It comes from the university antiquities department." Barth went digging in his backpack again and came up with a beat-up pair of sandals. "Blisters I can deal with," Barth went on. "I'm worried about insects, scorpions, the sun, but most of all the people—highway robbers and regional rivalries. Nobody will recognize me as their own and everybody will mistrust me as a stranger."

"You're going to need protection."

"And you want to protect me?"

"I just want to go. There's nothing here for me."

"What about my mission?"

"To save Chesua?"

"Yes, that's why I'm going."

"Sure."

"Don't give me 'sure' as in 'why not?'" Barth warned, "because I won't take you with me. I need somebody who wants this almost as much as I do."

"Don't get too picky, Professor. I'm here. Do you want my help or not?"

"Thank you," Barth answered, wiping the last of his tears from his eyes, "but I'd rather take my chances alone than go with someone who's only half-heartedly committed. TCIs are infrequent, but fairly precise. If you go with me, you stand a chance of changing future events. Maria might even live if there is to be an alternative future, but you will never come back to your present existence. If you come with me, you may give Maria life again—maybe a better life—and you'll be helping me accomplish a very important mission. Come for those reasons if you must. But you have to understand that you'll be leaving everything you've built—Forza, your friendships, your home—all gone. You might as well be dying."

"Sounds like what I need—a permanent vacation."

"Maybe not," the old man said, holding up his hand, emphasizing just a tiny gap between his first finger and thumb. "There's an ever-so-slight chance we can return. But if my calculations are flawed, or if we can't get back to the right place at the right time . . ."

"We're fucked."

"You could put it that way, yes."

To Barth's surprise and delight, Juve stepped up and engulfed him with a warm embrace. "You crazy old man," Juve said. "Get me to Judea and I'm as committed to your cause as I was to Forza Facia."

The powerful affection of Juve's embrace comforted Barth. "I've had a long life," he spoke quietly as they both began to gain composure, "a fruitful life. It's easy for me to go. And I'm going because there's something there I believe in. But for you, Juve, there's more. There's so much for you to live for. You're young. I'm not entirely sure what will happen with this damn TCI, but I know I've had a good run. You, on the other hand, have your whole life ahead of you."

Holding Barth at arm's length, Juve sighed. "Maria was going to be the mother of my child, Barth. I was going to be a father. I let down my crew, but Maria offered me a new life. I was going to live for something, for some-one—love her and the baby, nurture them, watch them as they slept. Even if I wanted to go back to Forza, I can't. Bellator and his assassins saw me. It's over. I don't ever want to come back. I'd rather die. And if this business of yours holds even the slightest chance of a new life for Maria and our child, I'll take it."

"Then the sooner we leave, the better. But there's a problem—" Barth began.

"My clothes?" Juve offered.

"No, I've got a few changes in my pack. They're plenty big. And I really don't need all of them."

"We've got to lose the pack," Juve interrupted. "We can wear several layers on our way in and deal with the extras when we arrive."

"Okay, but the problem is language," Barth explained. "I've got an Aramaic chip. I don't have time to get another one."

Juve thought for a moment. "Then, I'll be your mute son," he suggested, amused with the idea of Barth as his father. "Or nephew."

Barth considered Juve's suggestion, and then decided, "I'd rather have you do the talking. You can be more forceful, if you have to. You're more mobile, too. You can get in and out of places faster and easier if we need to eavesdrop. I can be your mute uncle."

"Okay, I guess you're right, but you know what questions to ask. You under-stand more about what's going on."

"I'll advise you when we're alone. You can speak for both of us when we're around other people. We'll develop some signals." Barth reached behind his right ear. "Remove your wayfone," he said as he pulled out a black wafer and handed it to Juve. "Replace it with this."

Juve did as he was told. In a few seconds, he was looking around the room experiencing a strange sense of transformation.

"Go ahead," Barth encouraged him, "say something in Aramaic."

Juve hesitated, then spoke slowly. " *'T'dlowshee . . . shema . . . daamtaa . . .* Holy shit!"

"I don't know about the last part, but the beginning sounded pretty good," Barth observed. "But then, I can only understand it when I'm wearing the chip."

Juve wandered around the room, amazed at the fact that he could look at something and not only know how to say it but understand what he was saying. Barth was amused. "I spent an hour doing what you're doing," he told Juve. "Your tongue and lips will have to get used to making a few new sounds, but other than that . . . Oh, yes, you should be able to read and write, too. Don't be surprised when you find yourself reading from right to left."

"Incredible!" Juve marveled. "And I can still understand you."

"We'll still be able to converse in Roma, like we're doing now. And there's a good chance we'll be able to understand Romans. Just be careful. We'll probably sound strange to them. They speak an old form of Roma called Latin, but it's basically the same language."

"I'm impressed."

"Yes, it is amazing. My friend Zachaias invented it," Barth said. "Another thing—your Aramaic vocabulary will be limited, especially at first. Keep that in mind. They don't have words like *wayfone* or *electricity*. So if you find yourself groping for a word, it's probably because you're trying to say something there's no word for. These people don't have a concept of the solar system, the planets, refrigeration, automobiles—those are obvious—but they also don't know about soap, chewing gum, plastic, even rubber. Just be circumspect. Pay attention to the way people behave and comport yourself accordingly. You don't have to do a lot of talking."

"Suits me. I'm not big on talking anyway. When do we leave?"

"Immediately. We have a four-hour journey just to get to the TCI."

"*Kepa . . . wabar . . . bayta . . . Yeshua,*" Juve said proudly.

"Okay, son, it's not a toy. Let's get going."

TIME CONTINUUM INTERSECTION

THE TCI WAS QUITE A BIT DIFFERENT THAN WHAT JUVE expected. He was prepared to step into some sort of booth or vehicle. Instead he was walking along a mist-crowned lake in a ragged robe far from home. He and Barth had flown from the city across the Roman Sea and landed somewhere in what was once Judea, where they had changed into their costumes. A few hours ago, as they flew over Greece, Barth had reminisced briefly on the wonder of the great civilization that had once flourished there. As they approached the desert, Juve had seen Barth succumb to a kind of awe for the land as it came into view. Barth had briefed him on the lay of the land, the sea, the Jordan River, and the westward way to Jerusalem. Then they walked for the better part of an hour. Now the sandals were blistering their feet. They arrived on the eastern shore of the Dead Sea facing a stream that led up into wooded hills.

"Welcome to the lowest point on Earth," Barth said as he looked pensively up into the woods rising away from the water. He pulled from his satchel on Juve's back a small instrument. After pointing the device in several directions and consulting each time, Barth pointed into the hills. "Up there. We're close."

The two men trudged up a crease in the hills cut by a stream. The air was warm and dry. After about a half hour of climbing they followed a smaller branch of briskly tumbling water up a cleavage of brown rocks. The route was deceptively long. Barth grew more and more impatient, going over all the possibilities they might face out loud. Juve, too, allowed the grueling trek to weaken his resolve. *Even if he is the world's greatest scientist*, he thought, *I've got to be nuts to go along with this.* The heat didn't help. Finally, Juve could stand the suspense no longer. "How long before we get into this thing?" he asked.

"It's not a thing, my boy," Barth replied as he calibrated and read the device in his hands. "We're looking for a place where . . ." The great scientist stopped in his tracks, fiddled with his device, and continued, "It's a place where threads in the fabric of space and time happen to interfere with each other."

"Why here?"

"Why here, indeed," Barth replied mysteriously. "It's pretty much just the way time and space ebb and flow. My discovery . . . what makes my discovery so important, you see, is that I associated earth masses with time waves. It sounds strange, but some energy is kind of ghostlike. I call it ghost energy, because it's sort of wildly anti-gravitational. Or at least it can—according to my predictions—open a dimension of space and permit . . ." Barth searched for words. "Just think of it as holes in space that connect to spots in time," he concluded.

"Sure," replied Juve, more confused than when the old man had begun to speak.

"It turns out that this ghostlike energy comprises exactly 74 percent of the universe. It's what gives the world its shape. So, when you get to know it as intimately as I have— mathematically—it doesn't take much more than elementary math to figure out where the traversable intersections will be and where—I should say, *when* they will take you."

"What if one of these intersections turns out to be in somebody's bathroom?"

"Excellent question, my boy. Excellent question!" Barth gave him an approving smile. "I wish I knew the answer." Barth pointed to a rock formation up ahead. "See that pile of rocks?" Juve nodded and Barth pointed in the opposite direction. "And that mass over there?"

"Sure. I can see them."

"Well, somewhere between them we should find a spot that makes these numbers double, maybe triple." He pointed to his device. "Right now, you see, we're at twenty-one. That's pretty normal for out here."

"So we're looking for numbers in the forties or sixties."

"Exactly," Barth replied as he took a sudden turn to his left, checked both rock formations, and bent back over his instrument. "Within the next fifteen minutes we've got to find an area about two to three meters in diameter and get into the middle of it. The event horizon, that is, the lip of the TCI, could be a little dangerous."

"What's 'a little dangerous' mean?" Juve inquired warily.

"Who knows?" Barth shrugged. "I've never actually observed a TCI, but my calculations suggest that the event horizon could sort of tear you apart."

Juve just shook his head as he walked. "What the hell am I getting into?"

"Amazing!" Barth suddenly exclaimed. "Look at this, Juve . . . 236!"

Juve looked over his partner's shoulder. Barth was perspiring heavily and Juve noticed for the first time that he actually smelled like an old man—the well-worn musk of old habits and loneliness. In his gnarly grasp, the device flashed numbers that fluctuated wildly in the two hundreds as Barth moved it about. He took a deep breath and announced confidently, "In the next ten minutes or so there will be a TCI, right around here!" He made a divot in the sand with his heel. "It may happen sooner, it may happen later, but we are not going to move from this position." Barth pushed Juve closer to the divot.

"Easy," Juve joked. "You're just my mute advisor. Let's practice a little respect."

Without acknowledging Juve's warning, Barth continued, as animated as a kid with a new toy. "Now when we arrive, we'll carry the locator in this sack. Don't let anyone see it. Who knows what the locals will make of it? And we'll need it to find our point of departure. In case we lose the locator, remember this—we depart exactly twenty-one days from the moment we arrive. We'll depart from the top of a hill alongside the eastern wall of Jerusalem. The people there call it Skull Hill." He looked Juve in the eyes. "Got that?"

"Skull Hill, twenty-one days. Got it," Juve answered as he felt a new sense of apprehension. He scanned the trees at the highest point on the horizon. Then he realized he was hearing the distant hum of aircraft.

"I don't know exactly where on Skull Hill, so let's not lose the locator," Barth advised adamantly. "If we do lose the locator, or if we lose each other, get to the hill on time, stand on the summit and hope for the best. If we've done our job, if we save Chesua, the TCI will bring you back to a very different place."

"When?"

"After we've saved Chesua," Barth replied with pronounced irritation.

"No, what time will it be?" Juve explained. "When will it be, what day, what hour?"

"It will be there, now," Barth said as if Juve should have known. "It will be as if nothing has happened, as if no time has passed."

"I hope you're right. What if I decide to stay?"

"Stay? Why would you want to stay? Why wouldn't you want to go back to a better world? The past is a pretty ugly place, and the future, if we succeed, could be a whole lot better. And it doesn't hurt to know that my discovery will never fall into the wrong hands."

Now it was clear to Juve what was approaching. "Any reason we should expect a couple of aeroprops out here?" he asked Barth.

"Aeroprops?" Barth remarked incredulously. "Hell, no. Why? Do you hear aeroprops?"

"Two Centaurs." He trained his eyes on the eastern edge of the hill that hid the aircraft from view. "They should be coming over those trees."

"I suppose . . . some kind of expedition," Barth suggested, then another thought struck him. "Maybe we've been spotted and they've sent a rescue squad."

Juve heard Barth, but he was more intent on spotting the aircraft. He cocked his head as the sound of the approaching aircraft changed. "They're splitting up. They'll be coming around each side of the rock."

"Not good," declared Barth. "Feels like interference."

Just as Juve predicted, two insectlike machines appeared, one to the left and one to the right. There was no doubt that they were focused on Barth and Juve as they slowly approached, facing each other, hovering over the trees.

Barth looked at Juve. "Remember, no matter what we have to do about these intruders, be back on this spot in five minutes. Don't leave if you don't have to. It could be three minutes. It could be ten." The occupants took their time lowering themselves from the hovering aircraft in harnesses. As they stepped onto the rocky crevice several hundred paces away, Barth remarked, "Let's hope it's a rescue. At least there's a chance we can stall them until the TCI happens."

"Armed rescuers," Juve replied as he noticed that in each party of two men, one carried an automatic weapon and wore a sidearm. "Get ready to do whatever I say without hesitation," Juve ordered. "Lean up against me. If I shove you, drop down with me. Understand?"

"Yes."

The heat from the rocky soil rose in waves and made the visitors appear to quiver as they approached. Juve arranged himself and Barth back to back, each watching one of the teams walk toward them. "Our only hope is that it happens now," Barth said. "Take your time," he told the visitors, knowing they couldn't hear him. The sun beat on the shoulders of the would-be time explorers as their uninvited guests came close enough to recognize. "Oh, shit," Barth spat angrily. "It's Zachaias."

"And Bellator," Juve replied. "Don't provoke them."

"Stay where you are," hollered Bellator, wiping his brow. He was thirty paces away and approaching.

"What does it mean that it's Zachaias and Bellator?" Juve questioned Barth.

"The language chip," Barth whispered. "Zachaias must have discovered the Aramaic chip missing."

At about ten paces, the intruders stopped. "Okay, then they know what we're here for. They want to stop us," Juve concluded.

Barth whispered over his shoulder, "There's no way I won't go, Juve. You've got to stop them."

"They need the chip," Juve tried to whisper without moving his lips, but with a quick motion of his right hand, Bellator ordered a line of bullets to rip up the hot rocks just two steps in front of Juve's feet. Barth jumped and gasped. The intruders were amused, except for Bellator. He put out his hand and his guard placed a sidearm in it. Bellator stepped toward Juve. The guard followed a few paces behind. The opposite team followed suit, approaching Barth from the other side.

"You killed my daughter," Bellator snarled as he brought the weapon to the level of Juve's face.

Juve trained his eyes on the muscles in Bellator's hand and replied, "And I'm on my way to bring her back to life."

"Not a chance," Zachaias scoffed from behind Juve.

Juve gave Bellator an expression that said, "Who do you believe?"

"I know a lot more about this than he does, Bellator," Barth advised.

"Why should I trust a traitor?" Bellator snapped.

"Because he's served you for seven decades," Juve suggested.

"Get them off that spot," Zachaias pleaded. "We can argue just as well someplace else."

"Go ahead," Juve challenged Bellator, "unless you don't want to see Maria. You know what Barth has invented. You just have to trust my intentions."

Bellator's hand trembled as he struggled to control his rage and indecision. Juve focused on the muscles in Bellator's hand, but the shaking made it difficult. He blinked away the sweat beginning to roll into his eyes. *Who does he believe? Barth or Zachaias? What does he want? The past or the future?*

"Down!" Juve barked as he dropped back against Barth. Just as he had directed, Barth easily toppled with him. Juve saw the flash of Bellator's pistol on his way down. Springing from the ground, Juve flew at Bellator and snatched his pistol as the guard's bullets ripped over his back. One shot from Juve killed Bellator's guard. He spun to aim at the other guard, surprised that his bullets weren't already flying. The other guard was already down. Bellator's bullet had found the far guard's neck, which was now relieving itself of blood. The sand drank it in thirstily.

Juve ordered Bellator to march toward the aeroprop harness. Then he grabbed the automatic weapon from Bellator's dead guard and told Barth to grab the other guard's weapon. As Barth passed Zachaias, he couldn't help but snicker, "Late again, eh, Zachaias?"

Enraged, Zachaias leaped at Barth and managed to wrestle him to the ground. The two old men rolled clumsily in the rocks and sand. Keeping an eye on the retreating Bellator, Juve walked toward the pitiful struggle, passing over the TCI on his way. "Get up, Zachaias," Juve barked, but the furious scientist refused. All of a sudden, Juve felt a sensation utterly new to him. It was as if the earth had become electrified. "The TCI!"

Juve jumped back to the appointed spot. His hair stood on end as he reached the focus of the strange, new energy. Bellator turned and froze, watching. Juve wanted to call out to Barth but the powerful force refused to let him. A fuzzy form followed and tackled Barth. It seemed that Barth was dragging Zachaias toward the TCI. Juve became more disoriented. *In a few seconds, I'll wake up a thousand years ago*, he told himself. The thought washed away all concern. To Juve the struggle was like a distant nightmare.

Barth reached into the TCI with Zachaias clinging desperately to his feet. Bellator looked on in horror as Juve faded from view and Barth, draped over the event horizon of the TCI, burst into flames that blew like fireworks in all directions. Zachaias screamed in agony, and then began whimpering. His arm had gone the way of his lifelong rival. Tumbling through the air went one of Barth's smoking sandals.

VILLA JOVIS

"YOU HANDLE IT, LUCIUS," TIBERIUS BARKED. "I'M NOT leaving Villa Jovis! Tell the Senate I will not agree to build their new amphitheater." As he spoke, the emperor distracted himself with his collection of insects suspended in amber. He picked up and admired his favorite pieces, carefully replacing each in its own cloth-covered berth of a large, multisectioned display case. "The games disgust me," he snarled at Lucius, directing his attention away from the collection and back to his ally from Rome. "There are plenty of more worthwhile ways to spend money. Figuring out how to feed Rome, for one."

Tiberius walked to the window overlooking the expanse of water between his island retreat and the coast of Italia. In the distance he could see the mountains forming the peninsula that divided the Bays of Salerno and Castellammare. To the north lay Campania and Neapolis. Farther up the coast, Ostia and the mouth of the Tiber River port, gateway to Rome. His thoughts wandered to the cramped little port and he contemplated several of the solutions that had crossed his desk since feeding the burgeoning city had become a serious problem.

"Rome is just growing too fast," remarked Flavius Aurelius, the other man in the room, who listened as he worked behind a table piled high with manuscripts. His thoughts often merged with those of his master, a skill Tiberius found almost indispensable in his most trusted advisor.

"Last winter was a disgrace," Tiberius agreed. "There's no excuse for squandering our resources on entertainment when people need to eat."

"But the harbor is inadequate," Lucius reminded Tiberius. "Unloading cargo at Ostia and transporting it overland will only take us so far, and the Tiber can only handle ships carrying up to three thousand containers."

"My point exactly. Widen the river as Julius Caesar proposed. Then we could draw ships twice as large. Augustus had plans for widening the river mouth. Tell the Senate I want them to turn their attention to Ostia and the river. If we can build an aqueduct all the way from the banks of Upper Arno, we can widen the Tiber. To hell with the amphitheater."

"I've never seen any plans," Lucius said.

"Of course you haven't, but they exist. See Marcus Fabius in the archives."

"It hardly matters," Flavius replied without looking up from his work. "The Senate is too weak and corrupt to stand up for what we need."

From the west a clap of thunder broke, approached, and slowly rolled above their heads. As the sound faded, Tiberius turned to Lucius and gripped him by the shoulders. "I need you to run things for me, Lucius, while I devote my time to giving Rome the moral foundation she so desperately needs. All these details, all the minutiae, take me away from real leadership. Flavius and I are remaking the Republic, but I can't ignore the day-to-day crap or it will bury me. I need you to handle Rome for me. Can you do it, Lucius?"

"Yes, Tiberius, you can count on me."

"I don't have to tell you to watch your back. There are men in Rome who would cut your throat as soon as look at you. My own mother is one of the worst."

Lucius smiled. "Unlike you, Tiberius, I look forward to the intrigue."

"Then have at it, my friend," Tiberius replied, taking his co-counsel's face in his hand. "If you love Rome and value its future, take on the beast and tame her. Just don't get greedy. I don't want to catch you trying to undermine my power."

"You can trust me, Tiberius," Lucius replied, looking Tiberius in the eyes and gripping his shoulder. Lucius turned and strode to the door. Before leaving he saluted Tiberius, who returned his gesture of loyalty. When the heavy door closed, Tiberius looked over toward Flavius, pointed two fingers at his own eyes, and then pointed at the door. Flavius nodded in agreement.

Tiberius smiled. "That's why I enjoy working with you, Flavius. We think in harmony—not the same thoughts, that would be redundant, but in harmony. Our work is the only thing that holds my interest these days. Let's get back to Empathia. Where do we stand on the harvest of ideas?"

"I've sent secretaries in every direction, sir. We'll have the Greek, Persian, and Babylonian reports within three months."

Thunder broke in the west again, and this time Tiberius cringed. "I'm not a religious man, Flavius, but when forces far beyond our understanding behave this way, I can't help it. I think . . . I'm reminded that we're at the mercy of great powers."

"All the more reason not to abuse the power we wield," Flavius offered.

Tiberius felt a warm wave of affection for his advisor, who had become as much a friend and colleague as an underling. Under Augustus, Flavius had begun work on a formula for pragmatic government. Augustus had been convinced that reasonable men could forego much of the time wasted on political intrigue if all could agree on an enlightened system of government. Flavius had already outlined the basic formula and had named the work *Empathia*, principally because it was based on understanding and incorporating into every law the needs of those who would be affected.

With the death of Augustus, Flavius had convinced Tiberius to let him continue his work on the Empathia system. Initially Tiberius authorized Flavius to continue simply because he could think of no reason not to. Eventually he called for a review of the project. Working under Tiberius, Flavius had redesigned Empathia to reflect the way Tiberius governed and to address the most pressing issues dogging his new patron. The review went better than Flavius had expected. At its conclusion, Tiberius stood and applauded what he called the inspired work of a Roman genius. In a matter of months, Tiberius ordered work to begin on the seaside retreat on the island of Capreae that he now called Villa Jovis. As soon as it was habitable, Tiberius and his most valued friends sequestered themselves in the new hermitage and devoted their time to the future of Rome.

"Isn't this exhilarating, Flavius?" Tiberius exclaimed. "While Rome is eating itself alive, we're on the verge of creating the first rationally compassionate and perfectly pragmatic government. How do you feel about where we are so far?"

"I know we're on the right track, sir. The more I gather from the work we're finding, the more firmly I believe Empathia will be the jewel of your legacy."

"Legacy?" Tiberius grumbled, furrowing his brow. "Why should I worry about my legacy? What'll my legacy ever do for me or anyone else? Empathia is worth working for its own sake. It's so beautifully simple—the idea of governing people the way they want to be governed. It not only has its own power, it guarantees its own success. It encourages the governed to improve themselves and govern themselves wisely. It removes such an incredible burden from those put in charge of operating the government. Power in the hands of one or a few has always been a situation begging for disaster. Elected or appointed, men can't help but become corrupt as they accumulate power. The true value of a government must be measured by how well it supports the genuine happiness of its people."

"Well put," Flavius remarked and added, "and all the more reason to watch Lucius."

"Yes, we should. Thank you for your concern, Flavius. I want to give you some of my latest thoughts, then you can show me what you've come up with on your harvest of ideas." Tiberius walked over to his desk and shuffled through several documents.

Flavius sat back and folded his arms, preparing himself to absorb whatever Tiberius had to say. "Good. I'm ready," he assured his patron.

Tiberius gathered up his notes as an even louder salvo of thunder cracked nearby. Rain was beginning to pelt Villa Jovis and both men could hear the sea punishing the rocky shore of the island. A steady breeze drove through the chamber. Below, attendants began shuttering windows. Tiberius loaded polished stones on the documents he left behind on his desk, and then strode over toward Flavius. He read from his notes. "The people are malleable . . . ," he began. "I'm not sure where to go with that," he added. "Oh, yes, it's the principal assumption behind the idea of government, isn't it? People need to be led. But we have to justify leading them, I think."

"Or help them govern themselves," Flavius added.

"Yes, because they will be governed one way or the other."

"I see two approaches: lead the people to self-assertion or build a system that precludes corruption." Flavius thought for a moment, then continued. "That sounds so naïve, but we want to make it impossible, or at least very difficult for a tyrant to do anything for personal gain, military glory, revenge, ambition, or his own advantage. As long as the reward comes from accumulating power and wealth . . . that is, what you can gain for yourself . . ."

Tiberius interrupted, buoyed by what Flavius had begun to say. "Right. As long as war and its spoils go to the generals and their friends in power . . . but how do we stop that? It's such a natural impulse to glorify conquest. What we need is an idea, an idea that people will embrace. An idea with rewards built in—rewards that come from seeing justice and happiness for one another. Something that uses the natural desire for justice in each one of us." Tiberius abandoned his documents to the floor near Flavius's desk and spoke as if to a hall full of senators. "That could be it, Flavius. Nothing's more powerful than people's desire for justice. When they come together and decide to right a wrong and their vision is clear, nothing can stop them! I've seen battalions of soldiers willing to give their lives with that unparalleled enthusiasm, but only when they are possessed with an unblemished conviction that what they were about to do was right."

Tiberius pointed at Flavius in mock accusation. "We've made a huge mistake in allowing enthusiasm for the state to wane, in dampening enthusiasm with the burdens we put on our people—burdens that fill our coffers, line our pockets, and make our lives more comfortable. But only for a while, only until we have to add cruelty to gain cooperation. That eventually kills all enthusiasm and breeds revolt."

He rested his hand on Flavius's shoulder, looking him squarely in the eye. "When we lose that passion, we lose the free and happy contributions of individuals. Add up the unhappy individuals we've managed to accumulate today. We have a population that requires more energy to subdue than they return. That not only tires our ruling class, it makes them mean and all the more corrupt. It's time to fix this, Flavius, before we exhaust ourselves."

Flavius nodded in agreement, smiling at the emperor's enthusiasm. Tiberius turned and considered the roaring storm outside for a few seconds, then spoke over his shoulder to Flavius. "Man's natural state is to be happy and productive. I want to capture and direct that natural force, Flavius. It's the most powerful force on earth."

"Consider this, then," Flavius began. "The mass of people go the way of certain individuals around them. And these people, when their leaders are just, reflect the spirit of those leaders. I think they are connected more closely than we have understood or at least ever admitted. We don't see the power of a movement until it is moving beyond our ability to check it."

"Exactly," Tiberius chimed in. "We need to inspire the people with people of quality. Unfortunately, people of quality don't last very long in positions of power, if they make it there at all."

"But the people have been inspired from time to time by rebels and prophets."

"So how can I capture that kind of spirit, Flavius? How can we build this into Empathia?" Tiberius shuddered suddenly as the storm thundered above him. "Where can I find an idea that inspires leaders with passion for the well-being of the people they lead?"

"Right now," Flavius answered, "the competitive sport of power in Rome is blind to the needs of the people. It brings the most powerful, the most clever, but also the most devious to the top."

"I am no exception," Tiberius snickered, "but at least I see that I'm part of an endless cycle of misery-making that destroys not only the poor and miserable but ourselves as well. I no longer respect men who shout for war from the comfort and shelter of the Senate floor. They talk of troop numbers and military budgets like they were similar commodities. I've heard the screams and moans of tortured men, Flavius. Their cries have never left me. With my own campaigns, my own example, I've helped make our people as power hungry as I have become, but I think I can stop the cycle. I want it to stop. Give me a principle that checks the passion for war before it can begin—anyone who votes for war, every senator who votes for war must vote with his own blood. He must have or offer one of his children in the fray, not in the command, on the ground. Of course, some of the senators I know would gladly sacrifice their own children."

"You know, we have had generous examples of exceptions to your rule," Flavius reminded Tiberius. "We have seen men who have given much and sacrificed so much of their energy to help our poor. Sadly they show up too late and can only do so much."

"I want to capture and make that spirit live as the rule," Tiberius roared back at the storm, now at the height of its rage. "Right now, caring for the people is a lonely and thankless enterprise. Our religions are little help. They provide dreams that work like opium, but the addiction is worse than the lack of religion. Our poets lick the hands of our generals with their songs of glory . . ." He asked Flavius directly, shouting to be heard over the storm, "Can we do this before we corrupt the next generation?"

"You have my undying support, sir."

"All right, then, let's get to the harvest. What have you found since last time?"

"One of my sources has identified an interesting prospect in Judea."

"Judea? That's where we found Hillel—'Whatever you hate, don't do it to your fellow man.'"

"Yes," Flavius replied. "We've already made that central to Empathia."

"So there's more from Judea? I expected more from the Greeks. We keep hitting gold there." Tiberius could tell by the look on the face of Flavius that his advisor was about to offer something interesting. "Go ahead. Tell me more."

"Hillel was almost twenty years ago. The Hebrews have a long tradition of legal scholarship, as you know. That's one of the reasons they're so difficult to control," Flavius explained. "At the same time, they bicker among themselves like spoiled children. Right now the poorest and most afflicted among them are becoming violently unhappy with their ruling class. They despise them almost as much as they despise the Roman occupation."

"And what is our friend Pilate doing about it?" Tiberius asked sarcastically.

"He's doing his best. He's dealt with a series of troublemakers in one form or another—some calling for insurrection, some just whipping up dissent—nothing Pilate can't handle. However, a certain rabbi has aroused my interest."

"Who would that be?"

"They call him Yeshua," Flavius answered, "a worker's son from Nazareth."

"What's he up to, organizing the workforce?"

"No, he's not that kind of agitator exactly, which could make him more dangerous. But that's not the issue. His ideas bear the mark of the Essenes."

"The Essenes, yes," Tiberius remarked, "the quiet ones."

"They live in caves along the west bank of the Dead Sea. All men. They renounce material comforts and devote their time to study and prayer."

"Sounds like a fun group."

"Here's what interests me," Flavius continued. "From what my people have gathered, the Essenes have already refined a lot of the ideas we've been struggling to perfect."

"Well, then, bring me one of these cave dwellers."

"Good idea."

Tiberius knew that Flavius was steering him toward a specific request and he loved to play along, watching the way his friend's mind worked. "Do you have a particular Essene in mind?"

"I recommend the man named Yeshua," Flavius answered. "He's an Essene or was one, but he offers more than a cave dweller, because he's been working their ideas among the people, on the street. He's been around, outside Judea. From what I hear, it sounds like he's blended ideas from the East and the Greeks . . . the point is, it comes out sounding a lot like what we're doing."

"I'm listening."

"Besides, you'll be doing Pilate a favor. He's going to have to deal with this man eventually. He sounds a lot like a Zealot sometimes."

"How urgent is this?"

"Last I heard, Yeshua was in trouble with the Hebrew power structure for blasphemy. It seems he claims to speak for their god."

"Why haven't they dealt with him?"

"I suppose they're concerned about his following. They say he performs wonders and cures disease."

"A crowd pleaser, eh?"

"Definitely. We've seen this kind of thing before. Any number of crowd pleasers, as you call them, seem to cure certain maladies under the right conditions, but this one also calls himself King of the Jews."

"The Sanhedrin can't ignore that for very long. It's a direct assault on their authority over there. They'll want Pilate to nail him up for sedition."

"We should bring him here. And pretty soon."

"Absolutely," Tiberius agreed. He opened the door and called for his secretary to send up the head of the Indomitable Lions.

"The problem is," Flavius continued, "we may leave behind a fairly substantial following. Some of them are Zealots, but I'm not sure how organized they are."

"Not a problem," Tiberius reassured Flavius. "We'll make Yeshua disappear. I've dealt with their kind before. Remove their leader and they scatter like roaches. We'll drop a handful of contradictory rumors regarding his fate among his principal followers. Trust me, they'll break into factions and run off like chaff in the wind." Tiberius pulled up his toga to reveal his left arm and a row of red spots. "We'll see what this wonder worker can do about my rash."

Lightning flashed within the chamber followed by a loud clap of thunder just as the door shook with a series of short, commanding raps. Visibly shaken by the odd coincidence, Tiberius commanded whoever was at the door to enter. The door swung open as thunder rolled away, out to the east. In strode the domineering figure of Gaius Marcellus, head of the Indomitable Lions assigned to Villa Jovis.

The raging storm still electrified the atmosphere in the room as Tiberius laid out the assignment to Gaius. "Take five Lions with you to Judea as soon as this storm passes and find a man named Yeshua of Nazareth. He's a popular rabbi and a rabble-rouser who calls himself King of the Jews."

"Shouldn't be too hard to find."

"Good. Then bring him to me—unharmed, or harmed as little as possible, but definitely alive. I want to talk with him at length."

"Sounds easy enough," Gaius replied.

"I know you're not crazy about leaving Villa Jovis for such a stinking, crowded little backwater, but I need to talk to this man."

"Consider it done, sir."

"Thank you, Gaius, I know I can count on you."

Gaius saluted and headed for the door, but Tiberius stopped him. "You may want to check in with Pontius Pilate, if only as a courtesy. He may already have plans for Yeshua, but don't let him interfere. Your orders come from the top."

"Of course, sir."

With another salute Gaius was gone. The storm was beginning to ease off toward the mainland, but it still pummeled Villa Jovis with a downpour of heavy rain, flashing light, and crashing thunder.

JUDEA

JUVE DROPPED TO HIS KNEES. THE EARTH HAD JUST SHIFTED beneath his feet. He was hit with a thunderous wave of otherworldly sounds as every tree in the time he had left was replaced with one of its ancestors. It felt several degrees cooler, and Juve shivered for a second. Fresh smells rode in on the cool, late afternoon breeze—hints of ripening fruit and the distinct scent of salt. Looking around at his new surroundings, he scanned the cypress and poplar trees along the tops of the hills on either side and then at the immediate area. Just as Barth had promised, Juve found himself within the same cleavage of brown rocks they had found and identified as the location of the TCI. *It certainly looks like the same place*, Juve thought, *but I'll know soon enough if Barth is on the mark.*

The thought of losing Barth troubled Juve. All he remembered was Barth and Zachaias, blurred by the effects of the TCI, approaching the spot where he had stood. Juve wondered what Bellator would do to Barth, and then how he would manage the mission without the professor to guide him. *How am I going to find Chesua? Forget about getting back—no locator. Twenty-one days to find Skull Hill.* Then he thought of Maria and braced himself against an even heavier wave of profound loneliness. Instinctively Juve shook off thoughts he knew would only diminish his chances of survival and success.

He began to survey and to assess his new environment. Down between the flanking rocks he noticed flowing water and decided to head toward it and follow it to whatever civilization he might find. He looked at his hands, quickly inspected the rest of his body, and then took a deep breath and a tentative step forward. Everything seemed to be okay, and he began to walk.

Juve ran through every option he had learned to consider in his Lion training. He began by building an itinerary of primary and contingency objectives and a list of immediate and secondary needs. Water was at the top of the list. The stream below looked more promising as he descended toward it. He could hear it gurgling gently over and through its bed of rocks. Soon Juve was following a trickle of water down the side of the hill. When he felt the stream had become wide enough, he knelt down, cupped his hand in the cold flow, and drank. The cooling effect lifted his spirits, and he continued to follow the stream downhill. Eventually the stream joined another. *I'm going to have to make something to carry water*, Juve reminded himself. He made finding people his next objective. *This part of the world is populated and water should be all I need until I find them.* Now he looked down a long pair of steeper and taller hills as he descended between them.

About an hour later, Juve saw a thin curtain of haze at the end of the little valley that opened into a large body of water shrouded in mist, but as he walked into the haze, he was struck by the fact that the air did not feel particularly humid, but rather warm and dry. *Just as it was and will be a thousand years from now*, he thought. The sun illuminated the fog as he approached the sea. He could almost taste the salt on the warm breeze. When he reached the water and tasted it, Juve realized that he was, indeed, back at the eastern shore of the Dead Sea. The water was thick with salt.

"The lowest point on Earth," he recalled Barth pointing out. *And here I am at the lowest point in my life. At least I know where I am. Soon I'll know whether this is really the past. It has to be. Everybody is gone. The aeroprops are gone. But it's still so difficult to believe.*

The sea stretched as far as Juve could see, north to south. Where was he? Near the top or bottom? How far to the northern shore where he would head west and cross the desert to Jerusalem? A subtle turbulence in his gut told Juve that it was time to eat. All along the eastern shore of the salty lake there would be vegetation and other streams of water. On the other side, across the

Jordan River, Juve knew he would face a long stretch of arid wilderness. He hoped to meet a settlement of people along the way, perhaps at the mouth of the Jordan. But he could not count on that chance. Juve planned to eat and to find a way to carry water before heading across the desert. After taking a long drink of water from the stream he left behind, he headed north.

An hour along the way, the disturbance in Juve's gut became a little stronger and more insistent. He considered wandering up into the hills on his right to forage. He was sure he would recognize the tree leaves or herbs that would settle his intestines, but he continued to follow the bank of the lake. It would be better, he thought, to rely on the care of the locals, when and if he found them. Meanwhile he walked and practiced speaking aloud in his new language. He concentrated on pronouncing the more unfamiliar sounds, such as the hard H. His language chip guided him and he allowed himself to rely on it, hearing himself improve as he put more and more of the great salty lake behind him.

But his gut didn't seem to want to make the trip with him. As he passed another stream feeding into the sea, he stopped to wet his face and hair. The tepid water made him shiver and his insides rebelled with a series of long, growling cramps. It occurred to Juve that he might have picked up something in the water that would make him sick. How sick? For how long? *My immunities come from another millennium. They may not be able to protect me here and now. What have I brought with me that might be at odds with the microbes around here? What will I bring back with me? This is riskier than I planned.*

Planned? He laughed out loud. *I didn't have time to plan anything. I may be in over my head.* Angry with himself for thinking negatively, Juve forced himself to banish thoughts that would compromise his survival. *I need a clear head. My brain is my main survival tool. I've got to keep it cool and optimistic.*

He splashed more water on his face, and then dipped his head in the stream. Again his gut responded, this time with wrenching spasms. He rose, his head swimming, headed for a clump of shrubbery, and relieved himself. The process was violent and convulsive. Juve was convinced he was sick—possibly very sick. He stripped off his clothes, staggered into the lake, and cleaned himself. The water felt greasy to his touch and so warm that he decided to rest in it for a little while. Strolling out into deeper water, he lay on his back and floated like a cork, amazed and delighted with the buoyancy of the inviting body of water. The mist obscured the sky and he began to feel suspended and out of touch with the world. *This isn't good*, he warned himself. But the warm water and the heavy atmosphere comforted and reassured him. He rolled on his belly and let the warm, briny water ease the pain for as long as he could hold his breath. On his back again he filled his lungs with the heavy air and blinked away the salty sting in his eyes. Juve floated, eyes closed, and let the lake convince him to drift a little longer.

Whispering voices echoed gently within Juve's first, foggy moments of consciousness. Even though the voices comforted him, he let himself drift away, back into oblivion. When Juve returned to the voices, he began to listen. He wanted to open his eyes, but his lids were heavy and his body lay like a huge stone on a hard surface. *Better to just listen*, he thought, as he concentrated on the sound. *It's a large room. Very large. Long echoes. Footsteps. The floor is rough or dirty. All men so far. Old and young. The older ones are definitely in charge.*

"God will make it clear to us."

"I tell you, it's clear. God has sent us the Babbling Preacher of Lies."

"That's impossible. He died ten years ago. Besides, this man's feet are so tender, they're blistered. He has not walked far."

"You heard him talking nonsense and blasphemy. Perhaps Satan carries him."

"Then it's a follower or his evil progeny."

"No! You saw his nakedness. He has no foreskin. This man has made his covenant with God."

"What covenant? He trims his beard."

"Why would a man of God display his nakedness in the desert?"

"He cursed the water. He may as well have cursed God."

"He may have been possessed by the evil one, but he is quiet now. We will wait and see."

I will wait and see as well, Juve told himself. *I must have wandered away from the lake. Naked, no less. Delirious, too.*

Juve wanted desperately to open his eyes, but he did not want to let on that he had regained consciousness. But as the debate continued, he carefully cracked his eyelids. In the momentary blur he caught a glimpse of at least seven bearded men dressed in long, white robes.

Where are the women? he wondered.

"I say he's Yeshua, the upstart from Nazareth."

"You were not with us, brother, when Yeshua was one of us. This is not Yeshua."

While the white-robed men continued to debate, Juve sank into a dream. He began to relive the sickness that overcame him by the banks of the Dead Sea. He moaned in a low, quiet tone. The men in white robes stopped talking and gathered around the dreaming stranger. Juve rolled his eyes under his closed eyelids and inhaled slowly and deeply. The room was silent as Juve, little by little, opened his eyes, focused on one of the men, and awoke with a start.

"Everything is all right," said one of the men on his left.

The oldest looking of the group, standing over Juve's head, explained, "We found you wandering near the Sea of the Dead."

"Naked," added a man near Juve's feet.

"You were badly burned by the sun," continued the old man. "We've taken care of you to the best of our ability."

A man on Juve's right gently lifted Juve's right arm and carefully pulled back the sleeve of his fresh, white robe. "You've healed nicely but your skin has grown very dark."

"All over," added the man at Juve's feet. Juve raised and turned his head to appraise all seven men. He let his head fall back on the hard surface and cleared his throat. One of the men stepped away and returned with a gourd and brought it to Juve's lips. Juve turned his face away, remembering what water had done to him.

"It's all right," said the man with the gourd in a kind and encouraging manner. "You've been drinking it for several days now. You're healed."

Juve looked into the bearded man's soft, dark eyes and noticed a small leather pouch on his forehead. Juve felt his own forehead and the man smiled. "Drink now, it will be good for you," he urged Juve. Juve allowed the man to spill a small amount of water into his mouth. It felt so refreshing and soothed his mouth. He swallowed, welcoming the water into his throat. Tilting his head up, Juve indicated that he wanted more water. "Not too much and not too fast," the man advised as he gave Juve a bigger drink.

Juve returned his head to the hard surface and took a deep breath. "Where . . . ?" he said, choking on his words. He had not spoken for some time.

The old man came around to Juve's right side and rested his hand on Juve's chest. "We are in the caves of Qumran, not far from where we found you," the man offered. "Where is your home, my son?" Juve pretended to have trouble speaking and the old man patted his chest and smiled reassuringly. "No need to talk until you've eaten and feel up to it. Rest now."

It was clear to Juve that at least two of the men did not approve of the older man's gentle, almost solicitous manner. It was also clear that the older man was in charge and that he intended to protect Juve. Closing his eyes, as if he were following the man's advice to sleep, Juve began to form his strategy. *I need to get out of here and find Chesua as soon as possible. How many days have I lost? Find out. But first, assess my strength. I need to spend a little more time absorbing the language and the way the men are expected to act around each other. Bad manners could give me away. These guys don't seem to be armed. No real threat. I'll align myself with the old man and his allies, find out what these people need, and how I can help out.*

Juve heard the men move back to where they had been huddled earlier. He stretched and pressed his arms against the surface below him. He realized he was much weaker than when he had arrived. Not good. But not bad either. He felt confident he could walk after flexing the muscles in his legs. *Best to follow the old man's orders,* he thought as he allowed himself to nap.

Juve woke and struggled against the stiffness in his body as he sat up and discovered he had been lying on a thick plank straddling two large rocks. His feet dangled over the edge. He slid down and landed on the floor, still holding onto the plank. The stone floor was cool and dry. Standing up straight, steadying himself, he took a step forward. He felt a good deal stronger than he had estimated and let out a deep sigh of relief and satisfaction.

The cave was darker than it had been when he met the white-robed men. Now, the only light came from a pair of oil lamps burning on either side of an opening in the cave wall. As Juve shuffled toward the chamber opening, his robe flowed loosely around his legs. Through the gap the chamber opened into a larger space, slightly warmer and dimly lit by the last remains of the day. Opposite the cave entrance, deeper in the chamber, Juve heard the peaceful chorus of snoring men and realized he could escape. *No*, he decided, *these men can help me. I need information and provisions. If I play it right, I might even score a guide, maybe even transportation . . .* He looked down at his bare feet. *And sandals.*

Stepping outside the cave Juve scanned the horizon. In the twilight a bright, nearly full moon illuminated the hills and, not far down their slopes, the sea as black as ink. "We call it the Sea of the Dead," said a voice from behind Juve. Before a thought crossed his mind, Juve had spun to face the speaker in a defensive posture, ready to attack if necessary.

"Easy, friend," the young man said, holding up his hands, palms forward. It was the man who had given him water from the gourd.

Juve relaxed and quickly composed himself, noticing that the leather pouch no longer hung from the man's forehead. "Yes, I know the name of the sea," he said.

"But you're not from around here," the man replied, puzzled.

"I heard the other men refer to it," Juve explained.

"Nothing lives in it. The salt kills even the fish that hazard in from the Jordan River."

"Seems you could find a cheerier place to settle."

"In this world?" the man almost chuckled.

"Yes," Juve countered confidently. "There are beautiful places in this world with fertile fields, and cool waters . . ."

"Our work requires a dry climate."

"Why is that?"

"We write. We write the word of God on animal skins. Here in our desert temple the skins do not deteriorate. The air is dry, as dry as you will ever find. Besides, we prefer to remind ourselves that we are not part of the world."

"How do you mean?"

"No matter where we go, we will always be like children camping on a stranger's land. When the stranger finds us, he will say, 'What are you doing here?' We will have to have an answer."

"I guess I know what you mean," Juve offered, reminding himself that his objective was to connect with these men, not argue with them. "This is not my home, either."

"What is your name?"

He knew it would happen eventually. Alone with this agreeable young man, Juve felt confident enough to try out his identity. "I am Juventus Trajan Carnifex."

"They call me Benjamin of Beersheba," the man replied, wrinkling his brow quizzically. "You are a Roman?"

"And a Jew," Juve added, then explained, "I was born in Rome. My father was a centurion. He met my mother in Jerusalem. She never told me where she was from. Growing up in Rome, I was often ridiculed for being a Jew."

Benjamin took a step away from Juve and turned to face him. There was a playful hint of curiosity in his expression. "Is it true that the Romans have built long passageways in the sky that bring water from the mountains into the city?"

"Yes," Juve answered confidently. He suddenly wished he had been a better student of history, so that he could answer the question that might follow. As for the aqueducts, he had visited several of those still in use.

"And does the water flow all day from great fountains?"

"Of course, beautiful fountains."

"And anyone can drink from them?"

"Certainly."

"And can you bathe in them?"

"No, you're not supposed to bathe in the public fountains, but there are public baths."

"For men and women—together?" Benjamin expressed this question more like a statement, and with definite disapproval.

"Yes, that's true."

Juve suddenly felt as if he were being cross-examined, but he was amused watching Benjamin. As the thin young man in his clean white robe formulated his next question, he paced in front of Juve with his hands held behind his back. "Is it true that Rome is full of men who spend their lives accumulating huge piles of worldly treasures?"

Juve considered the question. His hesitation pained Benjamin, who changed his tone. "Forgive me. My question troubles you."

"No, no, it's all right," Juve assured Benjamin, but the young man held up his hands to change the subject. So Juve complied. "I need to know how many days I have been with you."

"We nursed you for seven days, brother."

"Seven days!" Juve exclaimed.

"Yes, I'm sure," Benjamin assured him.

"Who knows how many days I floated in the sea . . . ," Juve began.

Concerned over Juve's sudden agitation, Benjamin tried to calm him. "You are our guest here. It is my duty to see that you receive what you need, but I can only guess how long you were in the water—a day, maybe two?"

Juve quickly estimated how much time he had left to complete his mission and find his way to Skull Hill and the return TCI. *I could have as little as eleven days left!* Juve realized. Benjamin sensed Juve's concern. "Tell me what you need, Juventus, and I will do my best to help you."

"I'm looking for a man named Yeshua." Juve startled himself with his own speech—he meant to say "Chesua," but it came out "Yeshua."

"I know him," Benjamin said with a pleasant sense of recognition mixed with mild suspicion. "In fact, you look a lot like him. I thought you might be his brother James." Juve was struck suddenly with an ominous feeling of dread, remembering his repeated dreams of the look-alike rabbi he never managed to save. "Please feel free to tell me what troubles you."

"It's nothing. Where do I find him?"

"I can tell you that he used to live among us, but that was years ago. He was a most unusual young man."

"Unusual? How so?"

"He lived with us and studied diligently. He was one of the most dutiful among us. But when it came his turn to speak, he proposed the most bewildering contradictions. And yet he spoke with such conviction that his most perplexing words rang true. Even though he's a poor man, he said he had studied in the synagogues and even in the temple in Jerusalem. Some of my brothers say he had traveled far to the east, where he sat at the feet of learned men."

"What kind of things did he say that perplexed you?"

"Many things. He made many predictions that upset the natural order of things. I still contemplate 'the first are last and the last are first.'"

"You could say that about anything."

"What do you mean?"

"You could say, the living are dead and the dead are alive. The light is dark and the dark is light. Or the tall shall be short and the short shall be tall . . ."

"Yes, I've meditated on that very idea. Not the tall and short version." The young man looked at Juve with a smile.

"I'm not big on riddles and contradictions."

"That's not all he said," Benjamin said, waving his hands for emphasis. "Many of his observations make much more sense. We would often debate the location of the kingdom. Some of us would claim it will be in the sky, others say in the sea. When we asked Yeshua, he said it can't be in the sky, because that would mean the birds would get there before we do. And not in the sea, because the fish would precede us. Then he laughed and said, 'Stop looking high and low, the Kingdom of God is within you.'"

"I like his sense of humor."

"Yes. So do I, except when he says strange things like hate your mother and father and then love them. Of course, the Torah says to honor your father and mother . . .'" Throwing up his hands, he concluded with exasperation, "I struggle with his ideas. The man was a mystery. He makes a strange kind of sense, but I wonder if I'm being tricked."

"I don't know if he was trying to trick you," Juve chuckled. "But he certainly handed you a lot of double talk." Thinking of his own parents, Juve suddenly realized that he loved his parents instinctively and hated them for abandoning him at the same time. The strange value of this contradiction gave him an eerie feeling as he stood above the dark salty sea.

"I think sometimes Yeshua's words do not contain the truth, but that thinking about them in a certain way reveals truth I would not have found without them. It's as if forcing yourself to think what can't be true opens the door to what is true." He tilted his head and asked Juve, "Does that make any sense?"

Feeling almost as if he had been awakened from a trance, Juve shook his head. "You're asking the wrong man. I don't spend too much time thinking about that kind of thing."

"Then why do you seek Yeshua?"

"He may be in danger. I've been sent to protect him."

"I see," Benjamin replied, thoughtfully regarding Juve. "I'm wondering if looking like Yeshua is going to help or hinder you."

"It's that bad?"

"I'll tell you this. When my brothers found you and brought you here, some of them thought Yeshua had returned."

"Will you help me find him?"

"Yes, I can take you to Jerusalem, at least."

"I would appreciate that, Benjamin."

"I know the shortest way. It's not as safe as the road, but we'll get there in four or five days. I have to ask permission, of course, but it's almost time to go into the city for supplies."

"I can help you, then," Juve offered, "but I'm afraid you'll be on your own coming back."

"Thank you. We have a cart. It would be much easier if we shared the pulling of the cart."

"And I would be happy to help you," Juve replied, looking forward to more conversations with Benjamin and happy to be able to head west soon, especially with so many days already lost. He adjusted his plans to the lost time, set his sights on the journey ahead, and determined to learn as much as he could, as quickly as possible, about Judea and Jerusalem.

It was clear that Benjamin happily anticipated his journey with Juve as well. As they began to plan their trip, Juve suggested that they rest. Benjamin agreed, withdrew into the cave, and returned with two thin, woolen blankets. They lay side by side as Benjamin described Jerusalem, its inhabitants, and the Roman occupation. Benjamin's complaints against the Hebrew aristocracy reminded him of the greedy Republic Leadership. He listened carefully to Benjamin's stories about Yeshua and pondered the teacher's parables as his new friend retold them. The two men talked late into the night and grew drowsy under the stars.

"I think I'm going to enjoy meeting Yeshua," Juve yawned.

"Many people do," Benjamin sighed sleepily. "He's full of stories."

QUMRAN

THE WOODEN, SQUARE-SAILED CORBITA RACED FROM ROME to Judea. Below the deck, a team of six Indomitable Lions pressed in around a well-worn table marked with furious graffiti. The shelves surrounding the men were crowded with baskets and bulging sacks crammed against terracotta and bronze containers full of provisions—drinking water, wine, oil, and foods—all held in place with thick leather straps. The small cabin reeked of dried meats, olives, fresh fruit, and the pungent manhood of its passengers. As the boat pitched, it swung the hanging oil lamp, which tossed their black shadows around the cabin. The Lions and their small, Ostia-based crew had covered half the distance between Capreae and the Judean port of Caesarea Maritima over the water they called Mare Nostrum. Now the Lions loudly rehearsed their newly forged plan to capture the rebel Yeshua. Each Lion repeated his role in the initial plan and through a handful of contingencies. They were as hard on themselves as they were on each other. They were six and they were one.

Gaius Marcellus raised his voice above the din. "With a good wind we'll be in Judea in a couple of days. Give us two days to reach Jerusalem, a week to find this rabble-rouser, a day to snatch him . . ." Gaius paused to calculate. "We'll be back in Villa Jovis in a matter of weeks."

"Why a week to find him?" challenged Sextus Vibius, the tallest Lion, his long legs cramped beneath the table.

"A lot depends on what cooperation we get from the population and from Pontius Pilate."

"Why wouldn't he cooperate?" asked Sextus. "We're taking a fucking subversive off his hands."

Gaius waited for the laughter to subside, and then explained: "Pontius Pilate needs to show he's in charge. His performance in Judea hasn't been exactly exemplary."

Quintus Salvius, the smallest of the group, spoke. "It's got to be one hell of a region to manage."

"Pilate's the fool who came marching into Jerusalem with Roman standards, right?" asked Decimus Livius, a huge man with a full red beard grown principally to cover his horribly pockmarked face.

"Yes, that was him."

"What a moron! He should have known Jews don't tolerate graven images."

"What are you talking about? I didn't know that," said Titus Valerius. Sitting next to Decimus, his own massive frame was dwarfed by his red-bearded neighbor.

"That's because you can't fucking read," Decimus said, shoving Titus.

"Right, as if you know anything about reading. All you look at is drawings of pimply faced boys."

The rest of the Lions delighted in the war of words and egged on both combatants.

"Any fool can read. Pictures just get me there faster."

"Go get a scroll. I'll beat you senseless with it."

Gaius watched as the two playfully lunged at each other and tumbled onto the floor. All the Lions jumped up and rooted for one or the other of their mates. When Gaius had had enough, he put his fingers up to his mouth and belted out a loud, sharp whistle. The men scrambled back to their seats and gave him their attention. "Be prepared for trouble from Pilate."

"What can Pilate say?" Titus interrupted as he pulled his tunic back into place and ran his fingers through his thick hair. "We're going in with orders from Tiberius."

"He'll cave when he reads the letter," Quintus added.

"Don't count on it," Gaius advised sternly. "And if he does, we may still have to go to plan three."

"Plan three is if he says no," objected Sextus.

"Right, but watch his reaction very carefully," Gaius squinted his eyes to emphasize his point. "He may say yes just to get us out of his sight, and then beat us to our target."

"So we should get a bead on Yeshua before we see Pilate," suggested Titus Valerius, demonstrating his value as a strategist. His superior intelligence showed in his mild, calm good looks.

The Lions expressed their agreement. Gaius paused as he checked each man's face for confirmation. He then added, "And remember, this is a quiet capture."

Marcus Arius, the youngest and newest member of the group, spoke. "You said this Yeshua is some kind of troublemaker, right?"

"That's right."

"Well, what kind? Is he armed? Does he have any fighters?"

"He preaches."

"Sounds like they should have sent our sisters instead," Sextus complained, winning sarcastic laughter from his comrades.

Gaius spoke more seriously, "His words agitate the people."

"I hear he works wonders," Marcus said, interrupting the laughter. "I even hear he raises the dead."

Quintus raised his voice in mockery. "Well, if he can raise himself, it won't matter if we bring him back dead or alive."

Gaius raised his powerful arms and signaled for the Lions to listen. "Yeshua is not the one we have to worry about. If we get to him, we can take him. This could be one of the easiest missions we've ever taken on." Gaius could feel the disappointment in his men. "But his followers could be a pain in the ass. They swarm him like gnats, thinking he will cure them of all their ills. We don't want to deal with an agitated mob. And if Pilate gets his hackles up like I think he will, we could be rumbling with the Judean division of the Roman army."

The Lions erupted in approval, pounding on the table, shoving and sparring with each other. Gaius watched them with paternal admiration and began to relish the thought of taking on an army.

* * *

Juve rose late in the morning to find Benjamin no longer at his side. The gentle murmur of men praying flowing from the cave reminded him of floating on the Dead Sea. He recalled now that he had drifted in and out of consciousness, each time electing to close his eyes and let the water soothe him. *It couldn't have been more than a day*, he hoped. *Why can't I recall being rescued?* Now Juve was angry with himself for losing track of time. He calmed himself with the voices of the men in the cave. Softened by reverberation, their words melded into a meaningless, comforting wave.

Juve stood, stretched, and began to go through a slower, abbreviated version of his morning workout. He rested, satisfied that his strength was returning in good speed.

Benjamin emerged from the cave and greeted his new friend. "I have the blessing of my brothers," he announced. "We can start for Jerusalem this morning if you're up to it."

"That's great," Juve replied. "I think I'm ready."

"We'll eat here, and then head for Qumran—not more than an hour or two away, pick up a cart and provisions there, and leave as the sun sets. Better to cross as much of the wilderness as possible in the coolness of the night."

An hour later, sitting on the cave floor with the small community, Juve watched as the oldest man prayed, "Let grace come to us and may this world pass away."

The rest of the men answered, "Come, Lord."

Their leader answered, "Amen."

Juve studied each of the men as they ate in silence. All were bearded. Their robes were clean and bright. Sandals gripped their feet and calves with crisscrossed leather straps. Each man, including Benjamin, wore a small leather pouch strapped to his forehead and another strapped to his left arm. Everyone, including Juve, ate a cold, grayish gruel from a wooden bowl using the fingers of their right hands. Though he was about to burst with the questions tumbling through his head, Juve politely observed the rule of silence. He smiled to himself as he recalled meals with Forza Facia—the boisterous horseplay and passionate rivalry. This contrasting quietness had an incredibly calming and clarifying effect on Juve. He decided that he would like to try one silent meal a week with his crew—when and if he returned.

After the meal, the men returned to pray while Juve waited at the mouth of the cave. *Pray and eat, pray and eat, pray and eat and sleep,* Juve thought. *I couldn't live like this. It takes a different kind of man. And where are the women?* He was compiling a long list of questions to ask Benjamin on their journey to Jerusalem, when Benjamin and the oldest of the men walked up to him.

Benjamin handed Juve a pair of sandals as the old man spoke. "We have offered our prayers for a safe journey. Your well-being is in the hands of God." Juve acknowledged the sandals and expressed his gratitude. "It's good to see you feeling well."

"I'm sure your kindness saved my life," Juve said.

The old man shook his head and replied, "No need to thank us, my son. It was God who saved your life." Then he handed Benjamin a small but heavy sack that appeared to be full of coins and withdrew into the cave. Juve's friend helped him lace up his sandals, and the two headed to the north and west.

After they had gone a short distance toward Qumran, Juve began to question Benjamin. He wanted to ask about the absence of women in the community, but he decided to start with the little leather pouches the men wore on their arms and foreheads.

"Phylacteries," Benjamin explained. "Surely as a Jew, you've learned of phylacteries."

"My mother was from Judea, but she didn't teach me about my heritage."

"In that case, we must begin your religious instruction," his companion replied.

For an hour or more, the two covered gently rising hills of rock and sand. The only contrasts to the barren earth were low-lying shrubs scattered about and occasionally a fleeing lizard. The air was heavy and dry, hot but cooled from time to time with lazy breezes. Juve learned that the leather pouches the men donned for morning prayers each contained a tiny scrap of parchment on which was inscribed words from the Torah. He learned that the Hebrew people saw themselves as set apart from the rest of the world. They were charged by their God to set an example to the world by living right and obeying a strict code of justice. It was as if Forza Facia had decided to stop disrupting authority and, instead, become a secret tribe of exemplary citizens. Juve learned that all over Judea groups of rebels, much more like Forza, resisted

Roman occupation in many different ways. It was no surprise to Juve that when the resistance was violent, Rome responded with quick and ruthless retribution. He had never heard of crucifixion, and when Benjamin described it, his blood grew hot with the desire for vengeance.

Benjamin sensed the heat of his new friend's empathy. "You are one of us, without a doubt, Juve. Now you may want to decide how completely you want to commit yourself to God. For me, it's all the way."

"I don't see how you can call living in a cave 'all the way,'" Juve said with as much confusion as disagreement. But rather than answer, Benjamin smiled and pointed down the other side of the hill they had climbed to a red-and-brown settlement in the valley below.

"God has given us safe passage to Qumran, my friend," Benjamin said. "You can join me if you like." Then he bowed his head, offered the palms of his hands to the sky, and prayed.

The people of Qumran welcomed Benjamin and his companion. While Benjamin discussed business with a man who seemed to be in charge, a young man named Amos took Juve on a tour of the community. They headed through a section of cattle pens situated alongside neat rows of tents and huts where the people of Qumran lived. Above and all around the settlement rose steep, red-brown walls of rock pocketed with natural caves and manmade cavities chiseled out of the barren edifices. Below, Juve and Amos approached the center of the rock and mud-brick community. There stood a collection of buildings huddled together and walled with stone. A canal of fresh, flowing water supplied a covered cistern. Facing away from the hills and caves in the northwest corner of the complex stood a tall watchtower. The main building contained a kitchen with a well-supplied pantry. Nearby was a pottery workshop with smoking kilns.

Of the greatest interest to Juve was the scriptorium. Sitting behind rows of desks, silent men scribbled earnestly with quills, which they dipped quickly and repeatedly into ink stands positioned alongside their desks. Juve watched a scribe roll up a scroll, walk to the back of the room, and place it carefully in a red earthenware jar that stood as high as the man's knees. Around the room were stacks of leather and papyrus, which Juve figured were writing material, alongside stacks of copper sheets. He asked Amos about the copper and learned that the scribes recorded on it as well. "Most of our work is written on animal hides," Amos explained, "which we prepare in the next room."

"What are they writing?"

"They're not writing," Amos replied with mild amusement. "They're copying."

Juve followed Amos into the next room. As they watched a pair of men clean a large animal hide, Benjamin walked up and informed Juve that it was time to go. He carried a large animal bladder full of fresh water. "We want to cross most of the wilderness tonight," he told Juve.

"You will be blessed with a clear sky and a bright moon tonight," Amos said with a smile that told them he was sincerely happy about their good fortune and wished them well. Juve and Benjamin bid farewell to Amos and walked out of the scriptorium, along the settlement wall, and arrived at the base of the watchtower. There Benjamin placed the sack of coins and the water in a wooden cart that several members of the community had prepared for their journey.

As they set out across the Judean wilderness to the west of Qumran, Juve asked more questions. He was genuinely eager to learn as much as he could about the gentle and generous people in Qumran. As the sun set and the air cooled, Benjamin gladly fed his curiosity.

"We've lived in this area for more than a hundred years . . ." As he recounted the history of the Essenes for Juve, the men moved through the desert darkness guided by a map of shimmering stars so entirely familiar to Juve that he found it hard to believe he had traveled in time. It was as if the night were a curtain. As they passed through, all that was unfamiliar about this time gradually seemed less and less strange. At the same time, what Juve had come to accept as ordinary, he now conspired with the night to leave behind. The moon, casting their shadows over the crusty floor of the Judean wilderness, was the same moon the pitifully demented prisoners of Zostok would howl at some day far in the future. Over his shoulder shone Sarenta, the star to which he prayed as an orphan and on his last night with Maria. He dared not look at it now and returned his attention to the words of his fellow traveler. "We have segregated ourselves from the rest of our people, because we want to prepare for the end of days."

"You are my friend, Benjamin," Juve said gravely, "so I have to tell you . . . let me put your mind at ease. This world will continue far beyond your lifetime."

Benjamin smiled and Juve could see his amusement. It was not a belittling smile but an expression of Benjamin's firm belief. Rather than engage in a debate that he could only hope to win by convincing the man at his side that he had traveled in time, Juve returned to asking about the end of the world.

"When it comes," Benjamin explained, "the wicked will be destroyed, and Israel will be freed from the oppression of the Romans. Because we are God's elect, he will save us from his visitation of justice and retribution. He will make flow from us the people of the future. We believe that when God brings on his justice, he will divide all people into two camps—the Sons of Light and the Sons of Darkness. Then the Prince of Light will lead us and the Angel of Darkness will command the Sons of Darkness."

"And that's why you deprive yourself of female companionship, good food, and the other pleasures of life?"

"All of the things you think we might miss and desire, we reject without the slightest care, because the Spirits of Truth and Perseverance fill us all with everything we need, each according to our need."

"Suppose I could see into the future and tell you . . . or just suppose you have miscalculated the end of days." Juve held up his hands to discourage Benjamin from interrupting. "Just suppose. Wouldn't your effort be better spent on helping make some small but real improvements to people's everyday lives? Helping them eat, helping them feed and teach their children?"

"Will the world be any better for my effort?"

"Yes, of course! Are you kidding?"

"Will men continue to undermine each other's good work?"

"Of course, but—"

"Is it true that Rome is full of men who fight each other over things that represent wealth?"

"Sure, you could say that."

"And they struggle to accumulate more than their neighbors?" Benjamin did not wait for an answer. "And that every treasure is gained at another's loss? And that, in the end, every one of us loses everything we accumulate?"

"True," Juve admitted, amused at Benjamin's ironic assessment.

"Will not the people of Rome continue to kill and rob from generation to generation?"

"Yes, but we can eliminate some of it."

"Should I be satisfied leaving behind a world like that?"

"What's the alternative? Will you be satisfied letting the rest of us improve our lives without your help?"

"You've got my help. When one person lives right, that means you have one less person to improve. Besides, you can't change anyone. Each person has to change himself. And as far as changing the world goes . . ." Benjamin threw up his hands in a gesture of futility. "Don't even try! It's difficult enough to change yourself. Leave changing the world to God."

"I don't know," Juve sighed. "I was raised without gods, but I know that things get better and worse and better again."

"And only God can put an end to that cycle." Benjamin looked off in the distance and turned the palms of his hands to the sky. "Nothing satisfies more than seeing God bring down his justice on this evil world. And even if God does not return in my lifetime, I know that I have helped to plant the seeds of the Spirit of Truth. I believe that goodness will always rise from whatever forces trample it down."

"I disagree, my friend, because my experience has been quite different," Juve said as he patted Benjamin on the shoulder. "If I've seen anything in my life, I've seen that goodness always manages to rise up, but only if we do something to help it."

"Goodness will persevere, Juventus. It will always emerge to inspire other men. No matter what we do. Whether the Zealots drive out the Romans or not. Whether you find Yeshua or not. Whether you and I make it to Jerusalem or not. It's all in God's hands."

"I think it's in our hands."

"Only because God is in us."

"Your idea of God is new to me, Benjamin."

"It's very simple," Benjamin said, waving one hand in a gesture that tossed away the idea of any difficulty Juve might have with what he was about to say. "When you know yourself, you know God. When you understand where your joy and sorrow come from, you understand God. If you follow this path of ideas, you will soon see that you and God are identical."

"That means you and God are identical, too."

"Yes. There is only one being, Juventus, and each one of us is a window of its soul."

"Then you and I are identical."

"You learn very quickly, my friend." Benjamin put his arm around Juve's shoulder in warm approval.

"That's because it's not much different from what I already believe."

"Unfortunately some people give little thought to their divinity. But when they hear about it, many accept it."

"And this is the message Yeshua is teaching?"

"Yes. He left our desert temple to spread the word."

"The word of God."

"Yes," Benjamin replied with a nod. "Yeshua is confident that the word will work wonders."

"Is it working wonders?"

"He has collected a following. Many accept the word and go on with their lives as if nothing has changed. Some stay by his side, devoted to him and his words. You see, his message is easy to believe but not so easy to hold in your heart. That takes practice. To live according to what you hold in your heart— that takes everything you can do and your whole life to accomplish."

"Benjamin," Juve said and paused before continuing, "what makes the word of Yeshua more important than my word or your word or anybody's word?"

"It's not Yeshua's word or your word," Benjamin explained with amused vexation. "It's God's word that Yeshua shares. It's God's word that we search for and record in writing for the ages."

"This is the part that puzzles me, then. If you and I are windows of God, as you say, why is our word any more or less the word of God than what Yeshua has to say?"

"It is not," Benjamin replied to Juve's surprise. "Every word you say is the word of God as far as it has risen in your heart." Benjamin stopped and took Juve by the shoulders. At that moment, a tiny lizard dashed across their path. Juve was taken by the fact that if Benjamin had not stopped he would have crushed the little animal. "The spirit of God is like water. Water is everywhere, even here in the desert, even in that rock on the side of the road. You can be full of it, like the sea that heaves and roars with it, or you can have so little that you bake in the sun like a stone." Benjamin resumed walking and Juve followed. "The point of life, Juventus, is to grow in your understanding of God and to reduce yourself as you grow in the understanding of God."

"So, then, what's the point of being Yeshua or Juventus Carnifex or Benjamin of Beersheba? If our purpose is to be less and less of what we are?"

The two men walked in silence for a while as Benjamin considered how to reply. He finally answered, "I'm afraid you'll just have to live and see."

BETHANY

JUST BEFORE DAWN ON THE FIFTH NIGHT OF THEIR journey, the two travelers rested. They had put the desert and the town of Bethany behind them. Jerusalem was several hours away. *My appointment at Skull Hill—maybe five days from now*, Juve estimated. Walking through the sleeping town, they had raised the attention of several dogs, but no one else seemed to care. Just beyond Bethany, Benjamin assured Juve that it would be worth waiting for the morning light in order to approach Jerusalem in the daylight. So they sheltered themselves under the cart and fell asleep.

Juve rose when the shadow of the cart no longer shaded his feet and he felt the morning sun warming his skin. Benjamin woke to the sound of Juve's morning workout. He watched, perplexed, as his new friend lay facedown on the ground and pushed his head and chest up over and over again. Benjamin furrowed his brow and shook his head. *A lot of work and motion to what end?* he wondered. Benjamin climbed out from under the cart and fed himself with dried fruit and water, while Juve stretched out on his back, put his hands behind his head, and sat up again and again. Benjamin watched and drank from the water bladder. Then Juve stood up, bent over forward, and placed his hands on the ground without bending his knees. Benjamin grimaced. Noticing his companion's bewilderment, Juve invited him. "Come here and try it."

Benjamin waved his hands, declining. "No, I'll just watch." He was puzzled by the glistening layer of perspiration that coated his friend's body. "You've lost more water than we have in our skins," he told Juve with a note of warning in his voice.

"Give it a try," Juve insisted, "it's good for you."

Benjamin shook his head with just enough lack of conviction to tell Juve that all the man needed was a little more nudging. So Juve walked over and offered Benjamin his hand. "Come on, you'll enjoy it." With a smile and a tug to Benjamin's arm, Juve instructed him to bend forward. "No, no, don't bend your knees," Juve said. "I'll hold them straight this time. Now bend down. Let your arms dangle. That's it . . ." Benjamin obeyed but could barely get his hands below his knees. "Ugh, you're in terrible shape!" Juve scolded. "Stay there and just relax. I'm going to put a little pressure on your back. Don't resist. Just relax." When Benjamin's hands reached his shins, he let out a miserable moan and Juve stopped pressing down on his back. "Keep trying while I run," Juve said.

"Where are you going?"

"Nowhere," Juve replied as he began to run—slowly at first, then faster and faster—while to Benjamin's surprise, the strange visitor from Rome stayed in the same place. Benjamin's wonder quickly turned to wariness as he spotted, behind Juve, a group of five men approaching from the direction of Bethany. Benjamin divided his attention between the approaching men and the running Juve. It looked to Benjamin as if the slowly walking men were catching up with his frantically fleeing friend. He would have laughed if not for the menace he sensed in the approaching men. At one point, one of the men pointed at Juve and made a comment that amused his friends.

Eventually Juve completed his routine and walked over to Benjamin. Still breathing heavily, he put out his hands to receive the bladder. "I'll have some of that, please."

Taking a drink, Juve followed Benjamin's gaze to the approaching strangers. He studied them for a few seconds. "Keep an eye on those men," Juve cautioned his companion, still a bit winded. "The way they walk tells me they're up to no good."

Apparently the barking dogs of Bethany had awoken some of her citizens in the night and aroused their curiosity. As the five approached with trouble in their smiles, it was clear they were the kind of men who regularly harassed travelers. Their garments were soiled. They obviously cared little about their appearance. The leader, the biggest man marching a step ahead as they approached, bore the scar of a vicious cut along the bottom of his jaw. The others showed signs of regular abuse as well. The oldest of the men had no teeth, which made his malicious smile the most disconcerting of all, despite his age. As the gang approached, the toothless old man suddenly showed signs of alarm. He tugged at the leader's garment, squinting hard to give his old eyes a clear image of Juve. The leader disregarded the tug and brushed the old man aside with his thick, muscular arm. "You guys are headed for the city today?" he asked in mock cordiality.

"Yes, we are," Benjamin answered meekly.

"From where do you come pulling this fine-looking cart?" The big man's sarcasm drew snickers of amusement from all but the toothless man.

"Qumran," Benjamin replied.

"Well," the leader said, "you wouldn't come all this way without something for us, would you?"

Juve stepped forward with the water bladder. "Yes, you are welcome to some of our water."

With a mean grin, revealing his blackened teeth, the man replied, "We have wells full of water in town. We want something we can really use."

Benjamin stepped toward the cart and began to reach inside, but Juve gently stopped him with his right arm. Taking a step forward, he spoke politely but firmly. "You can have water, but that's all you get today."

The men looked at each other, surprised and amused by Juve's confidence. They looked him over, reevaluating his strength. The toothless man was beside himself with alarm.

"We'll not only take your water," sneered a man with a huge nose and hard voice, "we'll take whatever else we want."

Juve was unfazed by the threat. "Have you had a good day so far?"

"Yes, it's been a good but uneventful day so far," the leader grinned, playing along, "and I think it's going to get a lot more interesting." All but the toothless man expressed approval of their leader's threat.

"I've rethought our offer," Juve replied with unmistakable authority. "You'll go now without our water. That's if you want to go in one piece."

The leader of the gang moved forward as the toothless man slipped behind the group. In six seconds Juve dispatched the four aggressors as the toothless man turned and ran down the road toward Jerusalem. Benjamin watched wide-eyed as Juve orchestrated and executed his attack. While his left arm took down the leader with a blow to the sternum, Juve watched another man stepping toward him on the right. His right foot was on its way to the man's chin as he planned how he would take care of the remaining two lumbering together toward him on his left. No sooner had Juve's attacking foot devastated the second man than his left foot flew in a wide arch across the third's head. Juve snatched the hair of the fourth and used the attacker's clumsy forward momentum to accelerate him headfirst into the side of the cart. The cart shuddered and the fourth man dropped like a felled tree. His face threw up little clouds of dust as it smacked the ground. Benjamin winced when he heard the unconscious man's huge nose crack. The leader twisted on the ground, grasping his chest, gasping for breath. The man Juve had kicked in the head also lay unconscious, while the fourth crawled toward town, moaning in agony. Neither of the conscious men paid attention to their toothless mate, running and calling back to them, "I knew we shouldn't have troubled him." His panting speech was almost comical with so many sounds impaired by his lack of teeth.

Benjamin bent down, picked up the water bag, and went to the leader with the injured throat. "Water?" The man looked up in pain and bewilderment. "Have some water," Benjamin urged him. The man struggled to his feet, waved off Benjamin, and staggered toward his crawling comrade.

"Leave them alone," Juve told his companion. "They'll get help in the city."

As Juve and Benjamin headed down the road, Benjamin pulled the cart. He still trembled with residual fear as he tried to comprehend what he had just witnessed. His agitation amused Juve. "They won't be bothering travelers for a while."

"I've never seen anything like that," Benjamin said.

"Like what? The way I fight?"

"Yes. Where did you learn to fight like that?"

"I was trained in Rome," Juve replied.

Benjamin shifted his hold on the wagon and said, "You take your need to help too far."

"What do you mean by that?"

"You should not have hurt those men, even though they bear the stain of paganism."

"What? And let them rob us and maybe hurt us?"

"If that was God's will."

"Well, apparently, today it wasn't God's will."

"What you did was your will."

"If God and I are the same, what's the difference?"

"You have a much longer road ahead of you than I thought, Juventus."

"What road are you talking about?"

"The way to knowing yourself."

"I know myself better than you think."

"Why do you find it necessary to stop injustice with your fists?"

"What are you talking about? It's just the right thing to do—to help the weak and protect the defenseless."

"I thought you understood that all people are one with God."

"Yes, but those guys weren't exactly acting like gods, were they? I may not be the ocean, but we just crushed a bunch of desert rocks." Juve saw Benjamin shake his head in frustration. "Benjamin, what's so hard to understand?" Juve almost pleaded. "If God is in me, it means he made me strong so that I could deal with these kinds of idiots."

"What happened to you?" Benjamin asked, looking into Juve's eyes. "Why are you so angry?" He watched closely for Juve's reaction. Juve was taken aback by Benjamin's words. It was clear to both of them that Benjamin had struck a chord.

Juve made a decision. As they walked, he told the story of his parents' betrayal, his loss of Maria and Auspex, their efforts to protect the defenseless—all carefully framed and adapted as if these events had taken place in the Rome of Benjamin's day. While it felt good to open his heart, Juve sensed that Benjamin knew he was not speaking freely.

"Are you making amends?" Benjamin asked.

"I haven't always protected the defenseless, Benjamin," he said as he looked down on the emerging city below. Jerusalem spread before them at the bottom of the hill. The sun illuminated magnificent structures—palaces, amphitheaters, temples—some buildings carved from pure white stone that glowed in the late morning light. "Yes, I'm making amends. I've hurt the weak. I've killed them."

Benjamin stopped and gazed at Jerusalem with reverence. "This is the city of David, the perfection of beauty, the joy of the world." He spoke the words like a prayer, stood transfixed for a moment, and then resumed his conversation with Juve as if it had not been interrupted. "That must be an awful burden to carry."

"Of course it is."

"How does hurting more people help you make amends?"

"I was helping us. They would have hurt us."

"But they are just as defenseless."

"Defenseless, my ass. Did you see the size of their leader?"

"Do you think they would prey on strangers if they had a better way?"

"So you're saying they are the weak ones?"

"Undoubtedly."

"Your ideas are interesting, Benjamin, but not practical. If we let the thugs of this world have their way, the world would be unfit for living."

"Who did you kill?"

"I killed a lot of people."

"Men, women, children?"

"Yes."

"I can't imagine carrying that burden, Juve."

"No, I don't think you can imagine the burden, Benjamin. The only thing that helps is knowing that I've stopped. And that I'm doing everything I can to make amends."

"It's good that you want to make amends. Does it help?"

"Yes, it does. But I'm still haunted by one face. Most of the time I did not see the faces of the people I killed. And when I did, I always saw fear or anger. But the last innocent man I killed looked at me and asked, "Why?" with his eyes. From then on, when I was ordered to kill people who I felt were good, I made them disappear. Until I tried to kill a man who turned out to be the father of the woman I love. It made me realize that I had lost the ability to tell the difference between who deserved to die and who I should protect."

The travelers became silent as they approached the city. Jerusalem was surrounded by a wall with a hundred towers or more. They faced three of the most impressive and prominent as they descended through groves of olive trees. "Hippicus, Phasaelus, and Mariamne," Benjamin remarked as he noticed Juve studying the towers. "King Herod named them after his wife and two of his friends killed in battle. He killed his own wife in a fit of jealousy."

Some distance down the hill Juve saw the toothless man stumbling from exhaustion, still trying to run to the city. Juve followed the line of the road and saw that it led to a flight of steep stone steps at the southern end of the wall. "Is that the only way in?" he asked, pointing to the steps.

"No," Benjamin replied. "There's a gate . . ." He strained to control the cart. "A gate on the eastern side." Juve smiled and relieved his friend of his rolling load.

"Walking downhill can be more difficult than pulling uphill sometimes." He got in front of the cart and leaned back into its weight to keep it from rolling downhill. As they neared the foot of the hill, they saw the toothless man moving with great effort up the steep steps.

"Don't be surprised if we find a crowd of Yeshua fans waiting to welcome us," Benjamin advised Juve, "or a squad of Roman soldiers."

JERUSALEM

A SLENDER AND STRIKINGLY BEAUTIFUL YOUNG WOMAN IN an ordinary white robe was buying oil in the marketplace outside the temple walls in Jerusalem when she noticed several young boys running to the south with bundles of palm fronds in their arms. *Someone important must be coming to town today,* she thought as she gathered the oil into her sack of goods and headed home. As she turned away from the oil merchant's stall, she collided with a young boy running with a pack of six or more. The woman and the boy tumbled to the pavement. The boy was up and running without a word. "These kids today," she said to the young man who was helping her to her feet, "they have no respect!"

"When I was a child," he agreed, "we wouldn't think of passing an older person without a 'beg your pardon,' much less knock a woman to the ground."

"What's all the hurry, anyway?" she asked the man, taking note of his kind, dark eyes, smooth skin, and easy smile.

"They say Yeshua is coming in by the east gate."

The young woman's eyes squinted in disbelief. "Are you sure? I don't expect him today."

"You know him?" he asked.

"I know him very well," she explained, following with her eyes a group of adolescent boys and girls shouting and running down the street where the young boys had disappeared, "but I don't expect him today."

"I'll walk with you to the gate if you like," the man offered, running his fingers through his thick, dark hair.

"Thank you. I suppose I should see if it is him."

"I've never seen him, but I've heard much about him."

"What have you heard?" she asked. They walked quickly, but they were still passed by another group of young people. Like the others, they waved palms and shouted after one another.

"That he performs wonders and stirs the people with his words."

"Well, I guess you could say that," she told the ruggedly handsome man at her side. "He's definitely going to turn things around."

"I am called Titus Valerius." He bowed slightly and allowed his new acquaintance to decide whether or not to complete the introduction.

"I am Mayam of Magdala," she said, nodding to Titus. There was no hesitation in her manner, even though she was a Jew meeting a Roman. Titus was charmed.

When Juve and Benjamin arrived at the eastern city gate, a crowd was waiting for them. A dozen of the youngest ran up the road to meet the travelers. The bigger boys fought over who would pull the cart. Eventually the two strongest wrested it from Juve and shared the load. They followed Benjamin and Juve, who followed the procession of boys as they danced and shouted, waving their palm fronds and kicking up dust. One of the oldest boys with little more than a cloth around his waist moved close to Juve and whispered, "Six Lions in town from Rome."

"What did you say?" a perplexed Juve asked. The boy seemed to realize he had made a mistake and ran back through the crowd and around a corner. "What was that?" Juve asked Benjamin.

"That's a messenger boy," Benjamin explained. "What did he say?"

"He said there are lions in the city."

"I doubt it," Benjamin chuckled. "They sell a lot of animals in the Temple market, but no lions."

As Juve and Benjamin made their way through the gate, the boys who pulled the wagon parked it and tried to maneuver Juve on top of it. The crowd drowned out Juve's protests and the boys finally positioned him atop the cart. The crowd roared in approval. Juve surveyed the group of fifty or so residents of Jerusalem—men and women, old and young, boys and girls—all from the ranks of the poor. Their robes were dirty, their hair matted, their faces, feet, and hands soiled. More were approaching. Toward the back of the crowd, Juve saw a man and a woman approach, observing him intently as they moved deliberately closer. Most of the people recognized the woman and let them through. The man followed her through the parting of the mass. Juve heard several people call the woman Mayam. At the same time, the crowd urged Juve to speak. They called him Rabbi and Master.

As he studied the adoration of their faces and the need in their eyes, he realized that he could say just about anything and, he was sure, they would approve. The thought of such power intrigued and alarmed him, but he was more interested in Mayam and her companion. There was cautious skepticism in the man's eyes, but Mayam watched him with questioning compassion. Juve could tell she did not think that he was Yeshua. *Maybe she knows Yeshua better than the others*, he thought. *That would explain the deference of the crowd toward them.*

Juve could not imagine how to tell the crowd that he was not their Rabbi. He opened his mouth several times to speak, but each time, the crowd increased the volume of their cheering and shouting. He looked down at Mayam and saw that she understood his predicament. She turned to the crowd and raised her arms, but the crowd was unmoved. She turned back to Juve and called up to him, "Raise your arms." He did as she suggested and within a few seconds, a hush rippled over the throng from front to back. Mayam reached her hand up to Juve and he pulled her up to his side. Without hesitating, she spoke to the people in a full, clear voice. "It's too early to celebrate, my brothers and sisters. You will see him in the next few days. I will send word. Now go on and let us make our way."

Disappointed but obedient, the crowd slowly dispersed. Most of them waved and saluted Juve as they walked away. Juve jumped down from the cart and lifted Mayam down and to his side. "Thank you," he said, admiring the sway she held with the crowd and the deftness of her authority.

"Who are you?" she asked.

"My name is Juventus Trajan Carnifex. And this is Benjamin of Beersheba, my companion from Qumran."

"They call me Mayam. And this is Titus. We've just met."

"I have come to Jerusalem to meet Yeshua," Juve told them.

"Then you will come with me, Juventus," Mayam offered. "I am going to meet him and his friends in Bethany." She smiled at Benjamin and added, "You will join us as well, Benjamin."

"Thank you," Benjamin replied politely, "but I have business in the city and have to be back in Qumran."

"I'm afraid I have to go as well," Titus chimed in, "but if you'll tell me when you plan to return to Jerusalem, I would very much like to see you again and meet Yeshua as well."

"We will be back before the Passover celebration, I'm sure."

Titus smiled and nodded pleasantly to the small group. "Until then," he said as he went off toward the center of the city. On his way to meet his fellow Lions at a house in Jerusalem, Titus wondered whether or not Juve, despite his and Mayam's denials, could be the Yeshua he and his team had come to fetch for Tiberius. After seeing the way the crowd had mobbed Juve, would it matter whether they came back with either man? *Of course it matters*, Titus reminded himself sternly. *You're an Indomitable Lion and honor-bound.*

The house was tucked away down a narrow alley with high walls on both sides. Its entrance faced a wall covered with crude political and pornographic graffiti. When Titus arrived, his comrades had already anointed the room with the heat and odor of their bodies. Dust and dirt from the streets of Jerusalem clung to their sweaty togas. The room roared with their debate. Everyone took notice of Titus as he entered. The youngest, Marcus Arius, hailed Titus warmly, and the others saluted him with different degrees of enthusiasm.

"I hope you did better than we did," Sextus Vibius, the tallest Lion, yelled to Titus over the heads of the others.

"As a matter of fact, I found two Yeshuas," Titus replied just loud enough to let everyone hear.

Red-bearded Decimus Livius took the bait. "Okay, let's hear it. What's the joke?"

Taking full advantage of everyone's attention, Titus began to spoon-feed his discoveries. "I met a woman in the marketplace named Mayam."

"Yeah, the woman who runs with Yeshua," Decimus shot back, waving his hand dismissively. "Tell us something we don't know."

"First of all, she's gorgeous."

This remark drew catcalls and lustful suggestions about Titus's intentions toward Mayam, which he ignored as he continued. "She and a guy named Juventus plan to meet Yeshua and his band on their way into town."

"Juventus," Marcus interjected. "That's not a Hebrew name."

"Let's go after them," the diminutive Quintus Salvius suggested. He was pleased to hear the rest of the Lions raise their voices in approval. But their leader Gaius Marcellus called for order.

"Not so fast! Let's hear the rest."

"Juventus is probably from Rome, but he looks just like Yeshua," Titus explained.

"How do you know?" Decimus sneered. "You've never seen Yeshua."

"He fooled a crowd into thinking he was Yeshua. He had them in the palm of his hand."

"We heard about that," Quintus said. "I sent Decimus and Sextus out, but when they got there, the crowd was gone." The criticism in Quintus's voice was clear, and the rest of the Lions jumped at the chance to mock Decimus and Sextus. Gaius slammed his fist on the table to restore order. "Let Titus finish."

"I think we should keep an eye on Juventus. At some point, we may be able to use him as a double for Yeshua," Titus explained.

"He'd be perfect for creating a diversion," agreed Marcus Arius.

Gaius Marcellus took in everything he heard, incorporating each man's discoveries into his plan, modifying it as they spoke. When he felt he had all the information he needed, he raised his arms and silenced his men. "All right then, here's the plan. We go see Pilate. Get him to arrest Yeshua and turn him over to us. If he shows any lack of enthusiasm, we'll intercept Yeshua—and Juventus as fallback. Someplace where they won't be surrounded by supporters." Gaius checked the faces of all his men. "Any questions?" The group acknowledged their approval of the plan. Then Gaius stood and said, "Let's go see Pilate. And afterwards we'll try some more of that horrible Hebrew wine."

* * *

In Jerusalem, after they said their goodbyes to Benjamin, Mayam had taken Juve with her as she collected provisions for Yeshua's arrival. Now Juve and Mayam walked together toward the town of Bethany. Juve was beginning to feel at home in this part of the world, and even at this point in the history of the world. He had begun to lose the feeling of being in some other time. It was just *now*. And even though he knew there was a future in which he had lived, today felt much like any other today. He had a destination and a mission.

His walk with Mayam began with an argument. They had quarreled over who would carry the provisions. She insisted on carrying everything, and so did Juve. Both found the other's insistence on shouldering the long, rough-cloth sack unthinkable. Eventually Juve won. For a while, Mayam defiantly brushed off the critical glances from people as they walked out of the city. Juve sensed that people were mocking him as well. He noticed several women hiding their snickers behind their hands and men mumbling comments to each other. Eventually Mayam vented, "See what you've done!"

"What have I done?"

"Why do you degrade yourself like that?"

"How am I degrading myself?" Juve asked in confusion. "It's only right that I carry our provisions."

"No, it's not proper for a man to carry for a woman. They were ridiculing us. This isn't Rome, you know. What are you trying to prove?"

Juve remembered Barth warning him to observe local customs. As he thought about what he had observed, it was clear he had become at ease and off guard a little too soon in this new world. No, he had never seen a man carry anything. Certainly not a man walking with a woman. "You certainly are more than capable of carrying this sack," Juve said, "but I am a good deal bigger and stronger. It's much easier for me to carry it." Juve watched Mayam's face tell him that he had made his point. He stopped in front of her, put his hands on her shoulders, and proposed a plan. "If we see anyone coming along the road, I'll let you carry the bag for as long as they can see us."

"Very well," Mayam said with a smile that told him he was making a positive impression on her. "You're very persuasive."

"Persuasive?" he asked.

"Good at convincing people to see things your way."

"I'm not trying to get my way," Juve explained a little defensively. "I just want to do what's right."

"I haven't met too many people from Rome . . ."

"How do you know I'm from Rome?"

"Juventus Trajan Carnifex."

"Of course."

"You must have seen great wonders there."

"Oh, it's . . ." Juve paused. He wanted to say something for which there were no Aramaic words—something about the "metropolitan" atmosphere. "It has more . . . It's like a bigger Jerusalem, more people, bigger buildings . . ."

"The streets are wider and covered with smooth stones, I hear."

Never having been to the Rome of Mayam's time, Juve groped through his memory of history lessons for things to describe. Mayam didn't wait for his answer. "What about the people? I've seen only Roman soldiers. Are all the people of Rome so strong and healthy?"

"Not everyone. We have poor people. I notice that a lot of people around here are much poorer than the poor people of Rome and not so well fed, nor as well dressed, either."

"I don't know anything else, so I don't think of us as poor. Some of us have more than others, but only the Romans and our own priests have more than they need."

"In Rome most have what they need, some have less, and a few have much more than they need."

"It seems to me that everybody would be a lot happier if those who had more would share with those who need more . . . ," Mayam began. She shook her head impatiently. "I've thought about this many times and I talk about it with Yeshua. We always come to the same conclusion." Mayam hesitated, and Juve pressed her for their conclusion. "I know it sounds simple, but it seems so right to make sure everyone has what they need. So why not try to live that way?"

"You mean to live the way the Essenes do?"

"No! Never." Mayam was emphatic. "Life offers too many pleasures. The best aren't sold in the market either." She smiled warmly at Juve. "I've always lived in Bethany. I've seen nothing of the rest of the world. I want to know more about how people live in Rome. You must have learned so much there."

"Let me tell you, Mayam. I've learned more here in Judea in the past few days than I've learned in the rest of my life."

"Goodness!" Mayam replied, surprised. "What kind of life have you lived that you learned so little?"

"Oh, I've learned a lot," Juve assured her. "Just all the wrong things."

"Don't be so hard on yourself, Juventus."

"Just before I came here I met a woman. I loved her more deeply . . ."

"You loved her? You mean you don't love her now?"

"She was killed."

"Oh, that's so sad!"

"Along with my best friend." Mayam covered her mouth with her hands and looked intently at Juve's face. "Maybe that's why everything here seems so new and good to me. I've lost everything I loved."

Mayam leaned against Juve as they walked. Their arms brushed and they easily found each other's hands. Resting her head on Juve's shoulder, she could feel a powerful need to cry welling in his chest—a muffled rush of breath, quickly restrained, then another. She squeezed his hand reassuringly and immediately felt his body begin to shake under his release of tears. She could feel the enormity of his loss. It seemed to darken everything around them. They walked for a long time, Juve sobbing freely and Mayam holding his hand. Her heart filled with his sorrow. A steady stream of tears rolled gently from her eyes. After a long time, when Juve's sobbing had subsided, Mayam tilted her head and gazed up at his face. He looked at her and smiled sadly. He showed no sign of embarrassment, but she could tell he wanted her to lead him away from his sorrow.

"Juventus, tell me about Rome," she said.

"I will, if you'll call me Juve."

"Juve," Mayam smiled, "tell me about Rome."

"What do you want to know?"

"If someone is dying, do they have ways to help them?"

"Yes, of course. Why do you ask?"

"My brother is dying," she replied.

"What do you mean?" Juve asked, suddenly concerned.

"He's asleep. I can barely feel his breath, but the rabbi says he's dead and he wants to bury him."

"Can the rabbi feel his breath?"

"No, but I don't think he tried very hard. He pretended to feel." Mayam shook her head. "I'm not sure he's all that interested."

Juve understood the rabbi's lack of interest in a poor woman's need for complicated, long-term attention. *He'd rather bury the brother and be done with it.* "Is there any color in his skin? Or has he gone pale?"

"Ashen," Mayam replied.

"Can you move his arms and legs?"

"Yes."

"How long has he been this way?"

"Eleven days."

"Without food?"

"My sister began to rub honey and olive oil on his tongue after the third or fourth day," Mayam explained. Then she asked, "Do you think he's alive?"

"If he were not alive, Mayam, you would smell death," Juve reassured her. "But I'm afraid he may not wake up . . . he may never wake up."

"We fear as much," she answered, shaking her head. "They say something similar happened to my grandfather, but I don't remember."

"Is he in Bethany?"

"Yes."

"I may be able to do something," Juve said, "but I can't promise anything." Juve put his arm around her shoulder.

"Thank you," she said. "I feel better."

"I feel better, too."

Mayam nestled into his embrace and he could feel her smile as she sighed, "It's difficult to let go of sorrow, isn't it?"

"I never thought of it that way, but yes."

"You can let go of your loved ones. They would want you to let go, so that you can appreciate what life you have left to live."

"It must be so much more difficult for you. Your brother is with you but not with you at the same time."

"Yes, we can't let go of him yet," Mayam admitted. "I thought he would go the way of my grandfather, but I wouldn't let myself believe it yet, even if it is true."

"The truth isn't always easy to accept."

"You're right," Mayam said. "But everyone wants the truth. It doesn't seem that way sometimes, but deep down, somewhere inside, we all want the truth." All of a sudden Mayam stepped free of Juve's embrace and beamed as she told him, "That's why I think you'll like Yeshua," she said, "and he'll like you, too." She walked alongside him now, extolling the virtues of the man she obviously admired. Juve learned the names of the other members of their group.

"Do they all care as easily as you do?" Juve asked.

"Caring is the easy part," she laughed. "It's living with love that thins our ranks."

"Where I come from, this kind of attention is rare," Juve told her. "You hardly know me and you've taken my concerns to heart immediately."

"Life is too precious," Mayam answered with uninhibited conviction. "I can't see wasting it wondering if you have permission to touch someone or waiting for the right moment to love them. I think our people are sick from the way affection is rationed."

"Yes, I agree. That's what I miss most about the people I've lost."

"Stay with us, then." Mayam pressed her face against Juve's shoulder.

"I have to go back . . . back to Rome."

"But why?"

"It's almost impossible to explain, but I'm not exactly from the Rome you know."

Mayam took a moment to consider Juve's strange reply. She understood that he was not ready to talk about the subject. "Well, it doesn't matter where you're from. It's where you're going that counts."

Juve looked at Mayam, and admitted to himself at last that she was stirring up emotions he hadn't allowed himself to feel since he had lost Maria.

YESHUA

THE SIX INDOMITABLE LIONS STRODE INTO PILATE'S RECEP-
tion room, confidently but without arrogance. However, they gave no hint to
any of the dozen men in the room that they were in any way impressed with
their official positions. Pilate was sitting at his desk, writing. He let them wait
until he was sure they understood his authority over them. Only then did
he rise and walk over to meet them. After greetings and pleasantries, Gaius
spoke, giving full rein to his deep, authoritative voice. "We are here to escort
the teacher and troublemaker Yeshua of Nazareth, son of Joseph, out of Judea
by order of the emperor Tiberius."

Pilate studied the impressive figure of Gaius Marcellus, holding an official
Roman document out to him. Without accepting the document, Pilate looked
Gaius in the eye and smiled. "Have you any idea what the emperor wants with
our Hebrew rabble-rouser?" A ripple of suppressed chuckling breezed through
Pilate's entourage of secretaries, advisors, and guards. The well-dressed group
stood in a loose crescent behind their superior, occasionally muttering to one
another. Some, no doubt, were betting on whether or not Pilate would stand
up against Tiberius, who had forced him on several occasions to back down.
After bowing to an order from Tiberius to remove a display of emblems, which

a group of Jews had found offensive, Pilate had sworn to his staff, "This is the last time that prick sticks his nose in my business!"

"The emperor wishes to consult with him," Gaius answered evenly.

There was another wave of muffled laughter. Now the five Lions standing with Gaius began to feel the threat of humiliation. Some of Pilate's men smirked ever-so-subtly at Gaius's men. The Lions returned steady glares of insolent defiance. The youngest, Marcus Arius, found it difficult to contain his brewing anger. He gritted his teeth behind closed lips and breathed deeply. His neighbor Quintus could hear him and nudged him. They exchanged sidelong glances and Quintus Salvius signaled Marcus to remain calm.

Then Pilate answered Gaius, clearly meaning to put his petitioner in his place. "I'm sorry you've come all the way from Rome. I could have saved you a lot of time and effort." He held his open right hand above his shoulder. One of his assistants stepped forward and placed a document in it. The governor of Judea unrolled the scroll and quickly scanned it. "I'm afraid you're too late. We have plans for your messiah. Plans that can no longer be changed."

Unfazed, Gaius cautioned, "Let me make sure I have made myself clear, Governor. I have orders from the emperor of Rome."

"You have made yourself perfectly clear, Gaius Marcellus," the governor replied firmly but without disrespect, "but I have the matter of Yeshua of Nazareth under control. There are more forces at work in this region than the emperor in his island hideaway has taken the time to consider. I understand the complexities far better than he." He paused and wrinkled his brow as he looked carefully over the small but intimidating force of Lions. It was clear to Pilate that Gaius was serious about extracting Yeshua. He suspected, in fact, that Gaius would simply take the rabbi if he refused to turn him over. Pilate rallied. "Before you leave tomorrow morning, Gaius Marcellus, please make yourself at home in our city. Be sure to avail yourself of our amenities." He motioned with his left hand to a thin, dark-eyed assistant, "Cassius Plautius will be happy to see that all of you have comfortable accommodations, plenty of our best food and wine, and a taste of the entertainment." With a nod to the Lions, Pilate announced, "This meeting has concluded." Gaius nodded respectfully, turned, and, signaling his men to follow, marched out of the room. When the door had closed behind the Lions, Pilate took Cassius aside.

"Follow those men. They'll lead you right to Yeshua. Bring him to me. Alive. And get the Lions on a boat back to Rome."

As Juve and Mayam approached Bethany, Juve let Mayam carry the sack to spare her any more embarrassment. It was nonsense, but it made her feel better, even as she labored and perspired under the weight. Juve wanted to explain things to Mayam from his time-bridging experience. He wanted to be as honest and open with Mayam as he had been with Maria, but something held him back. *How can I explain that I come from the future?*

He wondered if Yeshua might not be a time traveler, too. Certainly if it were possible for Barth to open the doors of time, then the future of his day might also send back visitors to adjust history. In this way, the human race would continually correct itself. *Maybe someday they'll get it right*, Juve mused. *Maybe I'll have many chances to meet Maria and bring our child into the world.* The more Juve thought about these strange possibilities, the more trouble he had holding his thoughts together. Instead he followed Mayam toward a gathering along the side of the road. "What's going on up there?" he asked Mayam as a man came up from behind and walked next to Juve.

"Yeshua is speaking," Mayam answered, smiling at the man as he passed. Juve and Mayam soon became part of the thickening mass of people. Yeshua faced what Juve thought must represent the entire town of Bethany. He seemed to be speaking, but Juve could not hear him. He stood above the crowd, probably on a large rock. Otherwise there was nothing about his appearance that made him stand out. He looked like all the other people around him. A group of a dozen or so men and women seemed to ring Yeshua in an effort to hold back the crowd. Soon Juve could hear Yeshua speak, but his words were muffled now and again by the admiring responses of the audience.

"What good . . . ," Yeshua said.

To which the crowd chanted back, "Without love."

There followed a series of such calls from Yeshua and replies from the crowd. "Love can never . . ."

"Profit from pain."

"Love can never . . ."

"Conspire to gain."

As Juve listened to the give and take he couldn't help but be drawn into the emotion. At his side, Mayam was thoroughly enjoying herself and encouraging him to join what Juve could only think of as a celebration. Soon the crowd was clapping and jumping and waving their arms. People were crying and hugging and kissing. Juve scanned the faces of the eager participants—men and women of all ages, many with their children in tow. They seemed possessed by some unseen power, their faces bearing a variety of otherworldly expressions. He had seen this kind of mass emotion at musical performances, except that this crowd was much more serene and cohesive, more in tune with the performer, Yeshua. He wasn't trying to entertain his audience. He was leading them but at the same time letting them lead him. Both the player and the played seemed to know what the other was going to say. It was obvious the crowd had seen Yeshua many times, or heard his message repeated by others.

Juve looked toward Yeshua, his head and shoulders just visible above the heads of the throng. Suddenly it seemed that Yeshua was talking only to him. The words were clearer now and they seemed to penetrate him in an unusual way. For the first time, he felt that he was a part of the crowd. It didn't even matter what Yeshua said. The feeling seemed to lift his heart and carry him into himself in a way he had thought gone.

It wasn't until someone offered Juve a loaf of bread that he realized he was hungry. Juve accepted the bread and thanked the woman who offered it. He broke off a piece for himself and gave the rest to Mayam. As he did, he spotted two little girls playing in the dirt at their feet. They were using water from an animal bladder to wet the dirt and form the mud into a pair of little bowls. Giggling and chatting, they pretended to feed each other. "Thank you," one said to the other as she accepted an imaginary morsel.

Eventually Yeshua allowed the excitement to wane. He exhorted the crowd to share the spirit of the meeting with everyone they met. His final words were "Love especially those who hate you." The idea struck Juve. It resonated in a way that brought to mind all at once the futility of every violent act he had ever committed. He shuddered suddenly at the thought of his attempt to kill Bellator. He saw the man's terrified eyes behind Maria's shoulder. Her astonishment, like a knife in his heart, wrenched his chest. As if in a dream, Juve saw again his dying Maria in his arms. Now Bellator's grief-stricken face at the scene of her death. Juve felt as if he were falling as he moved with the crowd.

"Juve?" It was Maria's voice. He could almost see her face and wanted desperately to answer her.

"Juventus," Mayam repeated. Juve opened his eyes to Mayam looking back at him as she led him through the crowd away from the spot where Yeshua had been teaching.

"Did you call me?" he asked.

"Yes," she replied, "follow me."

Rather than push against the crowd, Juve and Mayam followed the flow. Juve surveyed the dispersing mass of people. It was clear that they were all of humble means—the kind of people Forza Facia defended—yet a number of them made their way to Yeshua with offerings of food, coins, and clothing. Yeshua graciously accepted all the gifts, passing each offering to one of his crew. The faces of Caldi, Cela, and his other comrades flashed through Juve's mind. This momentary tinge of nostalgia made him eager to meet Yeshua. He looked back to where the man had spoken. Through the crowd he thought he spied a knot of well-wishers, hangers-on, the kind who are always last to leave a party. He looked at Mayam and she nodded in agreement.

Together they approached the group. Juve thought, "I can teach his body-guards a thing or two." At the edge of the smaller, inner circle, Juve could hear Yeshua talking with his entourage. Mayam took Juve by the arm and led him through the circle of followers. Each man moved aside when Mayam tapped one after the other on the shoulder.

When Yeshua saw Mayam, his face beamed with an elation that made Juve smile with him. He watched the two embrace. They sighed and exclaimed their delight for several seconds, then stood at arm's length looking each other over. "How good it is to see you, Mayam," Yeshua said at last.

Mayam moved her left arm around Yeshua's waist and tucked herself under his right arm. "Rabboni, I want you to meet Juve." With her other arm, she presented her new friend. Still smiling, Juve stood face to face with Yeshua.

"Juve . . . you seem surprised," Yeshua observed. It was the face of Yeshua that surprised Juve. It was the face of the rabbi in his dreams. It was his own dark face, his own long hair, just as he had studied in his mirror after his recurring dream. If Yeshua sensed the likeness, he didn't let his surprise show.

Miffed at himself for betraying his surprise to Yeshua, Juve breathed in, exhaled slowly, and replied coolly, "I've come a long way. You're not exactly what I expected."

"You wanted, maybe, Elias," Yeshua said loud enough for his crew to hear, and they laughed at his joke. He added to Juve, "It's okay, we're not laughing at you. It's a stupid inside joke. I'll let you in on it, but first, meet my crew." With a sweeping wave of his hand, Yeshua gathered his friends and introduced them, one by one, to Juve. "Let's welcome our new friend," Yeshua announced. Then he asked the man on his right, "What do people call me these days, Simon?"

"I hear it all," the tall, serious-faced man answered. "Yahiye the Baptist, Elias, one of the prophets. Name a prophet, you've been called it."

"And you say what?" Yeshua asked Simon.

"You're the anointed one," Simon replied.

"Just don't tell that to everyone," Yeshua admonished Simon playfully. He let go of Mayam and Juve, and waved everyone toward him. "Listen up. Seriously. Don't go adding fuel to the fire with the anointed business. Is that clear? I'm in for enough trouble as it is. The elders, the chief priests, and the scribes—they hate that kind of talk. If I get out of Jerusalem alive this time, we'll be lucky. You hear the rumors. They want me dead."

"If you keep thinking and talking like that," Simon snapped at Yeshua, "you're going to fall right into their trap."

"No, Simon, you listen to me." Yeshua looked at all the people around him now and they could see in his eyes a deep and warm affection. Then he cleared his throat and they became fixed on what he was about to say. "I know we've seen a lot of love from these crowds, but they can call for our heads as fast as they can sing our praises." Yeshua looked at Juve. "Have you seen these crowds before?"

"They thought I was you in Jerusalem," Juve said. "I felt I could have said anything and they would have believed me."

"See what I mean?" Yeshua said to the group. "We bring the truth and the truth is good. But they all want it easy. I know I'd like to have it easy. When you hear the truth and you feel it in your heart, it feels good! But you know how hard it can be to live by it." The others agreed with a murmur of affirmation. Yeshua explained to Juve, "People come out of the crowds. They come up to me saying they were blind and now they can see. But tomorrow, they'll be calling for my head. So if they do kill me, get out of town."

"What do you mean, get out of town!" Andareos complained. He was the biggest, most formidable-looking man in the group. "We're not dragging our asses all over Judea, just to watch you get killed."

Yeshua interrupted, "You think the world we want to make is just like the rest of the world, only with us in charge, but it's not." He cleared his throat and composed himself again. Everyone listened intently as he spoke. "If you want what I've got, if you want to see what I see, you have to get used to the idea that it's not like the rest of the world. It's not about gaining a place of honor and having people follow you. People are going to hate you. They're going to persecute you. All this adoration I'm getting right now—it won't last long. I come here to open the way to the truth that's inside of you. That's where you have to go. That's where you're going to find the way to change the world. And it's not going to be easy. You're going to have to deny yourself. Get ready for the pain, because it's coming. They could be getting ready to crucify me down in Jerusalem. So if you want to be like me, get under the same cross and follow me. If you want more of the life you left behind, go now. But if you want the new life I have to offer, get ready for some bad times. Try to save your life and you'll lose it. Give it up and you've got it." Then, as if what he had just said was of only everyday importance, Yeshua cocked his head to one side in a manner that was completely disarming. "Juve? What kind of name is that?"

"I'm called Juve. My name is Juventus Trajan Carnifex."

"Carnifex," Yeshua said with a smile. "I think we have room for an executioner." The men and women surrounding him laughed. "Join us, Juventus. Maybe you'll see what you expect eventually." Speaking to everyone, Yeshua waved his right arm toward the west. "We're on our way to Jerusalem."

The group gathered itself together and began to walk to the west. Mayam and Yeshua walked just ahead of Juve. The sun hovered above the distant hills. It was near the conclusion of a beautiful spring day. A little man with a ruddy face walked alongside Juve. He introduced himself as Yahuda the Dagger. "What do you think of our Messiah?"

"Do you really think he's headed for trouble in Jerusalem?"

"I'm sure of it." The man possessed a pair of lips that immediately distracted Juve. They protruded and seemed wetter than normal.

"I just came from there with Mayam and they gave me a very warm reception, just because I look like him."

"Wait till they see the real thing."

"What do you mean?" Juve asked, trying to ignore the fine mist of spit that flew from Yahuda's mouth.

"People—that is, ordinary, everyday people—they prefer the trappings to the real thing."

As Juve considered what Yahuda said, he couldn't help overhear Mayam. Was she crying? She walked under the comforting arm of Yeshua with her head on his shoulder. She was talking about her brother, crying and wondering if he would ever wake up. Yeshua simply listened and comforted her the way she had comforted him. Yahuda interrupted his thoughts with a question. "You're from Rome?"

"That's right."

"What are you doing in Judea?"

Juve didn't want to talk about his imaginary background, plus he was more interested in Mayam's troubles. "I'm here to help. Let's leave it at that," he said. Yahuda seemed unfazed by his abrupt reply. He produced a sack of wine from beneath his robe and offered Juve a swig. Juve declined with an offhand gesture. Yahuda lifted the wine and squeezed a stream into his mouth.

"Believe me," he assured Juve, "we can use all the help we can get." The wine apparently warmed his belly and encouraged his curiosity. "What was it like in Rome?"

Juve gave Yahuda a disarming smile, raised his eyebrows, and replied, "You wouldn't believe me if I told you."

Yahuda's eyes widened with interest. Juve gave him a knowing nod. "I'll have to tell you about it sometime," he said. Then he leaned toward Yahuda and whispered, "When we're alone." Yahuda took a long draft of wine and smiled with eager anticipation.

As the sun began to set, Juve noticed Simon shuffle up to Yeshua and Mayam. Simon spoke to them, gesturing toward a clearing off the side of the road. Then he jogged to the head of the procession and announced, "We stop here for the night." Without disengaging from their conversations, the crew followed Simon toward the clearing. A single fig tree shaded a smooth space in front of a large assemblage of rocks. The rocks stood as tall as a man and as wide as the meager earthen dwellings Juve had come to regard as familiar. He approved Simon's choice of this resting spot. The fig tree offered plenty of evening shade, and the rocks would protect them from the heat of the rising sun in the morning.

"I'll be right back," Yeshua said to Mayam, as he walked off and disappeared behind the rocks. His entourage began to make preparations for the evening as the sun settled down behind the horizon. One by one, those who had not met Juve welcomed him and invited him to settle down for the night with them. Someone produced another skin of wine and they all began to share the contents. Mayam and a few other women took care of most of the work, while the men arranged themselves in a circle of clusters around where the women prepared the food.

From a few paces off, everyone could hear the sound of Yeshua clearing his throat. Juve turned with the others to see Yeshua standing and waving his hand in front of his face. "Do not go behind that rock." The travelers burst out in laughter. Yeshua, smiling, still proud of his joke, sat next to Juve. As the colors changed slowly and subtly from bright orange to red to crimson, someone marveled aloud at the ease of nature's beauty.

"Juve, which do you prefer, the sunrise or the sunset?" Yeshua asked his newest recruit.

"Sunrise." Juve replied as he started to feel the effects of the strong and pungent wine. "It's the start of the day. Anything feels possible. Yes, the sunrise. What about you?"

"Sunset. It's the time to ask, 'What did the day bring? How did I make things better?' But most of all, I prefer the sunset, because it's happening now."

"So if I asked you in the morning, you'd say sunrise?"

"Ask me in the morning," Yeshua quipped as he nudged Juve in the ribs with his elbow. Then he raised his voice and rubbed his hands together. "Let's eat!"

Juve accepted one-upmanship from Yeshua because he sensed no malice from the man. He also realized it was something a leader had to do to the new recruit. He respected the confidence and one-mindedness of his strange new friend. And he was confident that Yeshua returned his respect. Juve also felt relieved now that he had found the man Barth had sent him to protect. He was even more excited about what he could learn from Yeshua as a leader. But his real work was about to begin. He had a job to do and only a few days to do it. Meanwhile, he ate heartily. The other men and women joked about the day and their times together, and Juve listened. Someone raised the issue of hand washing. Yeshua coaxed the fair-skinned man they called Yahiye into telling the story. Yahiye was a big, gentle-looking man with kind features that softened the solid, muscular frame of a fisherman.

"Okay, we were up around . . . ," Yahiye began. "Where was it?"

"Galilee," someone said.

"Maybe it was Galilee. Anyway, we've been out for I don't know how many days. The crowds were huge. Something like four or five thousand people. And they're all hungry. Nobody has any food except for this guy with some bread and fish."

"There were more people with food," a soft-spoken man named Tomas added as he worked a small knife around a piece of wood.

"That's not the point," Yahiye said to Tomas. "There were some Scribes in the group. This one Scribe . . . What was his name?"

"Just tell the story," Mayam urged good-naturedly as she rested next to Yeshua.

"This Scribe comes up to Yeshua and asks why we don't wash our dishes."

"What dishes?"

"Some people had plates," Yahiye insisted. "And another guy—I think he was a Pharisee—says, 'Why don't you wash your hands according to the tradition of the elders?' So Yeshua—you can see he's lost patience with this guy. He clears his voice the way he does . . ." With his audience in the palm of his hands, Yahiye stood up and spoke in his impression of Yeshua, "Tradition? You want to talk about tradition? You know what Isaias says about hypocrites like you?" Now, with the group egging him on, Yahiye launched into an impression of Yeshua doing an impression of Isaias. "'You people honor me with your lips, but your hearts are gone,' he says. 'What a waste, the way you teach the commandments of men! Because you forget the commandments of God. You hold the traditions of men—like pot washing and cup scrubbing—and you throw out the commandments of God—like honoring your father and your mother.'"

The little group of friends laughed loudly and applauded Yahiye as he acknowledged their approval and sat down. It was easy to see that Yeshua was pleased. He cleared his throat and raised his hands. In the spirit of the evening, his comrades wondered whether he meant to make a point or tell another joke. "Listen. I know you love that story, but please don't forget the point. There's nothing you can put into yourself that can defile you. It's what comes *out* of you that defiles you. What you eat doesn't enter your heart. It goes into your belly and out the way all food is purged."

Yahiye, still in the spirit of his success, rolled his eyes and waved his hand in front of his face. Yeshua saw the joke and smiled at Yahiye. "If you have ears, please hear me and understand," he continued soberly. "From within your heart come evil thoughts, adulteries, and murders. You can no more stop them from coming out than you can the other. Thieving, deceit, lust, pride, and foolishness—all of these things grow from within your heart. And these are what defile you."

It was suddenly quiet as Yeshua stopped speaking. He had put most of the others in a happy state of thoughtfulness. But the words of Yeshua made Juve wonder about the state of his heart. Juve felt new ideas clash and battle with principles he had learned as a Lion and burned into his heart. The force and cunning he had practiced and knew he might have to use to protect Yeshua seemed oddly out of place as he watched his new companions settle into the evening. Bursts of conversation rose and fell, laughter and stories merged with his thoughts.

This is how people should live all the time, Juve thought, *but how?* He decided that there might be some way to merge his physical power under the guidance of some of Yeshua's principles. Of course, he would have to learn so much more about the man's ideas. His plans delighted him as the night gathered in around the travelers. He lay down, stretched out, and gazed at the stars. He knew Sarenta was rising behind his head. He arranged himself so that he would not see it tonight. It would only bring on troubling memories of Maria. Instead he closed his eyes and listened to Yeshua and his crew. They sang songs between more recollections and stories. To Juve's surprise, Tomas sang a song with a beautifully clear and resonant voice that the night seemed to carry far away, over the mountains of Judea.

Three more days, maybe more, maybe less, Juve thought as he combed his fingers through his lengthening beard and drifted off to the laughter and warm, soothing voices congratulating Tomas and requesting another.

THE ROAD

THE MORNING FOUND THE FAMILY OF TRAVELERS IN THE cool shade of the rocks. Juve was among the first to rise. The other followers sat up, groggily easing themselves into wakefulness. One woman lazily petted a golden-haired dog. Juve walked away from the sleepers and began his morning exercise routine in private. As he exercised, he studied the landscape, associating each feature with something familiar to him in what he now thought of as his other life. That hill was like the factory along the Tiber where they made motosled engines. The shallow gorge running gently down its side reminded him of an aqueduct, but he couldn't remember where. It was another world, his future. He was more than a visitor here. This was more than a mission, he admitted to himself, it was a new life. With his workout completed, Juve rejoined the others. They shared their bread, dried fruit, nuts, and water with him without hesitation and spoke with him as if he were an old friend. He had been adopted by a family, quickly and without question.

Yet Juve could not bring himself to trust them entirely. *I'd never accept a new Forza recruit as quickly as they seem to have accepted me*, he thought. Nevertheless, as the morning developed, Juve mingled among the group, eager to learn all he could. Andareos and Simon were brothers. So were Yahiye and Yakob—that is, the larger Yakob, the one they called Big Yak. He was obviously the bank. Juve could hear his sack of coins jingling as he lumbered along. Andareos, Simon, Yahiye, and Big Yak had fished as a team for many years before following Yeshua. Some of the women seemed to be paired with men, but others preferred their own company. Now they all busied themselves among the men. As the group began to move down the road, each woman carried something, even the oldest, Miriam. Juve had learned that she was Yeshua's mother. She walked alongside one of the three men named Yakob—the one they called Yakob the Just, a brother of Yeshua. It angered Juve that Yakob did not relieve his own mother of her load, but he held his tongue.

With the sun still low in the sky behind them, the small group walked and talked. Juve could hear Yeshua promise a glorious future. He picked up his pace and drew nearer to Yeshua so that he could hear what he was saying.

"We have been happy together. But the time has come for us to do what we have been called to do," Yeshua told those around him. "We're going to Jerusalem to claim what is ours. We're not going to take it by force, but we're going to take it." Murmurs of excitement arose from those closest to Yeshua. Others moved closer, a few brushing Juve as they passed. "We are the children of God and Jerusalem is our city. It's our home." Seeing so many eager to hear what he had to say, Yeshua raised his voice. "We have been kept out of our Temple too long. The high priests have guarded the doors and have kept us from what is ours with laws that contradict the word of God and with taxes that close those doors to all but a few. They have filled the Temple with their records of debts—debts so heavy the poor can't bear them. We will destroy those debts by destroying those records."

A few voices rose in agreement, almost matching their leader's enthusiasm. "We will accept this deprivation no longer. Our God is the God of all our people." Someone near Yeshua must have mumbled a caution or objection, because now his voice rode over their heads, "There's nothing wrong with taking what is ours. It is our birthright." Most of the group agreed now as Yeshua continued, "So let's go together. Don't be afraid. The people of the city will welcome us and many will follow us. They can't hold back all of us."

This time Juve could hear the man they called Simon the Zealot revel in the idea of spilling blood. Yeshua corrected him immediately. "No, we're not going to take what is ours that way—the way they have taken it from us. If we did that, how would we be different from them? We would become oppressors like them. No, we won't be like them. Their way doesn't work." Yeshua motioned for the group to give him room. He walked over to a large rock on the side of the road, stood up on it, and motioned for everyone to gather around. When his audience was ready, he continued: "Remember who we are, brothers and sisters. Remember how we are."

Yeshua looked over his family, and a warm glow of affection settled on all of them. Juve could feel it. "If we fail, if we are pushed back, we will return again and again. I may not return with you the next time. There's a good chance they'll take me and make an example of me. But they cannot make an example of all of us." Yeshua smiled. "Who will tend the fields, make their sandals, and prepare their meals? There will always be more of us, so we must teach each generation our way. Eventually they will see that it is the better way. Soon they'll see that their way cannot work without our hands or without our hearts. They can beat our bodies into submission with their rods. They can test our determination with starvation, but only for so long. We make their wealth. They need us. If we rise up, they can gather their possessions close to them, but there is only so much they can hoard. It will run out when they can take no more from us. Then they'll start taking it from each other. And that's when they will begin to see that we are right, that our way is the only way people can live and work together in harmony. They'll say, 'Where are those people who work so well together? Those people we persecuted, those people who had the courage to stand up to us when they had no chance of winning—where are they? They stood up for what was right while we pushed them down. Let's try their way,' they'll say. And on that day, we will begin to show them the way."

Juve noticed that even Simon the Zealot and those who hung with him, including Yahuda, seemed willing to follow Yeshua's lead now, at least for a while, because they raised their voices in agreement with the rest. Yeshua raised his arms and commanded their attention again. "No!" He cleared his throat. "You will show them the way. I may not be with you after Passover, so don't forget what we've learned together."

As Yeshua stepped down from the rock and continued to lead the procession toward Jerusalem, Juve's mind began to spin. *This is where he gets killed,* he told himself. *I've got to keep him away from Jerusalem.* He began to think of ways to separate Yeshua from his entourage. He was struggling with the problem of how and where to take and hide the rabbi when the wet-lipped Yahuda sidled up alongside him.

"I don't like this talk of death," Yahuda confided. "If he keeps saying it's going to happen, it's just that much more likely to happen."

"You're right," Juve blurted, causing several heads to turn. He spoke to Yahuda in a more subdued voice. "He's resigning himself to something that doesn't have to happen."

"I agree," Yahuda replied.

"You said something last night that got me thinking. You said you were here to help, but the way you said it—as if you have your own plans, independent plans, if you know what I mean? Do you have independent plans, Yahuda?"

"I have plans, my own plans," Yahuda answered cautiously, "but good plans, good for Yeshua, good for all of us." He held Juve's arm just above his elbow and asked secretly, "Do you know something I don't know?"

Juve smiled ironically. "I know a lot of things you'd find difficult to believe, my friend. And I, too, want to put my forces toward Yeshua's benefit."

"Tell me a little bit more about yourself, stranger," Yahuda said, letting go of Juve's arm.

"Not much to tell," Juve replied. "I'm here from Rome on word that Yeshua might be in trouble."

"They've heard of Yeshua in Rome?" Yahuda said incredulously. "Who in Rome is concerned about him?"

"Certain people—people with good reason to protect him."

"I find that very difficult to believe, my friend," he muttered suspiciously. "So you want to take Yeshua to Rome?"

"To Rome?" Juve thought for a moment. "No, I don't think that's the answer." Then he turned the questions on Yahuda. "What's your story?"

"My story . . . ," the man began, pushing out his lower lip as he ordered his thoughts. "I'm a man with little patience for the kind of crap Yeshua is willing to take. See, I ran with the Zealots of Galilee for seven years. That's where I got my name, the Dagger." Juve saw Yahuda pat and adjust something hanging at his side, under his garment, and he chided himself for not noticing sooner that the man was armed. "Before that, I was a doctor. I've taken care of every kind of disease and discomfort you'll find in this godforsaken desert. I've traveled all over Judea and beyond. Never to Rome, though. There's no end to what needs to be done here. The misery of my people kept me going, working myself weak trying to relieve their misery. Rich and poor get sick, but the poor get no relief. Their miserable lives make them blind and lame. They rave as if evil spirits possess them. I find these maladies only in the poorest and dispossessed. The only way to cure them is to kill the makers of their discomfort." Yahuda looked for a clue of agreement in Juve's expression, but Juve gave no hint.

Instead, Juve asked, "Have you seen Mayam's brother?"

"Yes, I have."

"Do you know what's wrong with him?"

"I have an idea," Yahuda replied. "When I try to lift his eyelids, they're tight, as if he's resisting. That tells me he's not in an endless sleep. You know, the kind you get with some blows to the head."

"Have you tried to treat him?"

"Only to keep him comfortable." With a shrug of his shoulders, Yahuda added, "Sometimes they wake up gradually. Other times they come out of it suddenly."

Juve's suspicions were confirmed. He, too, had seen comas from head injury and states of incapacity brought on by an inability to cope with extreme stress. "I think you're doing the right thing," he said. "Has Yeshua tried to do anything?"

"No, I think he knows better," Yahuda answered with a shade of amusement. "I wouldn't mind learning how he does heal, but I know he can only heal those who believe he has the power to cure them."

"You've observed him, I see."

"I'm still a doctor at heart."

"If he's doing what I think he's doing, it's . . ." Juve tried to express what he understood about healing by suggestion, but he could not find the words in his new language.

Yahuda helped him. "It's the patient who's doing the curing."

"There's great power in allowing someone to think for you."

"Well, this power Yeshua uses to heal, it could be used to do almost anything."

"I'm afraid you're right."

"It's what our forefathers were doing when they wrote the Torah. They understood that a people with a single mind cannot be subjugated."

"Until they misuse that power and abuse their own people."

"Another reason for turning everything upside down." Yahuda spit to the side of the road. "The people at the top have to be on the bottom for a while."

"What are your plans?" Juve asked, now clearly expressing his keen interest. His companion leaned in and spoke just loud enough for Juve to hear. "I've got friends in the city ready to move on my signal. Know what I mean?" He looked up at Juve. "Zealots—the crew Yeshua and I used to run with in Galilee." With a nod of his head in Yeshua's direction, Yahuda continued, "He was serious about overthrowing the Temple back then, too. He talked like a real messiah in those days. He talks in circles now, ever since he hooked up with Mayam.

"But he's got a hell of a following now. I think he's up to something. I think he's working these people. He used to complain that the Zealots lost followers too quickly—that we scared them off. He left and I decided to follow him for a while, when I heard how well he was doing. At least to learn how he does it. If I could win a following of this size, I'd give it back to those sons of whores." Yahuda spat again. "I'm ready to spill their yellow blood. With the Zealots, we were lucky to get a dozen men willing to do what needed to be done. Now he's got scores willing to do whatever he says and all he says is the kind of crap you just heard." They walked for a little while before Yahuda continued. "We could use a man your size, Juve. And the fact that you look just like him—that gives me all sorts of ideas." He shook his head and with a sinister chuckle added, "Know what I mean?"

"I don't think so, Yahuda. I've spilled enough blood. I've killed with my bare hands and with weapons you couldn't possibly imagine. I've killed for money and I've killed for sport. I'm through with it." He waited for a reaction from his companion, then continued, resting his hand on Yahuda's shoulder. "Do what you have to do in Jerusalem. I won't get in your way."

"I can't believe he's got help all the way from Rome," Yahuda complained. "He had real fire once. Now he just confuses me."

"Just don't forget," Juve said. "I'm here to *protect* Yeshua." He reached his hand up the back of Yahuda's neck and gripped his head behind his ears.

Yahuda's knees buckled and he started to stumble, but Juve quickly released his debilitating grip and, holding Yahuda by the neck, gently set him back into his walking stride. Seeing that the stunned Yahuda took his meaning, Juve added, "That goes for Mayam, too."

"I'm glad we think alike," Yahuda replied, pulling himself together. "We have a lot more to talk about, but not now." He made a nervous motion with his eyes that encompassed the rest of the group. "They'll suspect something if we talk too long."

As Yahuda drifted away to another part of the entourage, Juve wrinkled his brow, reviewing what had just happened as the others walked and talked. They seemed to be just as confounded as he was. He knew he had to act soon. He was convinced that Yeshua was heading for the fate he had come to prevent. Unfortunately, it looked as if it might happen in a crowded city as part of a major disturbance. *That could be bad and good*, he thought. *Bad for control, good for cover*. Nothing worried Juve more, however, than the fact that he was on unfamiliar turf. He considered kidnapping Yeshua, but he had no idea where to take him or hide him. He knew now that he needed help. Yahuda was too ready to wet his knife with human blood. The others—few of them impressed Juve. There was some muscle but not enough craft. *Except for Mayam*, Juve concluded, *they're nothing like Forza*.

During his deliberations, a few of the family had eased their pace and let Yeshua and a few others gain some distance. Juve merged into a cluster populated by Tomas and Little Yak.

"I don't get it," Tomas complained. "One minute he's our messiah, the next he's dead." Tomas whittled furiously as he spoke. Juve realized now that it was Tomas he'd heard grousing about the rocks under his back last night. Mayam drifted back to see Juve. She threaded her arm around his and they walked arm-in-arm for a while. Soon they were talking about Yeshua. Tomas and the others nearby began to pepper Mayam with questions about Yeshua's gloomy predictions.

"How can he be our messiah if they're going to kill him before we even get started?" Tomas whined.

"What is it we love about him?" Mayam asked Tomas without expecting an answer. "His voice? His face? Certainly not the smell of him after three days on the road. These things we see and hear and smell—they don't matter. I've seen better-looking men. I've heard prettier voices." She let Tomas think for a moment. "It's his words, Tomas. It's what he has to say, not the sound of him saying it, that matters. His words don't ever have to die. If we take them to heart and remember them and pass them on, they never will die. We will have them forever. We will give them to our children. Our children will give them to their children."

"But why does he have to die?" Tomas protested with a sudden swipe of his knife. Juve saw that a four-legged animal was beginning to emerge from the piece of wood in Tomas's hand. "Why does he have to die now? What good will dying do?"

Simon noticed that the others were very interested in what Mayam had to say. He let himself drift back toward her group. Yahuda was just as keen as Simon to be in on the action. He also moved into Mayam's circle.

"If we spread his ideas," Mayam continued, "they will do the same good they do for us. In that way, at least, he lives forever."

"I know men," Simon argued. "I know what will happen. They will defile his words the way the Pharisees and Scribes try to twist them to their advantage now. They will, that is, if we don't get control and keep control of his message."

"You've already got him dead and buried," Mayam argued. "He's still alive, don't forget."

"You heard him," Simon countered. "His own death is all he talks about lately. If we want to carry on his message, we have to protect it the way a mother protects her young."

"We have a hard enough time keeping his words straight," Tomas chimed in, "How will we know which words to say when, if Yeshua isn't with us?"

"Tomas, you fret too much," Mayam told him. "Yeshua's words are living words. They sound strange and confuse us, because we've never heard them before. There has never been a heart as good as his from which such words could rise. Not since the prophets, anyway. If people defile his words, their words will sound empty, like all the dead words we hear every day. People will always recognize his words as living truth."

"And it's our job to keep them alive," added Yahuda, "and that's a practical matter." Yahuda looked at Juve and asked, "Am I right?"

"I'll tell you what I think," Juve answered Yahuda. "I think men should spend more time listening to women, instead of making them their slaves." Then he slipped his hand under the sack on Mayam's shoulder and smiled at her. She smiled back and allowed Juve to take the load from her shoulder. He shifted the sack over his shoulder. "Besides," Juve assured the group, "nobody's going to kill your master. Not while I'm around." Juve's threat raised a mixture of response—raised eyebrows, some raised in mock fear, but for the most part, silence.

"I believe Yeshua's prediction rather than yours," Simon replied dismissively. Then for the ears of the others, he added testily, "And if he's going to die on us, he'd better pick a successor. Otherwise, we'll be at each other's throats."

Yahiye challenged Simon. "The man's talking about dying and that's all you think about?" Rather than wait for Simon's reply, the huge man hurried ahead and walked next to Yeshua. As the discussion gathered steam, it attracted more listeners. In a little while, as Yeshua and Yahiye walked far ahead, arm-in-arm, the rest bickered about who was the most loyal, who would take over if and when Yeshua died, who would report to whom, and even who deserved the highest seat in the new kingdom. Juve's mind wandered toward Maria and Auspex. He wondered, if Auspex had lived, how he would have done leading Forza Facia.

As he watched Yeshua and Yahiye continue to put greater distance between themselves and the debaters, he assured himself that the men and women of Forza had a much clearer sense of mission. *They will do well*, he thought, and wondered if Yeshua would consider letting him whip this bunch of babies into shape. Just then he noticed a barefoot boy run up from the direction of Jerusalem and speak to Yeshua. It was the same boy who had whispered something about lions when he had come into Jerusalem with Benjamin. After a short discussion with Yeshua, the boy was back on his way to Jerusalem. Then Juve heard Simon say something that returned his attention to the group's discussion.

"And he told us that some of us will not taste death until we have seen the Kingdom of God." Juve realized he had missed the beginning of Simon's story—something about how Yeshua had taken Simon, Big Yak, and someone else aside and had spoken to them in private. But it seemed that there was more to it than just conversation. Simon seemed transfixed, even as he walked. "It wasn't only Yeshua who appeared as white and bright as the sun," he continued. "There was Elias and Moses with him. The master spoke with them. I was trembling and had no idea what to say . . ."

Big Yak interrupted, "I remember, when he said that, everything got so unreal."

"To me, it looked like Yeshua was the sun," Simon added, still looking skyward, as if he were witnessing the event all over again.

"I never saw anything that white," Big Yak continued. "He was brighter than the sun!"

Simon seemed annoyed that Big Yak felt the need to amplify the story. "I wanted to build a temple right on the spot," Simon told the group, looking at them, one at a time, trying to hold their attention.

But Yak was just as eager to relate the strange event. "There's some kind of power on that mountain. I heard a big voice. Something told me it was the voice of God."

The others gazed at Big Yak, waiting for him to tell them what the voice said. Now Simon interrupted, spread wide his arms, and imitated the voice of God. "It said, 'He is my son. Listen to him.'"

"Then Elias and Moses were gone," Big Yak continued, wide-eyed.

"But here's what you have to remember," Simon said, speaking in his most commanding voice. "We saw Elias. So Elias has come. And you know what that means."

Everyone except Juve seemed to understand the meaning of Elias coming. He hoped they would express it, because he knew he couldn't ask. He could tell it was something they all were supposed to know. But no one explained. Juve caught Mayam's eye. He could tell she sensed his confusion. She smiled reassuringly. Simon continued his story, warning his listeners not to repeat what he was about to tell them. Yeshua had sworn them to secrecy, he explained.

Juve was losing respect for Simon. Yeshua apparently trusted Simon enough to give him some inside information and Simon was using the information to demonstrate his special office. *What kind of man is this Simon*, he wondered, and became even more annoyed as the bickering ensued. He looked at Mayam. She smiled; the squabbling amused her. Then she rested her head on Juve's shoulder as they walked. Juve treasured Mayam's pure and warm affection, but the quarrelling ruined his mood. Again they were arguing about something Yeshua had said.

"I hate it when he says that," Tomas grimaced as he put away his knife and carved animal. "I don't know if I should try to be first and end up last so that I'll be first, or try to be last so that I'll end up first."

"Don't be such an idiot," Simon taunted. "Either way, you end up last."

"You say that because you want to be first," Tomas retorted, "but if I want to be last and end up first, I still won't get what I want."

"Maybe that's the idea," Simon replied sarcastically.

Juve had had enough. He stopped walking and warned them, "You men bicker like a bunch of . . ." He groped for an Aramaic word that meant "schoolgirls," but apparently his language chip didn't hold it. He had forgotten Barth's warning. The concept of "schoolgirl" had not come into their vocabulary yet. He felt the heat of embarrassment in his face. "Like a bunch of old women!" he concluded as emphatically as he could, having lost his tempo. Mayam raised her head from Juve's shoulder and looked at him quizzically. "Mayam's the only one equipped to lead this outfit."

Everyone looked at Juve as if he had fallen out of the sky. He could see a mixture of suspicion and resentment in their faces. Yahuda wrinkled his brow at Juve. Finally, Simon spoke. "We follow Yeshua, stranger. Just because you resemble him, don't get any ideas about trying to take his place. Besides, your beard's too short." Juve could tell that Simon spoke for all of them. He held his tongue.

THE FRUIT CART

THE ROAD FROM BETHANY TO JERUSALEM CARRIED MORE and more travelers as the morning progressed. Occasionally passers-by would entreat those surrounding Yeshua for a chance to see and touch him. They would also beg the group for food and money. Juve was surprised at how often they received what they requested. Two big men, struggling with a cart, passed Juve. As they continued to hustle past the others in Yeshua's family, they rudely shoved them out of their way whenever they seemed to feel it was necessary. The cart was overloaded with crates of fruit and food. The rickety vehicle creaked and lurched as one man strained to maneuver it down the grade. Remembering how he and Benjamin struggled with their load on this very road, Juve realized that the men had more on their hands than they could handle. Instinctively he made his way toward Yeshua, passing the men and their cart.

Reaching Yeshua's side, Juve looked back and saw that the men were losing control of their load. The thudding and bumping contraption had already begun to scatter the crowd as the loose cart rolled and tumbled toward Yeshua. Juve shoved Yeshua to the side and dove to brace him from his fall, landing with him in a bluster of dust and grunts.

"Are you hurt?" Juve asked Yeshua. Without waiting for an answer or explaining what had just happened, Juve stood just as one of the cart drivers came dashing after his errant cart. The two collided as the cart smashed into a tree a way off the side of the road.

"Now look what you've done, goat fucker!" the large man yelled at Juve, pointing to the collision of fruit and splintered wood.

Juve gave him a look of warning and answered, "Go take care of your mess and maybe I won't be fucking any goats today." He made it clear to the man that he was thinking of him as the goat.

As Juve turned back to check on Yeshua, the man gave Juve's shoulder an insulting push. "Don't disrespect me, fool." Juve smiled ever so slightly as he relished the oncoming contest. He saw that his smile had unnerved the man, but not enough to make him back down.

"Did you hear me?" the big man barked as he shoved Juve with both arms. Juve anticipated the shove and leaned into it with just the right amount of force to make the man feel like he had pushed a wall. Juve's new friends had gathered around and gasped as the man stumbled backwards. Juve cocked his head to one side as if to say *That was your last warning*. With slow, lumbering motion, the man stepped up and prepared to take a swing. Instinctively Juve prepared himself to block the punch and pull out the man's larynx, but just as he was adjusting his stance, he felt a hand blocking his arm.

"Don't do it," Yeshua commanded. As Juve turned his face to Yeshua, the brute's thick fist sank into the side of Juve's face. If the blow had been backed by a little training and better coordination, it would have done more damage. As it was, Juve stumbled back a step and stood facing his attacker's smug grin. The crowd waited for Juve's reaction. He raised his right hand, stuck his finger in his mouth, and ran it past all of his teeth. Then he spit out a small, bloody mass. The bewildered aggressor waited. Juve looked at Yeshua and grinned broadly, so that he could see his bloody but otherwise perfect set of teeth.

"Now I look like a goat fucker," Juve said to Yeshua.

"I'm proud of you," Yeshua replied with a smile. The other cart driver called for his companion from the scene of the wreck. Juve's attacker walked over to the wreckage with an air of victory. Mayam and most of Juve's new friends smiled as they gazed proudly at Juve's face—not at his injury but at his expression. They could see that he was enjoying an unfamiliar but incredibly satisfying sense of rightness.

Seeing their expressions, he felt suddenly more a part of the family. *I can live with this*, he told himself, pleased at the thought. Only Simon and Yahuda revealed their displeasure. Then Yeshua, with a turn of his head, sent Tomas, Yahiye, and a few others over to the cart wreckage. Big Yak reached under his garments and retrieved a sack of coins, reached into it, and as he followed the others, counted out what he thought they could afford to give the cart drivers. Juve was stunned.

Yeshua motioned for him to follow as he fell in behind Big Yak. He put his arm around Juve and spoke reassuringly. "My friend, if you want to walk with me, you must love your enemies." Then he gave Juve's shoulder a warm squeeze of reassurance and smiled as if to say, *I know you understand*.

Yeshua and most of his crew were salvaging fruit, while Andareos and Big Yak did their best to rig the cart to at least roll again. At first, the cart drivers were incredulous, but as the work proceeded, they took the help in stride. Even Juve was sorting fruit—placing the salvageable pieces in usable boxes and tossing the too badly damaged pieces off into the distance. He reached for another good piece of fruit just as another hand snatched it up. Juve followed the bruised knuckles of the hand. They belonged to the man who had bloodied his mouth. The men looked at each other. In his former enemy's face, Juve could see a bewildered sense of remorse. The man struggled to say something as his eyes grew wet with shame. Juve smiled, gripped the man's shoulder, and nodded his head gently, silently saying, "It's all right."

It was about a week before Passover and pilgrims flowed slowly from all corners of Judea to the city. Juve listened to the voices in the clusters of travelers they passed or from among those who passed them. At two different locations he spotted men coolly observing the crowd. One of them, a heavy man, sported an unmistakable red beard. Juve was not surprised that Yeshua might warrant the attention of spies. Judea, he was beginning to understand, stewed in a great furnace of spiritual fervor, which Yeshua stoked. A steady pulse of anticipation rippled through the people they encountered. On most faces he sensed degrees of expectation. Something had to happen. *If it doesn't happen*, Juve thought, *these people will make it happen*.

Yeshua was called upon to administer to the crowds from time to time as they made their way toward Jerusalem. They would make progress, the throngs would thicken, and they would have to stop. When Yeshua admonished and advised his audiences, Juve imagined what Forza might think of such ideas.

Eventually as dusk cooled the day and evening sent people off toward food and rest, Yeshua and his company arrived at a garden that overlooked the great city. The men reclined as Mayam, her sister Martha, and some of the other women began to prepare the evening meal. Tomas, sitting next to Juve, reached over and handed Juve the small figure of a goat—the animal he had been whittling ever since Juve had met him. Juve examined the goat, rolling it around in his hands. The significance of the goat and the thoughtfulness of the gift surprised and moved him so deeply that he forgot himself and said, "Thank you," in Roma. Coughing to cover his mistake, he repeated his gratitude in Aramaic.

Tomas let out a long and grateful sigh of fatigue. "If we hadn't helped clean up that fruit cart, I would have starved by now."

As Juve studied the details of the goat, Big Yak moaned as he sat against an olive tree and beat his dirty sandals against a nearby rock. Yeshua slept in the late evening shade alongside Yahiye and Little Yak. Juve stood and studied the city and its untidy arrangement of dwellings that stretched toward the horizon under the setting sun. Another day was fading away. *How many days left to reach Skull Hill? Two? Three? How will I save Yeshua? When? From what?*

After dinner, with most of the family lounging in the twilight, Mayam drew from under her clothing a small, alabaster box and took from it a tiny vial. She carefully opened the little container and immediately a glorious aroma filled the garden. The delicate essence alerted everyone's senses. Juve noticed what a stark contrast it presented against the thick and heavy body odors of all the travelers and the remains of the dried meat and fruit left for the dogs to finish. Across from Juve, Yahuda eyed the viscous liquid as Mayam carefully filled the cupped palm of one hand. He whispered something to Simon, who reclined at his side.

Mayam gave the empty container to Yeshua, oiled both of her palms, and began to massage his feet. Yeshua rested his head against a bundle of provisions, closed his eyes, brought the empty vile to his nose, and inhaled deeply. A soft smile lightened his entire face as Mayam kneaded her dearest friend's toes, arches, heels, and ankles. The others seemed to take vicarious pleasure in the anointment and the fragrance of the oil. After a generous amount of time,

Mayam bent over and gently wiped her hair along the top of Yeshua's feet. His sleepy eyebrows shifted slightly upwards and the corners of his lips extended his smile almost imperceptibly. Wrapping her hair under his feet, Mayam babied their soles. Her face was hidden in the tent of hair that enfolded the feet of Yeshua. Seated across from Yeshua, Simon seemed to take almost as much pleasure from Mayam's treatment. He watched his master's face with his own sleepy smile.

As if sensing Simon's attention, Yeshua raised his heavy eyelids and looked at Simon. Juve watched the silent communication. "It must be nice to be the leader," Simon seemed to say. In response, Yeshua tilted his head lazily to one side and shrugged. Then he closed his eyes. Little Yak could no longer contain his anger. "I hope you realize you could have sold that spikenard for twenty shekels and given it to the poor," he complained. Yeshua wasted no time delivering his reply. "Let her alone," he commanded without opening his eyes. "She's been saving this ointment for my burial, but I'd rather enjoy it now."

"I know what you're doing," Little Yak answered Yeshua angrily. "You keep saying you're going to die, so that when it happens you'll increase your credibility as a prophet." Yeshua chose not to respond.

Why doesn't he answer? Juve wondered. *What makes Little Yak so emotional all of a sudden? He must have an awful lot invested in the success of Yeshua,* Juve concluded. Juve began to drift off to the sound of a baby crying in another part of the garden. The day's events had exhausted him. He wondered again how he would protect Yeshua in Jerusalem, when he didn't even fully understand the threat. As he deliberated, his thoughts began to disconnect and made less and less sense. He drifted down and waded into a disquieting dream.

Juve and Auspex walked down a long, gray corridor. They passed a dark room. From inside, Juve heard a noise, like a dog digging in the dirt.

"Don't go in there," Auspex warned.

Juve looked inside and saw Maria rocking a baby, her kerchief-covered head and shoulders rubbing against the wall. She was comforting the child. Then he wasn't sure it was a child at all. No, it was just a blanket folded over something. No, it had to be a baby, because he could hear it. Then the child started to cry, first slowly and then with more intensity. Juve ran into the room and held out his arms, reaching for the baby. Maria, head down, bent to hand the child to someone else—another man in the room. The man revealed his face. It was Bellator!

"No! No!" Juve screamed, sitting up. "Don't do it, Maria!"

His scream woke everyone in the garden. Juve, in a sweat, sat up, shook his head, and rubbed his face. Yeshua opened his eyes and looked sleepily at Juve.

"Old enemies," he explained. Yeshua shook his head and dropped back off to sleep.

PASSOVER

ABRAHAM HAD GROWN WEARY OF MESSIAHS STIRRING UP
the people, making unrealistic promises. Now this Yeshua. Word had reached
the priest that the latest Hebrew messiah had collected more hangers-on than
most. It was not enough to worry Abraham when small groups of men wandered off with this or that vagabond or malcontent with a gift for oratory and
vague plans for a new Jewish kingdom. Most of them attempted to live celi-
bate lives, didn't work, and no longer helped raise their children. A bother but
not a major problem. They produced no more children. That was a blessing.

"It's difficult enough keeping the Romans off the backs of the people when
they go about their business," Abraham muttered angrily. He clenched his fists
and let loose a growl of wrath loud enough to make an approaching stranger
stop and step aside. When Abraham arrived at the Office of Hewn Stone next
to the Temple, he paused before entering and considered his options one
more time. *The Sanhedrin concerns itself with only the most difficult cases. Is this
rabble-rouser really worth our time?*

Yes, he answered himself.

Inside the Office of Hewn Stone, Abraham found Joshua waiting. He
greeted his former teacher and added, "Thank you for meeting me."

"It is nothing, my friend," Joshua replied. "What is it that troubles you?"

"Nothing? What nothing?" Abraham answered. "You have always been the beacon in my life, Joshua. You have honored me from the beginning and you never refused to guide me along my way."

"Enough groveling, Abraham," the older man replied. "Tell me how I can help you."

Abraham sat next to his mentor and sighed as he took in the simple grandeur of the great hall. "You know we continue to be pestered by these young men who take it upon themselves to preach and lead our people in unorthodox directions. Yahiye the Baptist, Joshua of Berea . . ." He watched for a sign of recognition in his friend's expression. "And now this Yeshua."

"Yes, I have come to respect something of what each of them has to say— when I can tell what they are saying. Harmless, for the most part, wouldn't you say?"

"For the most part."

"Our Essenes, for example, they live a clean and quiet, well-organized life. They share all their possessions. They are particularly scrupulous about the Sabbath, if I am not mistaken. And this Yeshua, his style is similar, is it not? Some say he lived with the Essenes for some time."

Adjusting himself in his chair, Abraham continued with a little more vehemence, "Except that he's attracting an inordinate amount of attention. He's collecting followers by the battalion. He's cleaned out the best part of the male population in some of our smaller hamlets."

"But they return?"

"Yes."

"And are they any worse off for having walked with a man who helped them look into their hearts?"

Even though no one else was around, Abraham leaned in to almost whisper to his teacher. "He says he's the Messiah."

"Is that so?" Joshua stroked his long, gray beard thoughtfully. "Does he actually call himself Messiah?"

"They say he does."

"Who says he does?"

"His followers. At least some people say they say he does . . ." Abraham checked himself and feigned an attitude of judiciousness. "I see where you're taking me, Joshua, but I also see what may be a more serious threat."

"And that is?"

"Some refer to this troublemaker as King of the Jews."

Joshua gave Abraham a look of mild reproach. "Again, does he actually call himself King of the Jews?"

"I haven't heard him call himself king," Abraham admitted, "but I think it would be wise for us to address this kind of provocation, if it is—"

"You know, Abraham, I have always felt that the truth has its own life and always finds its own way. Our people have been fooled and led astray so many times. But they always find their way home. And if they find truth in what Yeshua has to say, well, maybe we should at least find out what it is they find so appealing before we condemn him for preaching it. Many of the insights that find their way into Torah have been inspired by so-called madmen wandering in the desert. Your namesake, for example."

Abraham considered what his mentor was saying. Joshua, seeing that his former student was searching his heart, placed his hand on Abraham's shoulder. "My good friend, I advise you to let those in charge of such matters worry about these rebels. We in the Sanhedrin have many weightier matters to wrestle."

"I suppose you're right, as always, Joshua," Abraham said as he rose to go. The two men embraced and parted. Abraham walked back out into the sunlight and scanned the street. It swelled with people preparing to celebrate Passover. He could feel his heart move with affection for his people. And then it raced with hatred as he thought of the man who called himself Messiah and threatened the peace he had worked so long and so hard to manage throughout the insufferable Roman occupation. The pressure in his chest urged him to make a decision. *No time to waste*, he told himself as he descended the steps of the Office of Hewn Stone. *Yeshua must die!* Abraham stormed his way through the crowded streets, kicking up little gusts of dirt and gravel above the cobblestones with his determined march to the house of the chief priest Caiaphas.

As Yeshua and his company approached Jerusalem, all were abuzz with news of Mayam's brother. Juve quickly learned that Mayam and Yeshua had risen early and visited the sleeping man's house, not far from where they had spent the night. With a loud command from Yeshua, Mayam's brother had opened his eyes, stood up, and taken his first tentative steps. To little avail, Yeshua had urged the astonished family and friends to downplay the event.

Less impressed with what the rest were proclaiming as a miracle, Juve looked again across the Kidron valley between the travelers and the city, skirted by its hundred gleaming white towers. The most majestic faced him as he walked with Yeshua away from the garden. He recalled the story Benjamin told him about King Herod and the wife he killed.

On both sides of the path and across the face of the broad mount, Passover pilgrims were rising from their camps. As Juve descended the well-worn path into the valley, preoccupied with his thoughts, the young runner whose face Juve was now familiar with passed him again and stopped to speak with Yeshua. He listened intently, nodding now and then. After sending the young man back into Jerusalem, Yeshua motioned for the others to gather around. As the group stopped and rearranged themselves, Juve abandoned his reverie and joined them. "The people of Jerusalem eagerly await our arrival," Yeshua reported. Everyone but Juve began to cheer. Yeshua abruptly stopped them with raised hands. "We're going to use the enthusiasm of the people to open the doors of the Temple."

"Now that's more like it," Yahuda beamed as he sidled up to Juve.

"I'm going to start a disturbance in the marketplace," Yeshua explained. "Just follow me. Do what I do."

"That's not much of a plan," Yahuda muttered to Juve.

"We've got to stop him," Juve replied. "I assumed we'd make plans in Jerusalem, but he's ready to go! We need to stop him, Yahuda."

"Listen," Yeshua went on. "Some of the Sanhedrin are plotting to destroy me. They believe I'd make an excellent martyr . . ."

"Martyr?" Yahuda hissed. "What a waste!"

"My execution, they believe, will outrage the people. They say it will demonstrate the barbarity of the Romans."

"We don't need to demonstrate that," Yahuda objected loudly. "We've had their barbarity shoved in our faces and their taxes loaded on our backs." Yeshua raised his hands again, but Yahuda would not be silenced. "We need to riot all right, but we don't need any more martyrs. Especially you!"

"I've made up my mind, Yahuda," Yeshua shot back.

"What did Yahiye the Baptist's martyrdom get us?" Yahuda protested.

"I agree with Yahuda," Juve shouted. "We need to change directions. You're headed for disaster. Let's back off of Jerusalem for the time being, regroup, and come up with a smarter plan."

"No, Juve, this is the time. All the prophecies point to this place and this time. The momentum is building as we speak."

"Yes, I can feel it," Juve answered adamantly. "It's saying we're headed for a bad conclusion."

"This is nonsense!" exclaimed Simon, joining the fray. "The people are with you. Teach them. There's no reason to make yourself a martyr. Don't do this!"

Yahuda had already concluded that there was little hope in arguing with Yeshua anymore. He turned toward the city and began to walk. Juve grabbed him by the arm and signaled for him to wait. He complied and stood next to Juve. Simon eventually stopped arguing as well and Yeshua stood before them, his arms still in the air. "We're going in," Yeshua replied firmly as he let his arms drop to his sides. "It's God's will."

Yahiye, Yakob, and most of the others voiced their willingness to follow their master's lead. Simon grumbled and threw up his arms in despair but agreed reluctantly to follow as well. With him, all the rest fell in line as Yeshua walked toward the gate. Juve grabbed Simon and asked him to walk with Yahuda and himself. His mind was racing with ways to prevent Yeshua's march to martyrdom. His anger and frustration grew as he heard Yahiye repeating his support for Yeshua's mad, sacrificial plan. Juve tightened his fists as Yeshua pumped up his followers with more crazy promises. "When this is all over, we will take our place in the Temple." Then Yeshua asked Yahiye, "What would you like to be?" Juve allowed the others to gain ground as he racked his brains for a plan.

"I just want to be your right-hand man," he answered with childlike optimism. Yahiye seemed to walk in a trance. His obeisance infuriated Juve, making it impossible for him to plan. All of them were acting like sheep heading for slaughter and Juve felt utterly alone—except for Yahuda and maybe Simon. Only they had voiced any real objection so far.

"I want to judge the tribe of Zebulun," Big Yak announced from where he stood with Juve and Yahuda.

"You still don't get it, do you?" Yeshua admonished the huge man. "Do you think it's going to be easy following the way of life I have taught you?"

As Yeshua continued instructing the others, Juve spoke under his breath to Simon and Yahuda. "This riot," he began explaining, "we've got to divert the attention away from Yeshua." He checked their faces. Both men seemed to understand. "Whatever Yeshua does, do it bigger and do it away from him. I don't know how much rebellion he has in him, but I know I've got more. What about you?"

"I can kick it up ten notches," Simon bragged.

"You won't outdo me," Yahuda goaded him with a smile.

Juve turned toward the city gate. They could hear an uproar beyond the walls. Word had reached the crowd inside that Yeshua was about to enter the city. Simon, Yahuda, and Juve joined Yeshua and the others passed through the gates, into the midst of a jubilant throng cheering, "Free us! Free us!" waving branches and throwing their robes along the path beyond the enormous walls. Despite his reservations, Juve's spirits rose as he walked with Yeshua's men and women into the city, down streets lined with cheering crowds, and finally, between a colonnade of tall pillars. People were packed between the pillars, arms waving, voices pouring out hysterical praise. Juve looked up at the roof of cedar beams connecting the rows of soaring columns and down the length of the aisle to see where it ended. It seemed to go on forever. He felt trapped.

Juve knew a crowd could turn with the slightest provocation, and this crowd reminded him of the fickle crowd in his recurring dream. The same dirty robes, the same spellbound faces, the same blind compliance to the madness of the moment.

"Yeshua, Yeshua!" a young voice called from his right. Juve looked and saw a girl about ten years old jumping up and down, trying to get Yeshua's attention. When he looked her way, she pointed at the astonished girl next to her and yelled, "My sister loves you!" The other girl covered her face, and they both giggled hysterically.

As they moved beyond the giggling girls, Juve saw an opening at the end of the covered avenue. He recognized the great courtyard from his visit with Benjamin as it presented its view of the Temple. The great courtyard was also packed with ecstatic men—and only men—of all ages, their backs pressing into a ring of stalls populated with angry vendors unable to do business. Behind the vendors were lines of watchful Roman soldiers in iron helmets, gleaming breastplates, and stained leather kilts, with short swords suspended from their waists. Over the heads of the people on the right, Juve saw the hills east of the city from where they had traveled.

Out of the corner of his eye, he spotted an object flying from the crowd over the stalls. It landed with a loud clang on the helmet of a soldier. The soldier cursed. Another soldier gestured toward a group of teenage boys mocking them from a safe distance. The soldier pointed at the boys and shouted something. Juve smiled as he watched the taunts fly back and forth across the yard between the boys and the soldiers. He sensed that in a few moments this place was going to explode with commotion, and was happy to see Simon and Yahuda informing the others of his plan. From where Juve stood, it looked as if Simon's brother Andareos had agreed to assist as he moved to another part of the courtyard. Big Yak also seemed to embrace the plan and went in search of a place to do his damage. Little Yak was less enthusiastic but on board. Yahiye had chosen to stay outside the courtyard and look after Mayam and Miriam. In a few minutes, Juve felt he could depend on seven—Andareos, Simon, Big Yak, Philipos, Bartholomew, Little Yak, and Simon the Zealot.

Meanwhile, Yeshua made his way through the parting mob toward the vendors of cloth, tools, jewels and stones, fruits and vegetables. There were as many musicians and magicians. In a few moments Yeshua stood a dozen paces away from a line of stalls where men traded the currencies of Gaul, Egypt, Persia, and of places as far away as India and China. The dealers watched nervously as Yeshua, backed by the mob, faced them across the rectangle of open space. Yeshua raised his arms and the crowd hushed to hear what he would say. Several of the dealers began bagging and gathering up their coins. "Thieves!" Yeshua screamed with the full force of his voice and rushed forward toward the booth directly in front of him. Two dealers inside leaped out the back of their place of business, toppling tables and trays of coins. "You make your living robbing my people! Your time is up! Your reign is over! Make way for the new kingdom!"

In the next few minutes Yeshua and his crew ripped apart one cubicle after the other, tossing boxes and bowls into the air. Crates of doves crashed open and the birds fluttered wildly above the commotion. Pottery shattered on the stone and crunched beneath sandaled feet. Coins and precious stones rained down on the riot. Several coins landed near Juve. One bounced off his shoulder and he grabbed it. One side bore a crude bunch of grapes, the other, a man's face. Then something struck Juve on the head and fell at his feet. Without losing sight of Yeshua, he looked to where he had seen it fall and picked it up—a piece of amber. Inside the smooth stone an insect posed, suspended in a creamy, red-orange cloud. A bolt of recognition electrified Juve. He turned it over to see if it bore the mark of Tiberius. It was Maria's gift!

It took Juve barely a second to surmise that to take it would ruin his chance to give it to Maria in the future. His head spun with the implications of what he had just seen—keep it and bring it back to Maria or leave it to find its own way? "I've already disturbed the future," Juve told himself as he dropped the amber and forced himself to focus on protecting Yeshua.

He scanned the crowd for anyone who looked like they might want to harm the man he had crossed the boundaries of time to protect. Yeshua's voice, until now always calm and compassionate, had transformed into a raging fountain of vicious oaths and merciless condemnations. His words electrified the crowd. Men repeated the meanest of the messiah's curses as they plunged themselves wholeheartedly into the spirit and pitch of the riot. All had held their resentments long enough. Most had walked a long way to celebrate Passover, and their pent-up passions were ripe for release. The fact that falling money made its way into their pockets fueled the fires of their retribution. To a man it was clear—real rebellion had begun. Their king and messiah had blessed their revenge and the spoils were already flowing their way.

Juve noticed the man with the red beard again. He stood noticeably aloof, watching Yeshua intently, with little interest in the liberation of the currency. Not far from him, Juve recognized Titus, the man who had befriended Mayam when he and Benjamin had met her. He, too, was observing. Juve watched their eyes as he maneuvered himself between the two observers and Yeshua, sensing that they meant to take advantage of the commotion. Titus and the red-beard held their ground and looked at each other. Juve caught them signaling each other. The signals were familiar, oddly similar to the Lions' signals he had learned and adapted for Forza. Red-beard wanted to make the move they had planned but Titus wanted to abort. "Is he confused?" Juve wondered.

Roman soldiers were making headway against the raging crowd. Many rioters had filled their pockets and fled the courtyard. As the crowd thinned, the soldiers were making arrests. It was time to go. Juve knew it was time to corral Yeshua and the others and get them to safety. He looked around. Titus and the red-beard were gone. Soldiers were beating and subduing the crowd. Juve saw Simon, Yahuda, and Big Yak forming a crescent around Yeshua, forcing him to move with the fleeing population. He joined them.

On the other side of the great courtyard, beyond the Temple where smoke now poured from the windows, rose a tower with a clear view of the tumult in the courtyard. It was clear to the Roman soldiers inside watching the disturbance who was responsible. Below the tower, two men hurried through the narrow streets lined with the shops and booths of craftsmen, most of whom had abandoned their tools and wares to welcome the Messiah. As they passed, they reinforced each other's arguments. Both were convinced of the need to establish order as soon as possible. Now they rushed toward the upper-city headquarters of Pontius Pilate. "We have to make an example of him," Abraham demanded. "The people must see that this kind of behavior won't be tolerated."

"Leave it to me, Abraham," replied Caiaphas. "I will use everything in my power to see that we make an unmistakable example of this rabble-rouser."

Pontius Pilate's office buzzed with heated debate, interrupted by the coming and going of messengers. A reenactment of the chaos in the streets played itself out in the room full of government and military leaders. Occasionally Pilate's voice boomed above the din, followed by outbursts of dispute, then by rumbles of agreement, and again by the cacophony of argument. "What do you mean, you can't find him?" Pilate bellowed in frustration at the man in charge of finding Yeshua. "How hard can it be?"

In another part of the room lower-ranking officers hovered over a large map of the city. It was sprinkled with markers representing the boundaries of the riot and the positions of the military detachments working to quell the disturbance. Outside, the real edges of the melee were bloody. Rioters were beaten and left on the street, others hauled into custody. The more resourceful rioters who managed to escape the main body of combat rekindled unrest here and there around the city. Yet, all in all, the rebellion was coming slowly under control. Many citizens and pilgrims were content to escape with their fists full of coins. They made their way to places where they could buy wine and celebrate. This night would not be forgotten. It would live in the stories of hundreds of travelers for years to come.

Pilate had summoned the high priest and now word reached him that Caiaphas was waiting in the reception room. With a flick of his wrist, the governor of Judea ordered Caiaphas into the innermost sanctum of local Roman power. From the reception room, Abraham insisted that he be allowed to go along, but his pleas were summarily rejected and Caiaphas was led in alone.

The high priest took note of the huge room and all the activity. Though he had never ventured this far into the domain of Roman power, he had imagined much of what he saw now for the first time. Pilate motioned for one of his assistants to make room for the high priest. The Hebrew potentate took his place at Pilate's table.

"We've worked well together for many years, Caiaphas," Pilate began. "I trust we can find our way to the conclusion of this little uprising—one we both can live with."

"I have no doubt, your honor," Caiaphas answered with little more than due deference. He knew Pilate well enough to expect him to show courtesy and restraint as long as everything went just the way he wanted.

"Here's the way I see it," Pilate continued. "Your so-called messiah is not doing any of us or your people any favors. His behavior has qualified him for execution but his following—at least in their present state of rebellion—is formidable enough to warrant caution. We've been considering our options but I want to hear from you before we act."

Caiaphas surveyed the faces of the men grouped around Pilate—serious faces, every one of them. Before responding, he reconsidered the arguments Abraham had drilled into him on the way. His own mind warned him that Yeshua had far more influence than other renegade Essenes and even Yahiye the Baptist. The tales of his miracles alone made Yeshua a sensation across most of Judea, but his words had taken hold, it seemed, with more tenacity than those of the others. Despite Abraham's demands to put an end to Yeshua, Caiaphas felt inclined to find a middle ground. Still on the fence, he decided to fish for clues from Pilate. "If you are considering the elimination of Yeshua, understand that we have considered it as well. Despite his powerful grip on the hearts of our people, we think the way he sets himself above your authority, as well as ours, must not be taken lightly."

Pilate allowed himself a hint of a smile as he understood now that Caiaphas was willing to cooperate. "I have orders from Tiberius to deliver Yeshua to him."

"What could he possibly want with Yeshua?" Caiaphas asked, sincerely perplexed.

"What, indeed!" Pilate replied with obvious amusement. "It seems the prophet's words may have struck a chord with the head of all Rome. But I can't speculate any further than that."

"Why not give him to Rome, then?" Caiaphas asked.

Pilate stood up and paced away from the table and ran his hands over his bald head. His greatest fear was all-out rebellion. He didn't have the troops he needed to put down a full-blown revolt and he knew he could not count on military support from his neighbor Syria. Yet he had all but convinced himself that this uprising could give Tiberius good reason to end his career. *On the other hand*, he thought, *I could stick it to him—not deliver Yeshua to the Lions—and insulate myself from the wrath of Tiberius by eliminating a major bunch of troublemakers once and for all.* Pilate turned and walked back toward the high priest, his eyes fixed on the floor most of the way. Then, suddenly looking up and directly into the eyes of Caiaphas, "Would it be of any advantage for your people to see Yeshua crucified?" Before Caiaphas could answer, Pilate continued, "As a warning that his kind of defiance cannot be tolerated?"

"We have, as I'm sure you have . . ." Caiaphas hesitated as he carefully framed his words. "That is, I see you have considered the options, as we have, and in the end, we are willing to sacrifice one of our own if it will, as we believe it will, save our nation from more serious retribution."

"If we execute Yeshua, your people risk, as I'm sure you are aware, a more forceful response should they rise up in retribution for killing your Messiah."

"He's not our Messiah," Caiaphas assured Pilate, "and we will let it be known that he is not worth defending. But I doubt that they will need much persuasion. As Passover continues and as they lose themselves in the festivities, I think my people will not be inclined to focus on the hard business of revolution." As soon as he spoke, Caiaphas scolded himself for echoing the words of Abraham. It made him feel manipulated by both the judge and the governor.

Pilate assumed that the distaste he saw in the high priest's face was distaste for the business of death. "You're not losing one of your own, my friend," Pilate reassured Caiaphas with what appeared to be sincere compassion, "you're removing a splinter from your eye."

Caiaphas nodded in agreement, and then he added, "I strongly recommend that we take care of this before Passover begins."

"We think alike," Pilate said as he motioned that Caiaphas be dismissed.

THE GARDEN

YESHUA, JUVE, AND THE OTHERS, LED BY YAHUDA, ESCAPED
the boiling riot by ducking through a series of passageways both above and
below ground. Outside the city, they headed across the Kidron valley and back
up to the somewhat secluded garden where they had spent the night. They
could still see smoke from the Temple, still hear the simmering rebellion, not
yet dead, but not gaining any heat. As they threw themselves down on the
ground, exhausted, they let fly their mix of emotions. Simon the Zealot felt
that they had done a good job of igniting revolution. "But if we don't keep it
stoked," he was still arguing, "it will burn out by the morning."

Most of the other men and women were physically spent and weary of
fighting Simon. They lay near Yeshua and Mayam, no longer interested in the
debate. Yeshua fell asleep as the dispute went on around him. A half hour later
they were all asleep, except for Juve, reminding himself he had two days, if
that, to keep his appointment on Skull Hill. Now, though, he concluded cor-
rectly that they had been followed, and his keen senses told him exactly where
the intrusion was about to happen.

He feigned sleep as he monitored the stealthy movement behind the olive
trees surrounding them. Juve lay between Yeshua and the point from where
he was confident the strongest part of the force would intrude. *Their stalking*

technique is impressive, Juve admitted to himself. They—maybe five or six of them—reminded him of stalkers he had evaded in his early Lions training. These stalkers were at least as good as his training opponents. *These guys have to be Lions,* he concluded.

Then it happened. Juve was up and poised to fight as six men flew in from almost precisely where he had seen them in his mind. Before the others awoke, Juve had laid low two of the biggest men. With them on the ground, the remaining four quickly adapted their attack. They avoided Juve and grabbed two of the sleepers. Titus—the man Juve had met with Mayam in the market-place—held Andareos by the hair and held a knife to his throat. The red-beard and other man did the same to Yahiye and Simon, while their leader walked calmly up to Juve and spoke. "We're here to take Yeshua," he explained with measured authority in a version of Roma that shocked Juve's ears, after days of Aramaic. But as Barth had predicted, he was able to comprehend. "We won't harm him or anybody else, if all of you cooperate."

Juve quickly assessed the situation. Yeshua, Mayam, and the others rose groggily and slowly came to realize what was going on. Yahuda was standing next to the leader as if he was one of his men. He gave Juve a reassuring nod. Juve focused on the leader, who was waiting for his response. "You have no idea what you're getting yourself into," Juve warned him boldly. "Get out of here before you find yourself . . ."

"Unless you're willing to sacrifice the lives of your friends," the man inter-rupted, "give me Yeshua now."

"Here I am," Yeshua said, standing alongside Juve. The leader looked from one to the other, eyebrows raised. Then, as he motioned for Yeshua to come forward, there was a commotion on the road leading to the garden. The leader raised his hand for quiet and looked toward the road. Juve readied himself to take advantage of any opportunity the distraction might offer him, but the knives at the throats of his friends trumped any of his options.

Now everyone's attention was riveted to the noise on the road. It was clear that men were approaching—many men, with leather on their feet and metal on their bodies. Juve waited for the leader to make a move. The three stalkers still standing waited for a signal. Yeshua looked at Juve, who returned a quick nod of reassurance. Then a strong male voice barked a command, and the approaching force broke into a run and quickly surrounded the garden. One hundred or more Roman soldiers, Juve estimated as he watched their shadows surround him.

Juve looked at Yahuda, still standing next to the stalkers' leader. He seemed genuinely surprised. The leader was just as surprised, and gave a signal. The stalkers let go of their hostages and joined Juve in the center of the group. Juve grabbed Yeshua and brought him into the center of the big men. He reached out his hand for Mayam and signaled the others to join the protective circle. The two stalkers brought down by Juve still lay unconscious on the ground as the ring of Roman soldiers marched toward them from all sides.

No longer shadows, the armored soldiers stopped about twenty paces from their captives. Their commander walked up to the huddled circle, metal and leather rattling, and stopped, silent. A second later, the clatter of his equipment was silent, too.

"Yeshua of Nazareth," he called out, "step forward."

Within the huddled group, the other members of Yeshua's crew were paralyzed. The strangers watched Juve. There was only one way to save Yeshua now. Juve knew it would be little more than an act of desperation. The words of the commander still echoed in his ears as he stepped forward with Yeshua, almost in lockstep. In unison, they announced, "I am Yeshua of Nazareth."

Juve scanned the terrified eyes of the other disciples. Only Mayam seemed calm, at peace with what was taking place. *Predictable*, he thought. He'd seen plenty of people in their last moment of life. Self-preservation almost always outranked principle in the human chain of command. Still he was disappointed that Simon and Yahuda would crumble so quickly, so easily. He glanced at Yeshua. His friend stood serenely, thoughtfully, occasionally nodding to those disciples who dared make eye contact. With each glance he offered a slight smile of understanding, as if to say, "Don't worry, everything will be all right." Juve saw Yeshua's eyes rest, at last, on the eyes of Mayam. They seemed to feed each other courage.

On the march back into Jerusalem, Juve reprimanded himself mercilessly for his failure. Now he was chained to Yeshua, Titus, and the other attackers, whom he had identified as Lions. He wanted to laugh. Juventus Trajan Carnifex, linked to the ancestors of his profession, chained to the man Barth had sent him to protect, and headed for some unknown, unhappy fate. The city was a shambles. Broken furniture and earthenware littered the streets. Cries of drunken revelers reverberated in the distance. Dogs scavenged the garbage. Cleaning crews had begun their work as the prisoners were marched through the streets. *They won't be easy on us,* Juve thought.

The soldiers led their captives down an alley behind an imposing structure in the best part of the city. They entered a wide set of elaborately carved wooden doors set a few steps back from a heavy iron gate. As both barriers slammed behind them, Juve was already filing details of his new surroundings and planning their escape. As corrupt as it was in the Rome of his day, at least there were procedures that took time. Escape would take time. Juve wondered how long it would be before they were all tried, or if they would be tried, as the commander announced himself at the doors to Pilate's reception room. They were admitted and stood silently in front of the man who would decide their fate.

Pilate addressed the Lions first. "I see you failed to take my advice," he said to Gaius, grinning with sarcastic satisfaction. Gaius was silent and composed. Pilate seemed pleased with the man's dignified respect. He looked over his shoulder at his team of advisors and assistants. They nodded with approval at their leader's success. "Put them on a boat back to Rome," he ordered his guard, who instantly whisked the Lions out of the room.

Then Pilate turned his attention to the remaining prisoners. Looking from Yeshua to Juve, he seemed as amused as he was perplexed. "What's this?" he asked the commander. "I send you out to get the daring and dangerous Messiah and you bring me two?" Chuckles rose from Pilate's staff. "Your ambition is admirable, Appius, but I promoted you less than a month ago. That wasn't enough?"

"Yes, sir," replied the commander. "I mean, it was enough, sir," Appius added with a smile. He obviously enjoyed his superior's ribbing.

"Well, what are we going to do with two Hebrew kings?" Pilate asked nobody in particular.

"Let this man go," Yeshua said, indicating that Juve be spared. "I'm the one you want."

Immediately Juve demanded to be recognized as Yeshua the Messiah. "I started the riot," he declared, puffing up his chest. "Look at him, then look at me." Juve thrust his arms out from his sides and challenged Pilate. "Who do you think started the riot?" The room became suddenly and uncomfortably still as Pilate's men waited for his reaction. He turned to them, gave them a shrug of mock amazement, and they all let loose with mocking laughter.

"Why should I let either one of you go?" he asked Juve and Yeshua, not expecting an answer. With a wave of his hand he ordered, "Crucify both of them."

A pair of soldiers quickly led Yeshua and Juve out another door, down several steep flights of stairs, through a series of iron gates, and into a dark underground passageway lined with iron-gated cells. Every hundred paces or so, they passed through another gate. As each closed behind them, Juve felt his chances of escaping with Yeshua diminish. At each gate stood a sour-faced guard. Each vacant face seemed to possess less humanity than the one before. None seemed to notice their newest tenants. It was as if this kind of guard duty had been reserved for the weariest soldiers—those whose service had finally drained them of all ability to care about human life. The cells they guarded were crammed with filthy men draped in shredded rags. The place reeked of human waste and perspiration. Here and there men grumbled, snored, or wept. At last they came to a cell with only a half-dozen men inside. With a well-practiced series of clanking motions the escorts led Juve and Yeshua into their cell. Yeshua looked for a place to sit as Juve appraised their situation.

"All right, it's not going to be easy to get out of here," Juve said to Yeshua as he ran his hands over the stone walls and inspected in the dim light the way the iron gate was mounted.

"It's over," Yeshua replied. He sat quietly, strangely at peace, it seemed.

"No! You listen to me," Juve ordered in a loud whisper. He squatted, face to face with Yeshua. "I didn't come all this way to watch you die."

With the slightest hint of a smile, Yeshua replied, "I didn't come all this way to argue with you."

"Listen, Yeshua, we don't have much time. I need time to plan our break and I'll need your help when we do it. So just for the time being at least, forget all this messiah business. We can talk about it when we get out. And if you still feel like you have to . . ." Juve's words trailed off. He couldn't find the slightest sign of agreement in the face of his cellmate. Juve seated himself across from Yeshua, reached for his hands, and held them. They were warm and relaxed.

Juve looked into the eyes of the man and spoke softly. "Yeshua, these people are going to crucify us." The messiah's quiet countenance gave Juve a sense of calmness that, reason told him, had no place in their present circumstance. Yet it was contagious. It took a great deal of effort for Juve to continue pressing his case. "Your mission . . ." He squeezed the hands of Yeshua. "It will die with you." The thought of Yeshua's death gave Juve new energy. He took Yeshua by the shoulders. "Have you taken a good, hard look at your crew? Do you really think they have what it takes to carry on your mission? Do they even understand half of what you say?" Juve rose to his knees and continued. "Simon is a self-serving . . . the man is so full of himself and so wrapped up in promoting himself, you can't count on him. And he's the strongest you've got!" Juve's frustration grew with Yeshua's silence. "You put your mission in Simon's hands and it's finished."

"Do you understand my mission?" Yeshua asked Juve. There was no challenge in his tone. There was nothing rhetorical about the way he posed it. Juve sensed that Yeshua sincerely wanted to know.

"I think I'm getting the idea, but I need more time," Juve replied in the same spirit of sincerity. "I think I see what you're talking about, but the people of Judea need more time. The world needs more time. Ever since I spoke to Benjamin, the Essene I met near Qumran, I began to understand that there is another—at least one other—way to think about things, a completely different way for people to behave. It goes against all of our instincts, but . . ." Juve felt strangely at ease trying to express some of the new and mysterious things he had learned in the past few days, but he wouldn't allow himself to settle into the luxury of thinking about them now. Night after night, he had fallen asleep under the stars lulled by these thoughts, only to wake from disturbing dreams of a disastrous future. This moment demanded action, or else there would be no more starry-skied musings. "I think that if you and I . . ." He looked directly into Yeshua's eyes again. "I think if you and I and your people went away for a while, we could come up with a plan that had some chance of improving the future." Suddenly the futility of his predicament rained down on Juve. He was volunteering for a backup mission to spread the ideas of Yeshua, when he knew he had only two days, maybe one, to get back to the TCI on Skull Hill. Even if he and Yeshua could escape, if they could organize—even if they could do it all, he would never be able to enjoy the results. He could almost feel his confidence drain away.

"The idea doesn't need us, Juve." With Yeshua's words a strange peace began to settle over Juve. He took some time to consider what Yeshua had just said and attempted to put it in the context of other things he had said.

As a kind of last gasp, a final exhalation of his impoverished case, Juve sighed, "It needs more time. It needs a better example than a crucified trouble-maker." The thought of Yeshua facing a humiliating death roused his remaining defenses. "They're going to say they crucified you for starting a riot. And your would-be followers—many of them—will say you deserved it. They had a great time last night, but when they wake up and find they can't get their bread and cheese tomorrow, they'll change their minds. I know, because I've seen the future, Yeshua. It's empty and hollow without you."

"You are a prophet?"

"Yes, I am a prophet," Juve realized as he said it. The idea gave him new hope of reaching Yeshua with his knowledge of the future. "Yes, I've seen the future. The future from where I come—I don't think you can imagine the things I've seen. In the future from where I come, they're looking for you, but you've been forgotten. A small group of people are trying to find you. I was sent by them to keep you and your ideas alive. Now I've found you and I can't let you die."

"You certainly speak like a prophet," Yeshua said, showing a new interest in what Juve had to say. "You should have shared your prophecy with us."

"I should have done a lot of things," Juve replied dismissively. He wondered how he could have explained his future, electrified cities, flying vehicles, computing machines, the wayfone, the language chip in his head . . .

"And you've never felt compelled to tell me this until now?"

"I tried to tell you. I meant to tell you, but it was more important to act. I was still learning. I'm still learning. When I let that cart driver hit me and then went over to help him, I understood. I realize now that the only way for people to get along is to—each one of us—do what I did. And that's the problem, Yeshua. I can do it. You can certainly do it. Some of your crew can do it, but we're outnumbered."

"Yet there's no other way, is there?"

Juve ran the alternatives through his mind. "You're right. It just seems so futile and such a waste to sacrifice you."

"Listen, Juve. People may be moved by words and ideas, but it takes example to make them follow."

"Example? What kind of example is it to go to slaughter like an animal?"

"You saw how the cart driver was moved. There's power beyond what we understand and it reveals itself in the kind of love you showed. The power that moved the cart driver is bigger than us, Juve. It's beyond us. Let's let it find its own way now. We've done all we can do. We've done our best. I'm just a carpenter's son, remember. I have no army or council of elders. Simple, plain-speaking men and women follow me. But I follow the will of God and in the submission of my will, I find my strength."

"Yeshua," Juve began. He stopped to formulate what he wanted to say. "It's in you and me."

"Of course."

"What if it wants me to save you at all costs?"

"Does it?"

"Yes, that's why I'm here," Juve replied confidently. "I have seen the future and you're not in it. I come from a time deprived of your influence. I've lost everything that was dear to me. I have no reason to be here in Judea other than to stop what's about to happen. The world needs you. I cannot and I will not let you be killed. That much is not up for debate!"

"Juve," Yeshua said, calmly pointing to the gate of their cell, "if you can find a way out of here, then you might be right. Get us out of here and I will acknowledge that it's God's will for me to live."

Juve studied the man sitting across from him in the dank dungeon. He had faced death many times, but always with the conviction that he would survive. Now this man, with no apparent fighting skills, seemed perfectly content with certain death just hours away. It must be his connection with his god, Juve concluded. So, in his mind, he ran through the ancient gods of Rome he had studied in school. No one had suggested they actually existed. Yet no one had said they didn't. Juve closed his eyes and concentrated on his favorite—Jupiter. It wasn't long before the gates of his memory opened and he rode on bittersweet waves of childhood nostalgia. Jupiter ran with Juno, Venus, and Diana. He recalled their faces from the statues and images he had studied.

When he imagined Mars, it reawakened his youthful admiration for the god of war. Juve remembered how, when he was very young, he had imagined possessing the strength and fearsome invincibility of Mars as he played—before he was sent away to become an Indomitable Lion. Now he realized that his Lion training had shattered his dreams of the Roman gods. But even though he had stopped thinking of his gods as real, much of his strength and courage could be attributed to his childhood hero worship. *Maybe*, he thought, *maybe I need to know more about the Hebrew god Yeshua still reveres in order to understand his strength and courage.*

Juve opened his eyes and saw Yeshua resting his head on his knees, his hair draped on either side of his face. This was the man Barth had sent Juve to save, sleeping, resigned to his fate. Juve wondered if he had found the wrong man or if he had arrived in the wrong time. Barth had described a man of inspiring words and ideas. That much fit. But this man's message included resignation. Juve realized he would never come to terms with resignation. He would never give up his will to the will of a god—real or imagined. He had never let anyone take charge of his fate. Not even his Lion commanders. He traded his subservience then for the promised results. Never would he submit to a god. It was frightening enough to let Maria possess his heart. His heart ached for her as he sat in his dark, stinking cell, distracted by the sporadic cries and moans of men abandoned by all hope. What was there to do? He had counted seven iron gates and seven guards, who would happily smash him like a rat, given the chance. He estimated that he and Yeshua were six or more meters below the ground. *The city*, he surmised, *has an underground drainage and sewage system. But where? On the other side of which wall? Why wonder? There just isn't time. I've leaped through time. Now there's no time left.*

Disgusted, Gaius weighed his options with his heart. He had lost all respect for Pilate. The governor was crude and cruel and his guards were weak. Gaius's crew of six had escaped easily from Pilate's contingent of his twelve best. Each of the Lions disappeared separately into the shadows of Jerusalem with plans to reconvene that night. All were on the lookout for Roman guards and any of the followers of Yeshua who, Gaius predicted, would be released after questioning. Gaius had developed respect for Yeshua and especially Juve, which made him that much more determined to carry out the mission that had brought him from Rome. A new plan was forming in his mind just as he spied Yahuda at the other end of a courtyard. Gaius made his way toward him and signaled him to approach the alcove in which he hid. Warily Yahuda walked over and heard Gaius ask him, "Do you want Yeshua to live?"

SKULL HILL

YAHUDA FOUND MAYAM AND THE OTHER DISCIPLES WHERE
they had planned to meet that night, the home of a friend of Simon. Everyone
had eaten except Yahuda, and Mayam made sure that he was fed before she
allowed anyone to question him. He had left the custody of Pilate with the
others but had promised to come back with some way to help Yeshua and Juve.
With no idea of what kind of plan or help he would furnish or where he would
find it, he had blindly followed his feet. Now with the real plan in mind, the
one Gaius had proposed in the alcove, he was eager to lay it out in front of his
family of followers.

"The men who accosted us in the garden—the first six," Yahuda explained,
"their leader has a plan to spring Yeshua and Juve tomorrow morning. All we
need to do . . ."

Yahuda could no longer be heard over the objections. "Why should we
trust them? What do they want with Yeshua?" The harder he tried to silence
them, the louder they objected. Mayam finally managed to quiet them. The
most vocal, Simon the Zealot, got in the last word, "What are you getting out
of this, Yahuda?" before Mayam ordered him to sit down and listen. Once
more Yahuda tried to lay out the plan, but the objections and suspicions made
it a laborious process. The frightened men and women, bereft of their leader

and the strange Romans who had appeared lately to protect them, quarreled late into the night. Some fell asleep.

"We have always depended on Yeshua, and he has taught us to be patient, to rely on our father in Heaven, who tends to our fate," Mayam offered to those who listened.

"Even if that means letting Yeshua die at the hands of the Romans?" Yahuda asked.

"If we had our own plan," Mayam suggested, "I think we might try it."

"All we have to do is create a diversion," Yahuda explained again. "We're going to be there anyway, aren't we?"

"Yes," Mayam assured him, "we will be there, but you've heard from most of us. No one wants to take part in a Roman plan."

Yahuda had also explained again and again that the plan came from the heart of a man who had come to respect and even admire Yeshua, but no one seemed to care. Still he tried again. "Of course, they have their own reasons for helping. What does that matter? We both want Yeshua to live. The Romans want him dead. If this man and his crew help us, they're not helping the Romans."

"And Juve?"

"Yes, of course, Juve, too."

"The Romans have their way," Mayam said in a manner that seemed to conclude the matter, "we have ours. We will depend on the way Yeshua has taught us."

It was quiet for a while and the remaining debaters, exhausted, reclined with the others. Then, out of nowhere, Simon's sleepy voice was heard. "What do you think Yeshua would want us to do?"

"Nothing, I'm afraid," Yahuda replied bitterly, when he saw that Simon's eyes were closed. "He'd say whatever happens is God's will."

After another spell of silence, Tomas asked, "What would Juve do?"

The next morning, citizens and pilgrims had begun to stake out their places along the road. They had become familiar with the crucifixion ritual. Reserved for the most treasonous criminals, a crucifixion guaranteed a ghastly spectacle. Victims would come, bloodied and humiliated, dragging the timber on which they would be suspended and displayed until dead, until their bodies had been torn apart and consumed by scavengers. The crowd collected themselves into groups, shoved, jostled for better views, and bickered among themselves. Fights broke out, stones flew back and forth, but as the sun rose above the eastern hills, they threw only taunts. Andareos and Simon were in the crowd, but kept their distance from the path Yeshua and Juve would tread. In the distance, toward the place where the condemned had spent the night imprisoned, there arose a clamor as the first to see them expressed their delight and pity. They were the first, also, to see that two men were indeed dragging the huge timbers from which they would soon be suspended.

The morning had been a treat for the soldiers who prepared the victims. Since sunrise both had been bloodied and bruised into hideous mockeries of themselves. No one would have noticed the resemblance the two once shared. As Yeshua and Juve plodded along the way to their executions, they remained silent. During the night, in the depths of his despair, Juve had given himself up to a dumb and simple trust that whatever happened was beyond his control and in the power of everything that goes on between time and eternity. It was nebulous, but it brought relief. At the end of the horrible abuse, as the huge timber was dropped on his shoulder, it hardly equaled the huge weight he had laid down during the night. Now Juve, with Yeshua several steps behind, turned and exited through the city walls. New voices cheered and jeered. The noise blurred into a single dull roar and Juve found it difficult to understand what they said. The language chip behind his ear had been smashed and compromised with blood and bits of bone. *People*, he thought with equal pity and disgust, *who will ever tame them? These men may have beaten us and they are certainly going to kill us, but they would be impotent without the pure pleasure they give the people. Look how they welcome it!*

Still, as he trudged along, he was watching instinctively for a way out, looking for a way to prove to Yeshua that his mission, not Yeshua's, was the right one. As the two condemned men trudged and turned left, around a corner Juve looked up and caught the eyes of a man. It was Gaius, the leader of the Lion party sent to export Yeshua to Rome. Juve looked again but the man was gone. Beyond the spot where he stood, the earth rose and formed itself into a prominence that clearly resembled a human skull. Suddenly the weight was also gone from his shoulder. He straightened himself and looked around. The Lions were battering the Roman guards. Two Lions used Yeshua's timber to hold back the crowd. Relieved of his burden, Yeshua stood and began to protest as two Lions drew knives and stabbed the guards at either side of the Messiah. Juve could watch no longer.

I can still make it! he told himself, as he grabbed a soldier about to draw his sword on the giant Decimus and delivered him to the ground with a deadly punch. The crowd cheered on the combatants, drowning out the dissent from Yeshua. He was almost comical in his ironic insistence that the violence end. In the midst of the melee, Juve came nose to nose with Gaius.

"I thought they sent you back to Rome," Juve said. Gaius looked quizzically at Juve. Unable to understand Juve's strange-sounding words, Gaius grinned at Juve before taking down two more Roman solders. Juve was soon occupied with putting away Romans, when he noticed two Lions wrapping Yeshua in a large gray blanket, which instantly began to bloom with the blood of its angry contents. As Yeshua struggled to escape, three Lions disappeared with their captive into the crowd. Down the road from where Yeshua and Juve had dragged their timbers, the sound of marching feet grew louder with every step as Roman reinforcements hurried to the scene.

Gaius stepped up to Juve. "We're no match for forty Roman escorts." Juve returned Gaius's smile as the remaining Lions gathered, urging Gaius to leave.

Juve slammed his fist against his heart. "The Lions' way!"

Gaius and the Lions gave Juve a look of perplexed delight. Each of them returned the Lions' signal, then followed the trail of Yeshua's blood into the mob. Juve followed just as the crowd parted for the Roman reinforcements on the opposite side. Several soldiers dashed after Juve and the Lions. From over his shoulder, Juve noticed another disturbance off to his left. The Lions carrying Yeshua had run into a throng of forty or more men who seemed to be following the orders of a wild-eyed Simon the Zealot. Then, to the right, Juve saw Romans with drawn swords hurrying toward him. He knew that, unless he stopped to slow them down, they would certainly catch up with the Lions, the Zealots, and Yeshua. Surprising the first of the soldiers with a blow to the face, Juve stood fast and brought down a second and a third, but the soldiers kept coming. Every move opened another wound on Juve's back or arms. For the first time in his lifetime of hand-to-hand combat, defeat crossed his mind. And the soldiers kept coming.

Finally four strapping soldiers subdued Juve and held him, one at each limb. In a few seconds, the captain of the detachment stood facing him. "So this is the new Hebrew Messiah?" The soldier on the captain's right muttered something to him. "Got away? Then, who's this?" Juve could not understand their words, but he understood their intentions as all four of his captors let loose loud, derisive cries. "Well, someone's gonna get crucified," the captain sneered, then smiled and smashed Juve's nose with his fist. Juve saw it coming and almost welcomed the darkness that made the jeering roar of the crowd fade gently away.

Two young boys inched their way up Skull Hill. The sun was setting and they took full advantage of the gathering darkness. Each boy was armed with a sack full of stones. Two Roman sentries of the lowest rank paced around the base of the crucifix, complaining about their superiors, who lolled lazily farther down the hill. "When I'm promoted," groused the smaller of the two, "I'm going to give that Melius his due."

"What promotion?" the other snarled cynically. "You'll be on shit duty till the day you die."

"Fuck you, Flaccus," grumbled the soldier.

The coarse voices nudged Juve from unconsciousness. Through his delirium he realized that he had been nailed to the huge timber on top of Skull Hill. He had hung silently long enough to give Flaccus the idea that he could soon go home and leave the crucified Jew to the dogs creeping closer in the dark. The two soldiers had grown tired of throwing rocks at them to kill the boredom, while Juve sank in and out of awareness. In response to the voices below, Juve groaned.

"Now look what you did," he complained. "You woke him up, Scrofa."

"What's the difference?" Scrofa sneered.

"The poor bastard feels no pain when he's out cold," Flaccus explained testily. "Let him die in his sleep. He's had a bad day." Just then a stone whizzed by Scrofa's ear and hit Juve on the ankle with a dull smack. The pain shot through Juve, but his body could react with only a subtle shudder.

"You little turds!" Scrofa cried. He ran blindly several strides in the direction of the sound of the laughing boys scrambling away, proud of their success.

Juve groaned again as Scrofa shuffled back up the hill. Flaccus attempted to comfort Juve, "Just let it go, my friend. Quit fighting it."

In another minute, Juve was falling back into oblivion. Throughout the next hour, he rose from silence to suddenly sputter deliriously in bouts of giddy hope and fearful rage. On his way in and out of consciousness, he dreamed his way through walls, underwater, over cities, around his enemies, and among those he loved. Drained of all but his last few breaths now, Juve swam in and out of sweet, foggy scenes of Barth in the outfit he had improvised for his trip to the TCI. He saw Maria and their baby playing in Forum Fountain. In one lucid moment, Juve opened his eyes and realized where he was, why he was dying, and that his indomitable will was the only thing keeping him alive. Once more his well-honed inner strength gave him a fresh sense of calmness and pride. He had luxuriated in his power many times throughout his life, but he was ready to give it up now.

Suddenly, at his feet, he saw Yeshua—the man who had challenged his convictions about strength and action, the man Barth had sent him to rescue. Doubting his senses, he blinked his eyes. Yeshua had been wrapped up and carried away. *This is another annoying dream*, Juve concluded and consoled himself with the conviction that the man who would make the world better for some other future with Maria was still alive. What did it matter if Yeshua actually stood below now or was recovering from Roman abuse? Yeshua was alive and that meant Maria and their baby might live—or at least have a chance to avoid death at her father's hand—whatever the future, certainly it would be better.

"Let's put him out of his misery," Flaccus said as he moved toward Juve. Scrofa stood in his way and crossed spears with him.

"Regulations," he sneered. "This is a political criminal. He goes natural all the way. He's the king of the Jews, after all." Scrofa spoke over his shoulder to Juve, "Where's your army, King?"

"Leave him alone," Flaccus demanded.

"No, I want to know when the king's army's gonna show up," Scrofa insisted. He looked up at the dying man and watched him try to raise his head as if to speak. "What kind of king are you anyway? How come your army is nowhere to be seen?"

Juve looked down at Scrofa. Unable to understand his words, he clearly took his meaning. With all the strength Juve could muster, he smiled.

"Insolent Jew!" Scrofa snarled as Flaccus pushed him aside, preparing to thrust his own spear up under Juve's sternum as a spear sank into his own back. Scrofa spun toward the dull thud as another spear found its mark in the center of his chest. With both guards mortally bleeding on the ground below Juve, Gaius and Decimus ran up and retrieved their weapons. Then Gaius helped Decimus climb up the timber to Juve. Atop the horizontal beam, Decimus worked Juve's hands from the nails. Gaius prepared to catch the body as Decimus loosened Juve's feet. Holding Juve just below the knees, Gaius waited for the release of Juve's other hand. In another moment, Gaius was holding him at the waist as Decimus dangled the nearly lifeless body as carefully as possible by the wrist.

"It's Gaius," he whispered to Juve, happy to see that his fellow Lion remained unconscious. Juve groaned as he dropped and sank into the arms of Gaius.

"I couldn't leave a fellow Lion like this, Juve." With these words Juve opened his eyes and turned his head to Gaius. He blinked and focused. A twitch of a smile flashed and faded from his face. "I'm going to get you to someplace quiet," Gaius promised, as he cradled Juve and started down Skull Hill. Little rocks crunched under his feet and threatened to make the powerful man stumble, but Gaius strode more carefully now with his comrade. "I'll stay with you as long as I can, brother, but I have orders. The Zealots wrested Yeshua from us. They've got him hidden somewhere. I have to deliver him to Tiberius."

Juve raised his head and opened his mouth. Gaius halted and waited for what he sensed would be Juve's last words. Juve looked into the eyes of his rescuer and spoke in the language they shared, "Let it go."

FAITH

SIMON'S VOICE ECHOED SOFTLY OFF THE WALLS OF THE cave. "If we don't tell his story, it's going to be told by somebody else. They're already getting it wrong out there," he argued, pointing to the opening of the cave. "We have to keep Yeshua's story out of the wrong hands . . ."

Mayam wiped away a tear from her cheek as she interrupted, "Yeshua's story will live, Simon." She continued to wash dirt and dried blood from the right arm of the battered body at her knees. "It doesn't need our help." Assisted by Tomas, Mayam had washed and dried most of Yeshua's body, one part at a time. She kept him covered with garments gathered from the other members of the family now surrounding their beloved teacher. The gashes and bruises staining Yeshua's face had surrendered most of their swelling fury. As he lay supine, the insults to his flesh served only to discolor him with an awful collage of purple, black, red, and olive hues. Simon and Mayam had been debating for an hour or more, interrupted now and then by deep, tortured breaths from their Messiah. Each elevation of his chest was followed by a troubled attempt to speak.

It's as if he's gathering strength for his final words, Simon had told himself. On that assumption, he reasoned as persuasively as possible, certainly for the benefit of those who had also managed to escape to the cave, but more in the hope that Yeshua would endorse his impassioned case for organization.

"Have you heard what they're saying?" Simon challenged Mayam.

She replied calmly as she gently arranged Yeshua's right arm under the motley pile of garments. "I'm not the least bit interested in what they're saying, Simon."

"Well, you should care, because the same people who followed him and believed his promises of eternal life in an everlasting kingdom are quickly losing confidence in us." Mayam and the others could see that Simon wanted to scream. His face raged red with frustration.

"He's not even dead," Tomas complained, "and already you're making excuses for his death."

"I don't want him to die, Tomas! I want him to live as much as you do. But if he dies, I just want to make sure we have a plan."

"If he dies . . ." Tomas paused to swallow the lump in his throat. "If he dies, I believe he will come back, just as he promised. Do you believe his promise or not?"

"If our beloved brother lives, I will follow like him like a lamb." Simon searched the faces of the four men and three women huddled around Yeshua. "If he awakes and appoints his successor before he dies, I will obey whomever he commands me to follow." Looking squarely at Mayam, he added, "Even you." Then Simon looked around at the others. "But if he dies, we have to answer the question that's dogging each one of us."

Mayam addressed the family. "Let's make sure we all understand Simon's question." Then she spoke with a clear challenge in her voice. "What is the question, Simon?"

Simon used the silence to preface the words he framed carefully now. He had run them through his head many times since Yeshua had been captured. They had begun to tease their way into his thoughts the day Yeshua spoke of dying for the first time. He had rehearsed revealing them to just this kind of assembly. "I don't believe Yeshua will live," he began. "And if I'm right and he dies, and if he does not rise, then he is no more the son of God than you or I." Simon pointed, but not without reverence, to Yeshua. "Because if he cannot overcome the eternal darkness, he is just another prophet . . . No!"

he corrected himself in a slightly raised voice, "he is *the* prophet of our time. But his words will languish just as the sun sets on our days, just as the words of Ezekiel have fallen by the wayside. I refuse to let that happen." Simon clenched his fist and shook it as he emphasized his conclusion. "I want his story to survive!" He paused and rested the palm of his right hand on Yeshua's chest and leaned toward his face, whispering reverently in a voice all could hear, "My sweet Yeshua, I promise you that I will carry your word to the ends of the earth." Without lifting his hand, he paused ceremoniously, and then he addressed his family. "And I will lead anyone who will follow me."

If Simon had expected his words to elicit a response from his master, he failed. Yeshua's chest raised Simon's hand, but just as slightly, it descended. Mayam spoke with quiet confidence. "If Yeshua dies, Simon, what story will you tell?"

Simon lifted his hand from Yeshua's chest, brought his hands together in front of himself. "I will tell whatever I have to tell. The past is a parchment on which we must write the future." Simon checked the eyes of his family to measure the resonance of his words. "I gave up everything to follow Yeshua. I love him more than my mother and father. And I will find a way to keep him alive."

With a sigh, not of resignation but of pained patience, Mayam countered. "Your faith is only in your words, Simon. What does it matter if a hundred years from now people say Yeshua died or Yeshua rose from the dead or Yeshua sat down and wrote his instructions on a scroll? As long as the word that nourishes us today reaches the generations that come after us, we've done our part."

"No," Simon grumbled, "if the story is not a story of hope . . ."

"Hope?" Mayam exclaimed. "Yeshua's story is full of hope!"

"Not if it ends like this. We've got to make it resound with—"

"Do not . . ." They all took a quick breath as they heard Yeshua manage to speak. ". . . build my kingdom . . . on lies." Watching Yeshua's chest fall, the eight feared that it might not rise again.

A young mother walked her first and only child down the steps of a church. She and her three-year-old son had just attended their first religious service together. The boy had been fascinated with the burlap wall hangings, each casually decorated with brightly colored words and crudely cut silhouettes of birds, hands, cups, and rays of light. Throughout the service, he had identified with unabashed pride a bird, a sun, and the letter C. For some time he stared, frowning at the huge crucifix suspended from the ceiling over the sanctuary. "What happened to that man?" he had whispered to his mother. It was at this point that she questioned her decision to bring him to this church. After the divorce—after she was dropped, angry and disappointed, into single-motherhood, joint custody, and more complications than she had anticipated—she had thought it wise to give her son a spiritual grounding, *a moral compass*, she had called it. Now as they left the air-conditioned confines of the beige-brick box, he insisted, "Is he dead, Mommy?"

"Yes."

"Why did he die?"

She dug quickly into her religious training as a young girl. Her parents, too, had brought her to church just long enough to equip her with the basics. As an adolescent, like most of her friends, she had rejected what she had been taught and composed for herself a unique portfolio of spiritual attitudes.

"So we could go to Heaven, sweetheart."

The boy furrowed his brow as they moved among the other congregants and made their way across the blacktop parking lot. She had chosen the church because it was close, because they could walk the tree-lined block on Sunday mornings like this one, filled with birdsong, cool in the early morning before the hot summer sun began to bake the comfort out of the day. "Did he cry when they put the nails in his hands?"

Irritation edged her reply. "I don't know." Regretting her choice of churches, she let patience return to her voice. "Probably." She had attended church as a child, but she had been appalled when she entered this one and came face-to-face with the crucified figure looming over the altar.

They were half a block away when the boy asked, "Was there lots of blood?"

She realized now that it was time for her to make some sense of what her son had witnessed this morning. "Some people believe that when people do bad things, somebody has to make it better. So that's what the man did—he died for our sins—and now it's all better."

"Do I have a sin?"

The mother looked down along her arm to the tiny hand gripping two of her fingers. His arm, fully extended, reached just above his ear. He was distracted now by a squirrel darting behind a tree. She marvelled at the instinctive way he pointed at the tree, his index finger straight, his other fingers curled into his palm. *No one taught him how to point with his hand,* she realized. Suddenly she felt the miracle of life delight her as a rush of gooseflesh rippled along her arms. She stopped, sat on her heels, and held her little boy by the shoulders. His eyes opened happily at her unexpected turn of attention. "No! Baby, you don't have any sins. And don't ever let anyone tell you you're bad. Okay?"

"I'm good," he affirmed, and she could see that he was remembering. She chose her words carefully. "Just be good to people and everything will be fine." The boy nodded and she decided not to turn the lesson into a sermon. She stood and they continued to walk hand in hand.

"Mommy?"

"Yes?"

"Why did that squirrel run away from me?"